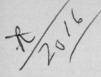

MURDER
AT THE
CASTLE

MURDER AT THE CASTLE

JEANNE M. DAMS

WORLDWIDE.

TORONTO • NEW YORK • LONDON
AMSTERDAM • PARIS • SYDNEY • HAMBURG
STOCKHOLM • ATHENS • TOKYO • MILAN
MADRID • WARSAW • BUDAPEST • AUCKLAND

Recycling programs
for this product may
not exist in your area.

Murder at the Castle

A Worldwide Mystery/April 2016

First published by Severn House Publishers Ltd.

ISBN-13: 978-0-373-26989-1

Printed in U.S.A.

Acknowledgments

Some of the people and places in this book are real; others are fictitious. I'm happy to say that Tower Wales is a real B and B, and Charles and Mairi Wynne-Eyton are real people, and both house and hosts are every bit as charming as I've described them. (Mairi is Scottish, and her name is pronounced Maw-ree, accent on the first syllable.) Flint Castle, on the other hand, has for centuries been only a ruin. For my own purposes I've rebuilt it at some distance from its real site, basing its design on an amalgam of Beaumaris and Conwy Castles, marvellous survivors from the time of King Edward I.

I am deeply indebted to the Wynne-Eytons for making my stay in Wales so pleasant and so informative, for introducing me to the Llangollen canal boats, and for their patient answers to my many questions. I thank my friend and mentor Bob Demaree for his expertise on matters related to choral music, especially that of Joseph Haydn. Tuck Langland also gave me excellent advice about opera, and my dear friend Christine Seitz was kind enough to read the whole manuscript and make some valuable suggestions. I also owe a debt of gratitude to Lise Hull and the other contributors to the extremely attractive and informative website www.castlewales.com. I spent entirely too many hours happily perusing the site when I ought to have been writing!

PROLOGUE

June 2003

ONE

'YOU LOOK BEAUTIFUL, Delia. Is that a new dress?'

She frowned and sighed. 'Always you say the same thing. You are not observant, John. I have worn this gown at least twice before, and every time you ask is it new.'

He turned away to adjust his black tie, and to hide his face from her. It was true. He did always say the same thing, or if not the same, always the wrong thing. He must try harder. Sixteen days. They had sixteen days together. If it was to begin with an argument, it might go on that way, and this might be their last chance.

'I'm sorry, darling. I'm blinded by your beauty!' He took her in his arms and kissed her.

'Take care! I wish to look fresh when we go down.' She pushed him off and smoothed the flounces of her crimson skirt. 'This first night is important. I wish everyone to say, "Who is she? So beautiful, so well dressed, such jewels…she must be someone important." And later I will sing, just a little, you understand. I will sing along with the dance music, as if to myself, and those around me will hear and will ask me to sing with the orchestra, and they will be amazed.'

To John it sounded a little like the plot of an old Andy Hardy movie: 'I know! Let's put on a show!' But this cruise was his final desperate attempt to put his marriage back together. He said only, 'You'll knock them for six, darling. Shall we?'

He bowed her through the door of their stateroom, then offered his arm, but she ignored it. 'My dear girl!' he murmured. 'The motion of the ship…your shoes…you wouldn't want to break an ankle, your very first day out.'

'I have perfect balance, and there is nothing wrong with my shoes. You forget that I am also a dancer.'

He'd said the wrong thing again. There was, in his opinion, everything wrong with her shoes. The four-inch heels were far too thin, the straps holding them on were far too insubstantial, and they were far too bright a gold. She might have got by with them—just—if she'd worn them over sheer, expensive stockings. On bare feet with crimson-varnished toenails they were…he winced at the word, even in his mind, but they really *were* unmistakably vulgar.

There was a time when he would have said so. Now he shrugged, but only mentally. 'Mind how you go, then,' he said, and followed her to the lift. The restaurant was several decks below their luxurious suite, and she should definitely not risk those heels on the perforated metal 'ladders' that were the only stairs provided for the first two flights. 'Perfect balance' or not.

Delia had taken a tour of the ship as soon as they had boarded that morning, securing, with a ravishing smile, the services of one of the overworked crew to lead her around while John unpacked. Now she pressed a button in the lift with assurance.

'I believe the restaurant is on the next deck down, darling.'

'Two decks. It is below the ballroom. There is a grand staircase down to the ballroom. I will make my entrance there.'

The combo playing in the ballroom lounge sat where they had an excellent view of the grand staircase. They paid Delia the tribute of a sudden silence, and then struck up a lively Latin tune as she glided down the last few steps.

She is so lovely, he thought. Then he amended it. *She looks so lovely*.

It was her incredible beauty that had first pulled him under till he drowned. Oh, her voice was very nice, though untrained, a warm natural mezzo brimming with fire and *brio*. She had auditioned for him on an aria from *Boris Godunov,* and he was lost. Some of the notes had been flat, some of the text garbled, but the passion of it! The bravura! She was young for the piece, her voice a bit light, but she put her soul into it, and John was enchanted.

It didn't occur to him until much later that it was an odd piece to choose when one was auditioning for an oratorio. But by that time he understood that Delia had also been auditioning for quite a different role.

She got both roles, of course. She sang the oratorio adequately, and her self-confidence and stage presence convinced almost everyone that she had been brilliant. And a month later Delia Lopez and John Warner were married in the little parish church where he had been christened twenty-eight years before. She wore a white lace mantilla that emphasized her lustrous black hair and smooth olive skin and made her look, to John's adoring eyes, like the Madonna. She was just nineteen.

There hadn't been time for a honeymoon. Big celebrations were planned all over the world for the Millennium, with music featured at many of them. John had performances scheduled every weekend, with rehearsals daily. His name as a choral conductor was already one to be conjured with, and Delia's reputation as a singer began to grow along with John's fame.

Delia's was not, perhaps, an untarnished reputation. She had somewhat more of the infamous artistic temperament than was quite justified by her abilities, according to some critics. But they were careful not to say so in John's hearing. His was as equable a temper as one was apt to find in a first-class conductor, but he would tolerate no criticism of his wife.

Maybe that was his big mistake, he thought as he followed her down the stairs. Should he have let her take her knocks and learn to deal with the real world? But how could he? She didn't take criticism at all well. The few times he had ventured to offer gentle direction of his own, she had either dismissed it with an airy wave of her hand or flown into a rage. The time she had thrown the small Henry Moore sculpture out of the window, narrowly missing a passer-by before it shattered on the pavement, was his last attempt to guide her.

The last attempt until now. He followed her to the bar, where she seated herself with a graceful swirl of skirts and looked up at him with an angelic smile.

'What would you like, love?'

'Something rich and dark and sweet.'

'Like you,' he answered, but his answer came too pat. She frowned. She was the better actor, and she could say the line as if newly minted. His response sounded as automatic as it was.

He bit his lip and asked the bar steward for a planter's punch for Delia. 'Do you have Myers's rum?' And at the man's nod, 'A double shot, then, please.'

'Certainly, sir. And for yourself?'

'Small whisky and soda. Er...scotch and soda, that is.'

'Of course, sir.' The steward sounded mildly affronted. 'Sorry...your accent... I wasn't sure...'

'I am from Bermuda, sir. I grew up with the English.'

'So of course you know that "whisky" means to us what some of the world calls "scotch".'

'Indeed, sir. Here you are, sir. Madam.'

Delia took a sip of her drink and then gave the steward a long, smouldering look. 'It is delicious. You are very good.'

'A lovely drink for a lovely lady.' He returned the look, with interest, and then had to turn away to serve another couple.

John gulped down his drink and wished he had another as he waited for Delia to finish hers. But the bar had become very busy, and though both Delia and John tried (for different reasons) to catch the steward's eye, he didn't return to their end of the room.

John was suddenly sick of the game. 'Let's go and eat, Delia. I'm hungry.'

She looked at him in irritated surprise. 'I am not. You may go if you wish.'

'I do wish. And I wish you to come with me.'

He could see her thoughts chasing across her face. A frown, then a pout, then the angelic smile. *Shall I make a scene? Perhaps not in so public a place. I will wheedle, instead. But no, that is his iron face. I will do as he wishes. For now.*

He laughed in genuine amusement and took her arm. 'Never, never take up poker, my darling wife.'

That was met with blank incomprehension.

The evening proceeded as planned. As Delia had planned, at least. She came, she was seen, she conquered. They had no sooner been seated at their table for two than the steward reappeared. 'I am so sorry, sir, for the mistake. The Captain invites you and your lady to dine with him.'

John would have liked to beg off. He had a fixed dislike of 'social' meals, preferring to eat in peace. But Delia was already on her feet and following the steward, her face alight with satisfaction. It was another rung on the ladder.

The meal was indeed a social occasion, and Delia made the most of it. She was brilliant at this sort of thing. She made every man at the table, even including her husband, feel he was a bit wittier than usual, a bit better-looking. Somehow, with subtle lifts of her eyebrows and little private smiles, she even managed to keep the women from being jealous. They were made to feel part of a minor conspiracy, we-girls-together, and quite clever to have landed men so dashing, yet so easily manipulated.

After dinner they went up to the ballroom, and again Delia sparkled. She danced every dance with one partner after another, the staid waltzes and two-steps as well as the Latin numbers that the orchestra played, John was sure, especially for her.

John wasn't a dancer. He sat watching her, her lovely head held high, her body as proud and taut as a flamenco dancer's, her face aglow as she moved through the intricate steps. She exuded excitement, sexuality, animal passion.

I am not the right man for her, he thought, sunk in something like despair. *I can never make her happy. I should never have married her. I'm not old, but around her I feel old. Old and stodgy.*

As she danced she began to hum, and finally to sing quietly. She manoeuvred close to the orchestra, without letting her partner know she was leading him. She sang a little louder. The conductor heard her. With a

broad smile he brought the rumba to a premature end
and pulled the microphone closer to him.

'Ladies and gentlemen, we have a very fine singer in
our midst. Come here, my dear.'

With a shy smile, Delia apologized to her partner and
approached the conductor.

'What is your name, lovely lady?'

'Delia Lopez, sir.'

'I hope you will consent to sing for us, Delia. Your
voice is as beautiful as you are.'

'Well…if you would like me to sing…'

The men in the audience applauded enthusiastically.

'Then do you know "Granada"?'

The orchestra knew 'Granada'. It is a song meant for a
man, but most of the audience didn't know that, and certainly Delia's dramatic mezzo voice suited it well. She
sang in the original Spanish, and when she had finished
the delighted audience demanded more. She obliged.

What seemed to John like hours later, the orchestra
finally stopped playing and she came back to the table,
breathless and exhilarated. 'They will not play any more,
those boring men. What shall we do now?'

John roused himself. He had been nearly asleep. 'We
go to bed. It's nearly two, and we made a very early start
this morning.'

She stamped her foot. 'I do not want to go to bed!
I am not sleepy. I want to sing some more, but I am
thirsty.'

'Delia, the bar is closed. The orchestra is finished for
the night. Come to bed.'

The room was clearing, but several people lingered,
a few of them eager to talk to Delia, to congratulate her
on her performance. One young man who had partnered
her for several dances spoke now, in an American ac-

cent. 'I'd be glad to take you for a walk around the decks, ma'am, if your husband doesn't mind. It sure is a beautiful night, and the stars are something to see out here in the middle of nowhere.'

Delia smiled beguilingly up at John. 'Please, John? It will be only for a moment. Do you mind?'

Anger rose in John for a moment. It was all an act, of course, Delia's sweet submission put on for the boy's benefit. Then his anger fled. The boy, he thought. I think of him as a boy. He must be just about Delia's age. Children, both of them.

He smiled and kissed Delia's perfect cheek. 'Stay as long as you like, darling. It is indeed a beautiful night.'

He went back to the stateroom, crawled wearily into the supremely comfortable bed, and prepared for a long night. He tried to read, but after lying for half an hour without turning a page, he gave up, turned off the light, and simply waited.

The sky and the sea had taken on their pearly predawn hues before Delia crept back into the cabin and John could at last sleep.

The next day they arrived at their first port of call, Santorini. They had docked long before Delia awoke, and she was cross when John brought her coffee.

'Always you wake me before I am ready! I do not want to get up. I am sleepy!'

'We're at Santorini, darling. I didn't want you to miss it. We're here only through the afternoon, you know.'

'What does one do at this place?'

'It's not so much a place to do as to see. There really are the most beautiful churches, all white outside, with blue domes, and ancient mosaics inside, icons, you know, and the views all over the island...'

He had lost her, he could see. She turned over and buried her face in the pillow.

'Later. Perhaps.'

He poured the coffee away, made sure he had his passport and camera, and gently closed the door behind him.

The island was as beautiful as he remembered from past visits. He found a taverna a bit off the beaten track that wasn't overrun with tourists, and had a tiny cup of coffee so dark and strong it furred the tongue, and a pastry with nuts and honey. He sat thinking until the place became crowded and his seat was needed.

Wandering aimlessly, he found himself in front of the most famous of Santorini's many churches, Panagia Episkopi. He paused, and then went inside.

He got back to the ship just in time; he had wandered farther than he had realized. Delia was not in the stateroom, so after a quick shower he went looking for her. He found her in the bar, surrounded by men. She was flirting, laughing, singing a phrase or two now and then.

She was having a wonderful time. John stayed at the edge of the room for a moment, and then quietly went back to the room and ordered a whisky and soda. He was sitting nursing it when Delia opened the door to their sitting room.

'There you are, John! You were away all day. Did you have a good time?' Delia whisked into the room and began to pull off her bright orange blouse.

'Sit down for a moment, Delia. We have plenty of time to dress for dinner.'

'But it is tonight the Captain's cocktail party, and I must look wonderful!'

'Please sit down.'

There it was again, his iron face. She shrugged and

flounced down into a plush armchair, swinging one bare
foot impatiently.

'Delia, why did you marry me?'

The foot stopped. 'What do you mean?'

'What I say. I want to know why you married me. You
don't care about the things that interest me. You find
me boring. You prefer the company of younger men. I
don't blame you for any of these things, but I would like
to know why you wanted me.'

'Because I wanted to be your wife, of course!'

'Yes, you wanted to be my wife. You pursued me. I
didn't see it at the time, but I do now. Don't lose your
temper, my dear. It's true and we both know it's true, so
there's no point in making a scene about it.'

He had never talked to her like this before. She didn't
like it, and she didn't know how to cope with it. Naked
honesty was not her way of dealing with him. Her foot
started swinging again.

'I would like an answer, Delia.' And then suddenly
he knew. 'It was the music, wasn't it? Your real passion.
Not me, the music.'

'All right! Yes!' She sprang to her feet. 'You are a
famous conductor. I was an unknown singer. Now the
world begins to know me. I am good, and I get better
all the time. This you have helped me do!'

He had not thought the pain would be so great. He
had thought she had killed his love for her. It was a moment before he could say, very gently and quietly, 'Do
you want a divorce, my dear? Now that I've given you
the start you wanted?'

'Divorce! No! Not ever! It would make a scandal!
And besides…' She stopped abruptly.

'Ah.' He paused again, until he had his voice under
control. 'I see. I am your security. You don't make

enough money yet to support yourself, at least not…'
He made a gesture that took in their luxurious surroundings.

'You married me! You made promises. Now you wish
to break your promises, to throw me out on the street?'
She stamped her foot. 'Never will I allow you to do this!'

John struggled to remain calm. 'I will not throw you
out on the street. I will, and I do, ask you to remember
that you, too, made some promises.'

'I have been faithful to you! Do not dare to accuse
me—'

He held up his hand and, amazingly, she stopped
in mid-tantrum. 'Technically, perhaps, you have been
faithful to me. In every other way you have shown me,
and everyone else, how little you care for me.' Again he
struggled for control. 'Delia, we made a bad bargain,
you and I. I believed I could bring you to love me. You
believed you could endure me for the sake of what you
wanted: wealth and fame. We were both wrong.'

He waited for her to speak. She was silent.

'I made a decision this afternoon, Delia. We can't go
on this way. I don't care for divorce, but if you wanted
one, I was prepared to give it to you. Since you don't,
there is another solution. It is best if we live separately.
When we get home, I will take steps to set up a legal
separation.'

She opened her mouth, her colour rising. Again he
held up his hand, and again she subsided.

'I will make sure you have enough to live comfortably. Not, perhaps, as comfortably as we have been living, but well enough. You will soon earn enough to
make up the difference, and we will both be much happier living apart.' He stood. 'Now, we won't talk about

it any more tonight. Go and get dressed for the Captain's party, my dear, and enjoy yourself.'

Without a word she turned and went into the bedroom, slamming the door behind her.

TWO

THEY AVOIDED EACH other at the Captain's party. It was not the sort of entertainment that John enjoyed. He knew no one on board, except Delia, and she was, as usual, the centre of an admiring crowd of men. John sat at a distant table, sipping at a very pale drink made with inferior whisky, and heartily wished this ill-conceived voyage were over.

'Who is that girl, anyway?' A middle-aged woman garbed in unflattering sequins sat down at the table. American by accent, she was in a belligerent mood.

She is my wife. John didn't say it. 'I believe she is a singer of some fame.'

'Hmph! A hussy, that's what she is. And if that's an old-fashioned word, it's the right one, anyway. Every young man on the boat's buzzing around her like bees to honey.'

'She is very beautiful,' said John neutrally.

'Beautiful is as—What was *that*?'

A hard shudder rattled the room. John's glass slid off the table and crashed to the floor. The string quartet in the corner, inaudible until now over the party babble, continued with a few wavering chords and then stopped playing.

A man in uniform stepped up to the microphone. 'Ladies and gentlemen, the Captain has asked me to make his apologies. He has gone to the bridge to see what is the matter. Though it's unlikely in the extreme that there is any danger, he asks you all to remain calm, return to your cabins, and wait for further instructions. I'm sorry to say that dinner may be slightly delayed, but please help yourself to more hors d'oeuvres on your way out of the room.'

That light-hearted remark did much to allay the passengers' fears. There was a good deal of 'But what's happened?' and general grumbling, but John's trained ear didn't pick up the rising note that would indicate panic.

The woman who had spoken to him about Delia had vanished, presumably back to her cabin as requested. John looked around for Delia, but couldn't find her in the crowd that was heading for the rapidly emptying hors d'oeuvre tables and then for the doors.

He hesitated, then headed for the stairs. Delia was not easily frightened, and she could make her way back to the stateroom without him. He only hoped she had the sense to take the stairs. The lifts were going to be in heavy use.

As he passed them, however, he saw that stewards were directing everyone to the stairs. 'A precaution, ladies and gentlemen, only a precaution. In case the electrical service might be temporarily interrupted.'

John felt the first pang of unease. Under what circumstances might the electrical service be interrupted? A fire?

Nonsense. Something untoward had probably happened in the engine room. A misbehaving engine might very well make a shudder like that, and since the engines presumably generated the electricity, they might have to shut it off for a moment or two.

He went up a few steps and then turned to take another look around for Delia. Ah, there she was! She was still in the ballroom, still surrounded by admirers. They were shepherding her toward the stairs. She seemed reluctant to go. He waved to try to catch her attention, but she was laughing and talking and didn't see him.

He went on up to the stateroom, where they had a balcony. He opened the door and went out.

There was a good deal of shouting on deck, which increased John's anxiety by another notch. The crew on a luxury cruise ship did not shout. He could see nothing amiss, except that the ship seemed to have stopped, but on reflection, he went back into the room and quickly changed from his dress suit into slacks and a warm sweater. Then he went to the closet and, feeling more than a little foolish, took out two life jackets.

He wished Delia would come. Probably she'd be there in a few minutes.

He stepped across to the stateroom door, and stumbled. Surely there had been a bit of a lurch? That was odd. They weren't moving.

But they *were* moving. John watched as the carafe of ice water slid slowly across the bedside table, stopping against the low barrier that edged the table.

An alarm sounded, a hideous electronic noise that penetrated to his very soul. After a moment it stopped and a voice came over the public address system.

'This is the captain speaking. All passengers are to bring life jackets and report to the boat deck immediately. Repeat: all passengers report to the boat deck with life jackets immediately. Do not put on your life jacket until you reach the boat deck. This is not a drill. Repeat: this is not a drill.'

Feeling disoriented and somehow empty, John took one more look from his balcony. The crew members were still shouting, but this time their shouts were purposeful. They were removing the covers from the lifeboats and preparing to launch them. And as John watched, the boat gave another lurch. It was now noticeably listing to port.

Where was Delia? Frantically he tried to decide what to do. Wait here for her? Take her life jacket and try to find her?

She had heard the announcement. Would she come back here or head straight for the boat deck? There were extra life jackets, weren't there?

Another lurch made him realize there was no time to waste. He took the pad by the bedside table, wasted precious moments searching for the pen, which had rolled off, and quickly scribbled: 'Delia. Gone to boat deck. Have your jacket. Come at once!'

He affixed it to the door with one of the brooches from her jewel box and hurried to the stairs.

He thought he'd never get down to the boat deck. The metal stairs from his deck were in truth little more than the ladders they were officially called, and they were jammed with people. Many had ignored instructions and donned their life jackets, and were having trouble manoeuvring the bulk through tight places. It didn't help that the treads were tilting markedly, and many of the women still had on their high heels.

Stewards did their best to keep the crowd moving, but now that high note of hysteria was beginning to sound clearly. *God help us*, John said under his breath, not certain whether it was exclamation or prayer.

'I can't!' It was a shrill scream, coming from the woman in front of him. She was, he saw, the woman who had spoken with him at the party. She was at the head of the ladder down to the boat deck, and she was paralyzed with fright.

'Here, I'll help you,' he said, with all the calm he

could muster. 'Take off your shoes. It'll be easier. And I'll be right behind you. I won't let you fall. Is your life jacket fastened securely? Then I'll hold on to the back straps. You won't fall.'

It meant he had to put on his own. He couldn't carry it, hold the railing, and hold the woman at the same time. It also meant he must drop Delia's life jacket.

He gave a despairing look around for her, but the scene by now was utter chaos. The crew was having trouble lowering the lifeboats on the starboard side, with the ship now listing heavily to port.

He took a firm grasp of the woman's life jacket and followed her, cajoling, soothing, talking her down the ladder.

Once on the deck, he was at a loss. The passengers were being loaded on to the boats as fast as it could be managed. Many were refusing to board. The boats certainly didn't look very safe, hanging as they now did against the side of the ship. How could they be safely lowered to the water?

And he couldn't board yet. He must find Delia.

'This way, sir.'

'I can't. My wife—'

'Someone will look after your wife. There's no time, sir! She's going down!'

'You don't understand! I must—'

And then the lights went out.

Screams. Panic. The press of bodies. The stink of fear. Then…nothing.

PART ONE

Ten years later

ONE

'How WOULD YOU like to go to a Welsh music festival?'

'An eisteddfod? Or however you pronounce it. I find the Welsh language even more difficult than most Celtic tongues.'

Nigel grinned. 'Well, you're close, except that double d is pronounced *th* and the *f* is a *v*.' He pronounced it correctly.

It was the hard *th* as in *them* and *there*. 'Ice-teth-vawd,' I imitated tentatively.

'Yes, well…anyway, this isn't a real eisteddfod I'm inviting you to. They focus on solo competitions, largely, and include a good deal of poetry reading. Usually in Welsh.' He grinned again, more broadly, at the expression on my face. 'No, this one is much more to your taste, I'd think. There'll be music of all kinds, solo and ensemble, but it isn't a competition, just a festival. It's in aid of the RNLI—'

'What's that?' I interrupted.

'Sorry, the Royal National Lifeboat Institution. You know, the ones who do sea rescue.'

'Okay, yes, I just didn't know what they were called. And I still find it odd that that's a charity here. Back in the States the Coastguard does that. But go ahead. A festival to raise money for the RNLI…'

'*And* it's to be held in a castle, an honest medieval castle, not one of your Victorian fakes.'

'Well, that seals our fate,' said Alan. 'Dorothy is totally unable to resist castles. When is this extravaganza to take place? We'll need to decide what to do about Watson.'

We were sitting in our parlour after dinner, Alan and I, Nigel Evans, his wife Inga and little Nigel Peter, our godson. Rising three, he had been almost too active throughout our meal, but was now contentedly asleep on the hearthrug, guarded by Watson, our mostly-spaniel, and the two cats Samantha and Esmeralda. The fire, which had kept the blustery February night outside where it belonged, had died down to pleasantly glowing coals, and I was feeling cosy and comfortable.

Inga responded to Alan. 'It's not until June, but we need to reserve seats for you now, if you plan to go. Oh, I do hope you will! You see, there's to be a selection of opera scenes, not staged, of course, but a concert version. And Nigel won't tell you himself, so I have to say it for him, he's to be the tenor soloist.'

'Oh, Nigel! Congratulations!'

Colour rushed into his face. Nigel may have inherited his formidable musical ability from his Welsh father, but his colouring and his temperament sprang mostly from his English mother. 'It'll be fun. Now, it's for a week, and I'm afraid Watson can't come. We'll all be staying at a perfectly lovely B&B called Tower Wales, quite near Flint Castle where the festival is being held. The Wynne-Eytons, who own the place, have several dogs of their own, and one never knows…'

'Indeed.' I hesitated. 'Maybe we should find a place where we could take him?'

'You'd have to leave him behind all day, Dorothy,' said Alan sensibly. 'One can hardly take a dog to a concert. Particularly one that sings along.'

For it was Watson's occasional habit to show his appreciation of music by howling loudly. Nigel cleared his throat, took a deep breath, and launched into *Nessun dorma*, perhaps the most famous tenor aria of them all. Neither the baby nor the cats paid the slightest attention. Watson stirred, cocked an ear, opened his eyes, and gave voice.

'Nigel, stop! Between the two of you, you'll wake the baby!' Inga's indignant voice stopped Nigel mid-note.

'Okay, okay, you've made your point,' I said, laughing. 'So tell us what this place is like.'

'You'll like it, Dorothy.' Inga took Nigel's hand to show she forgave him for showing off. 'You Americans are all potty about old places, and Tower is over five hundred years old. It's a fortified border house, if you know what that is.'

I turned to Alan.

'They go back to the days when the Welsh and the English were on rather unfriendly terms,' he began. 'You know about Edward the First and his campaigns?'

'No, but I'll look it up, or you can tell me later. Give me the pared-down version.'

Alan sighed histrionically. 'Very well. The Welsh living along the border in troubled times built strongly fortified houses, to defend themselves against the rapacious English. I had thought that most of them were ruined long ago.'

'They were,' Inga replied. 'Almost all except this one, which is perfectly preserved. It really is quite interesting. The walls in the oldest part, the tower itself, are five feet thick. You can't use your mobile or Wi-Fi! And the great hall has a nice grisly bit of history. The house is not far from Chester, on the other side of the border, and in some century or other there was a little disagreement with the mayor of Chester, who was promptly hanged in the great hall.'

Alan raised his eyebrows. 'I trust he does not disturb the present occupants?'

'I've never heard any stories,' said Nigel, with that casual acceptance of the idea of ghosts that I find so typically British, 'and we've neither seen nor heard him when we've stayed there.'

'Darn,' I said mildly. 'A ghost would have made it perfect, but I guess we'll just have to do without. Give us the dates, and get us festival tickets, and we'll make arrangements about the animals.'

NIGEL AND INGA kept us apprised of the festival programme as it developed, and in April gave us copies of the beautifully printed brochure. 'Good heavens,' I said, scanning the cover page. 'Sir John Warner! Nigel, I'm even more impressed that you're a part of this. You never told us he was the organizer.'

'We wanted to save that for a nice surprise,' he said.

For Sir John was in the very first rank of English choral conductors, right up there with Stephen Cleobury and John Rutter. His knighthood was recent, but I had gathered that, among his fellow musicians, he was felt to have earned it long ago. 'He's amazing. After that terrible accident, when he lost his wife and nearly died himself, to come so far…'

'He is the most sensitive conductor I've ever worked with,' said Nigel with enthusiasm. 'And a truly fine person to boot.'

'I didn't know you had worked with him. You never sang with the Camerata of London, did you?'

'No, but I knew him at King's, and he's been guest conductor for a few concerts with choral societies here and there. I've sung with him twice. He knows exactly the sound he wants, and knows how to get it. Firm but so good that one doesn't mind being bossed.'

'And I suppose you soloed for him, and that's how you got picked for this festival.'

'Not at all! At least, yes, I did a solo or two, and he did mention that the festival was coming up and a quartet was needed, and told me about the auditions. But the auditions were blind. I mean, he didn't just choose singers he liked…'

He trailed off, in danger of saying something that sounded like self-praise. The English half coming out again. I tactfully went back to the brochure. 'Oh, they're doing the "Lord Nelson Mass"! That's one of my favourites. I do love the Haydn Masses. And ending with a real barn-burner, *Carmina Burana*. And the opera bits, let's see… *Lucia*, *Barber*, *Butterfly*, *Traviata*, *Carmen*— an embarrassment of riches! And that wonderful chorus from *Nabucco*, too. I think that's one of the loveliest bits of all opera. Haunting.'

Nigel began singing it softly. '*Va, pensiero…*' And I, whose Italian is limited to terms like *al dente*, hummed along happily until he stopped in the middle. 'This is where it goes into parts, and I'm afraid I know only the tenor, which sounds rather strange by itself.'

'You really are a wonderful singer, Nigel. Are the other soloists as good as you?'

'Oh, I'm sure they're splendid. I've not met any of them yet, but they all have great reputations.'

I looked at the names, none of them familiar to me. 'Well, if they're all that good, the festival must have a pretty healthy budget.'

Nigel turned slightly pink and muttered something about the money not being the important part, from which I gathered that his own stipend might not be terribly impressive. Well, he was an amateur, after all. Very talented, and well trained at King's College years ago, but a computer specialist, not a professional singer who made his living that way. I let the subject drop. 'Will Sir John bring his wife and family, do you think?'

'The twins are a bit young for concerts, only Nigel Peter's age, and I don't know that Lady Cynthia will want to leave them with the nanny for a whole week. Then there's her own career. She's a pianist, you know, and is off doing her own thing quite a lot of the time. I think the family sometimes do travel with him, but they stay out of the limelight. She might come for a concert or two. You'd enjoy meeting her, I think. She's very pleasant.'

'Then we'll hope she can come.' I went back to perusing the programme of delights that would be in store in a couple of months.

JUNE CAME AT LAST. We'd had a cold, wet spring, and I'd despaired of summer ever breaking through, but when it came, it came in splendour. '"What is so rare as a day in June?"' I declaimed as we packed the car with luggage for a two-week stay in Wales.

'Is that a question or a quotation?' asked Alan mildly.

'A quotation. As you knew perfectly well, since I spout it regularly at this time of the year. James Russell Lowell, American poet, nineteenth century,' I added, the schoolteacher in me holding forth. 'And one of my father's favourite lines.'

'Your father had a point. Days like this are indeed rare. Especially in England.'

'Now, now! You're the one who's always telling me that I slander English weather!'

Nigel, who with Inga had gone a week earlier for rehearsals, had given us detailed directions for Tower Wales, our B&B just outside the unfortunately named Welsh town of Mold. We stopped for supper at a pleasant pub in Chester, near the Welsh border, and then drove through the long summer evening to find our beds for the next ten days.

We had called ahead to say we were on our way, and when we got to the top of the long drive, Nigel and Inga were waiting for us by the open gate. 'You can park around back once you've unloaded your things, but we wanted you to see the front of the house first thing,' said Inga. 'We think it's rather nice.'

Her dimple was much in evidence. I realized she was teasing me.

'"Rather nice" indeed! It's magnificent, and you know it!'

'Ah, but you know we English don't tend toward the superlative.' We all laughed, and she said, 'All right, it's brilliant. That's the oldest bit there, the part with the five-foot walls.' She pointed to the square tower to the left of the front door. 'Mid-1400s, but they don't know exactly when. Just drive on through, and you can meet Charles and Mairi. They'll tell you all about it. We'll close the gate and be right behind you.'

The Wynne-Eytons were graciousness personified, welcoming us to their home with as much warmth as if we'd been friends for years. After we'd been shown to our room, next to Nigel and Inga's in that amazing square tower, Charles said, 'I'd be happy to show you around the house, if you like, but I imagine you'd rather wait until morning for that?'

We agreed. It had been a long day.

'And breakfast?'

Nigel said, 'The rehearsals tomorrow are all orchestral, so I've got the day off, and I've an idea for a little excursion you two might enjoy. If we got a fairly early start...'

Alan nodded. 'Breakfast at nine, then?'

We took the time to unpack, and exclaim a bit over our large and elegant bedroom and Gothic-arched bathroom, before tumbling exhausted into the superbly comfortable bed. My last thought before sleep overtook me was how utterly still and peaceful the country was.

TWO

BREAKFAST WAS ONE of those calorie-and-cholesterol-laden feasts that I've come to expect in a first-class English hostelry. Of course this one was Welsh, but the menu was much the same. Mairi served us and explained that Charles was the grill cook and also made the marmalade, which was far and away the best I'd ever tasted.

'So what is this expedition you have planned for us?' I asked Nigel when I'd eaten enough to choke a horse, or at least a Great Dane. I poured myself another cup of excellent coffee and furtively spread another piece of toast with butter and marmalade.

'Have you ever travelled on the inland waterways?'

'The canals? No. Alan and I have thought about it, but navigating the locks and all sounds a little complicated.'

'Well, you're going to today. On a tour boat out of Llangollen.'

I couldn't begin to reproduce the way Nigel pronounced that name, and I didn't intend to try. It seemed to involve a lot of sounds that don't exist in English.

'A tour?' Alan raised one eyebrow. 'We're not overly fond of tours, being averse to being herded around with a lot of other people.'

'It's not like that,' said Nigel, and Inga nodded. 'This one is special. Actually, the boat goes *to* Llangollen, not from. It starts at...' He patted his pockets. 'Oh, I have it here someplace. At any rate, you board the boat, and it takes you to Llangollen through some very pretty country, but the exciting part is, you go over the oldest and highest aqueduct in Britain. You see, the canal crosses the River Dee, but at a height of almost a hundred and thirty feet, and you won't believe how odd it feels to be in a boat that far up in the air.'

'But…is it safe? I mean, if it's a couple of thousand years old…'

Alan roared at that, and Nigel and Inga laughed somewhat more politely.

'What's so funny?' I said indignantly. 'I know the Romans were wonderful builders and all that, but surely—'

'The Romans weren't the only ones who built aqueducts, dear heart,' said Alan, still chuckling. 'They were very popular with Victorian engineers as well, and many have been converted into railway bridges. I seem to remember, Nigel, that this one is a Telford creation?'

So I got a history lesson, all about the famous Victorian engineer Thomas Telford and his iron bridges that everyone said would never stand, hailed now as the work of genius—and still standing. This one, which rejoiced in the totally unpronounceable name of the Pontcysyllte Aqueduct, was well over 200 years old and still structurally sound and in daily use.

'All right, I'm game, as long as you don't make me try to say it,' I said when they had finished lecturing me. 'But when this trip is over and we're back home, I swear I'm going to make the Welsh a gift of a large package of vowels.'

Before we took off for the day, while Inga and Nigel made their daily call home to check on their son, Charles showed us over the house. It wasn't large, as country houses go. None of your Blenheim Palace, with its acres of elaborate rooms, or even Chartwell. No, this was a home, comfortable, easy to navigate—and something over 500 years old.

'I understand from Nigel that you don't know exactly when the house was built,' I said when he had showed us the great hall of mayor-hanging fame.

'No, unfortunately my ancestors didn't keep proper records, or else they've been lost over the years. We're not even sure when the various bits were added on, though we're trying to find out. It's a fascinating quest, if rather frustrating.'

We talked a little about the difficulties of living in an old house and trying to keep it in good repair. Ours, at least a hundred years younger than this one, presents new problems almost weekly, but we wouldn't live anywhere else.

Nigel was trying to curb his impatience, without much success. So we piled into his car and took off for Llangollen.

I had heard for years about the Welsh mountains. I'm afraid I'd been somewhat condescending about them. When you're from a country that boasts the Rockies, you tend to designate as hills anything short of the Alps. I had assumed that the Welsh mountains were like our Smokies: pretty, but low, rounded, old.

I was drastically wrong. Nigel drove us over something called Horseshoe Pass (which sounds like it should belong in the American West), and I was blown away. 'But these are *real* mountains! Rugged, sharp, high… and absolutely beautiful!'

'Yes, we thought you might enjoy the view,' said Inga sedately from the back seat. 'This is a bit out of our way, but we had some idea you didn't quite understand about these mountains.'

I turned around and stuck my tongue out at her.

It didn't take us long after that to reach Llangollen, a town that would have been lovely if it hadn't been quite so crowded.

'Goodness! Wall to wall people! What's the big attraction?'

'A big international Eisteddfod is held here every year?' Inga's inflection made a question of it, and I nodded to indicate that I knew that.

'Well, it's to be only a few weeks from now, about a month, I think, so lots of people are here for the preparations.'

'It's a huge festival, you know, quite unlike our little one,' said Nigel. 'A lot of folk music of various kinds, country dance, poetry, that sort of thing. But all sorts, really, from pop to classical. One year they did bits of *Noye's Fludde*. It was brilliant!'

I know the Britten opera only by reputation, but I tried to look intelligent.

'And highly competitive,' Nigel went on. 'Groups and soloists come from all over the world. I think last year something like forty countries were represented. Ours is small beer by comparison.'

'Not from what you tell me about the musicians,' I said firmly.

Nigel found, at last, a place to park the car, and we strolled the crowded streets, glancing in the shops and admiring the gardens and listening to the many languages and accents among the passers-by.

'There's a café in Paris, on the Rue de la Paix, I believe, of which it used to be said that if one sat there long enough, the whole world would pass by.' I gestured around us. 'Not quite Paris, but a pretty fair sampling of the whole world, wouldn't you say?'

The booking office for the canal boat rides was at the

top of a steep hill. Nigel planted the three of us at a hotel restaurant near the bottom of the climb. 'Look, we've lashings of time, and I don't know about you, but I'm starving. Why don't I nip up and get the tickets while you lot order lunch? Anything will do for me, Inga.'

'Right. Off you go.'

We had a pleasant, if unremarkable lunch. The dessert trolley was, however, laden with temptations, and after I had made my way through some sort of delectable steamed pudding (called on the menu 'Pwdin Eryri', whatever that may be), I staggered to my feet and said, 'Nigel, it was sweet of you to get our tickets, but I do think it would have been easier to climb that hill *before* lunch.'

'But you see, we don't have to climb the hill. We wait down here, just the other side of the street, for the bus that takes us to the embarkation point. A bit convoluted, I know, but I gather there's not a large car park at that end.'

Alan nodded in acquiescence, so I hid my shrug. I ought to have learned by now that they do things somewhat differently on this side of the pond. A bus ride to take a boat ride to get back where you started. Okay.

We hadn't long to wait for the bus, and the ride was quite pleasant, through beautiful country. Several of the passengers seemed to know each other; there was a good deal of conversation and laughter at the back. It didn't take long to get to the place where we were to catch the boat, and as we had been the last to board the bus, we were first off, and therefore first to board the boat.

It was an interesting craft. Barely wide enough to seat two plus one across, with a narrow aisle, it had windows on both sides and at the front (the prow, I suppose), with a minute sort of refreshment bar at the back, opposite the door. We were put aboard in what seemed like an odd fashion, with empty seats between passengers, until I realized that a small boat had to be balanced, side to side and front to back. But eventually all had boarded and we took off.

After a brief announcement about the available refreshments, the man at the microphone left the passengers to get acquainted, and we began to look around. Nigel knew several of the other passengers.

'Well, not to say *know*, but I recognize them. That chap over there is in the chorus for the *Va, pensiero*. Fine baritone; he'll make a soloist one day. Those two women near the tea bar are in the *Carmen* chorus, and there's about a row of Haydn sopranos back there by the door.'

'Hmm. I'll expect you all to break into the "Skye Boat Song" any minute now.'

With a mischievous look Nigel stepped into the aisle and stood up. 'Good afternoon to you all and especially to my fellow musicians. There are quite a number of us, and though we've rehearsed various pieces, there are two I'm sure we all know. In English or Welsh, your choice. First our famous hymn.' He hummed a few bars of the end, paused a beat and then launched into the great Welsh hymn that I know as 'Guide Me, O Thou Great Jehovah'.

The Welsh have a great choral tradition. Their men's choirs are famous throughout the world, and this particular hymn, written by a Welshman, has become sort of an 'anthem' at rugby games. I remember it well from William and Kate's wedding, and hearing it sung in four-part harmony by those beautiful, well-trained voices, some using the English words and some the Welsh, brought a lump to my throat. Many of the other passengers joined in, but I couldn't get out a single note.

Then, after a pause, Nigel sang three notes, and the group began the most famous Welsh song of them all, 'All Through the Night'.

That time I had to root in my handbag for tissues.

When they had finished, Nigel turned back to see the passing scene, and I took a few last sniffs and wiped my eyes. 'Nigel, that was so lovely! All that gorgeous harmony!'

'Yes, well, I just wish there were a little more harmony in rehearsals.'

'They're not going well? I would have thought musicians of this calibre...'

'Oh, it's not the music, exactly. That's going well enough, although there was more enthusiasm shown just now than we've had in rehearsal. It's...undercurrents. I don't know what's going on, but there's tension—'

He was interrupted by our guide. 'We've all enjoyed the music, friends, but now I want to draw your attention to some points of interest.' He went on to talk amusingly about the canal, the rules of the 'road', and some of the passing scene.

'We've enough musicians on board that you'll be interested in this next house, on your right. It's been turned into a luxury hotel, and was the favourite place for Luciano Pavarotti to stay when he came to these parts. Pavarotti and his bed, that is. He travelled with his own.'

'Given his size,' I whispered to Alan, 'I'll bet the innkeepers were delighted. Saved them broken springs.'

'And now, ladies and gentlemen, we come to the highlight of our trip, the passage over the Pontcysyllte Aqueduct. The aqueduct is one thousand and seven feet long and eleven feet wide, counting the towpath. It passes over the River Dee at a height of a hundred and twenty-six feet. It was completed in 1805, making it over two hundred years old, and is a World Heritage Site. We're not allowed to stop the boat as we go over, but we'll ask the skipper to slow her down as much as possible, so you can take pictures. Mind you don't drop the camera overboard!'

Many of the passengers stood, and the boat rocked a little. 'Careful, now,' said the guide. 'Perfectly good view out the windows; we can't have everyone at the door. Careful, there. Don't crowd!'

For despite his words, many of the younger passengers knotted around the door, which was open, with only a rope barring the way.

I clutched Alan's arm. 'Alan, they mustn't—there's no guard rail!'

There was a scuffle, a confusion of voices. A sound, something vaguely familiar…a scream, more screams.

The boat rocked as everyone rose and tried to see what had happened.

'Quiet, everyone!' The voice wasn't loud, but it was commanding. 'This is the skipper. There's been an accident. We'll stop as soon as possible, and meanwhile I'll push her as fast as is safe. Please sit down and remain seated until you're told you may move.'

'But what *happened*?' questioned voices all over the boat.

A pause. Voices from the front sounded like a private consultation between guide and skipper. Then the guide cleared his throat and told us in a shaky voice what we all, in our hearts, knew already. 'One of the passengers has fallen overboard. We know no more than that. Please be patient until we reach a stopping place.'

THREE

'WHAT HAPPENS NOW?' I asked Alan in an undertone.

'I'm not sure exactly what the procedures are in Wales,' he replied. 'In England it would be turned over to the local police, who would find and identify the victim and try to determine how he, or she, happened to fall.'

I shuddered. 'There's no chance at all, I suppose, that...'

'I'm afraid not, love. A fall of well over a hundred feet...'

'But the river was below. If he—she—whoever could swim...'

'The Dee is not terribly deep just here, my love. And it is very rocky.'

He took my hand in a comforting grip and we sat in silence until the skipper spoke again.

'We'll stop just ahead. There's no mooring, but the canal is wide enough there that we can pull to the side. I've phoned Llangollen to explain, and they'll stop our tour boats and phone the other companies. There's nothing to be done about private boats except stop them one by one.'

'But why must we stay here? Why can we not get on another boat and go on to...to wherever we are going?' It was a rich female voice, foreign in accent and peevish in tone, and others joined in her query.

'There has been an accident. Accidents must be investigated. The police will want to speak to anyone who might shed some light on the matter.' The skipper sounded weary, but very much in command. This might be only a small canal boat, but he was as much master of it as the captain of the *Queen Mary* was of that huge liner, and he intended to keep control of his passengers.

We bumped up against the side of the canal. Several of the passengers rose. Our guide, less genial than he had been before, reminded them rather sharply that they were to keep their seats. He also took a stance in the doorway (the hatch, I suppose it was properly called), with a muscular arm braced on either side.

'He doesn't intend to let any of the malcontents make a break for it, does he?'

'And quite right, too,' said Alan rather grimly. 'There are a good many foreigners on this boat, if I'm any judge of accents, and one never knows how they'll behave.'

It lightened the moment for me. In fact, I had to hide a smile. Alan is as free of prejudice as anyone I know, but at odd moments a Rule Britannia streak shows up. The English, even perhaps the Welsh, could be counted upon to behave themselves in a crisis and do as they were told. Denizens of other nations were unpredictable. Such was the faith that underlay his remark. I thought briefly about football riots, in contradiction of his theory, and then about the orderly throng that made its sedate way up the Mall after the wedding of William and Catherine, held back only by a few policemen, and decided that just perhaps he had a point.

Was it a pressing crowd of 'foreigners' that forced the poor soul out of the boat to his or her death?

The lighter moment passed. Who had fallen?

It must have been someone who was travelling alone, or a companion would be prostrated, and looking around, I saw no sign of that. Distress, of course. It was a terrible thing to witness. Some of the women were crying, and the men were sober, but I could see no evidence of personal grief. In fact, if I were to be uncharitable, some passengers seemed to be more upset by the ruination of their pleasant afternoon than the loss of someone's life.

The wait for the police seemed endless. We tried to make conversation, the four of us, but no one was in the mood for small talk. I did ask Nigel what effect, if any, this tragedy was going to have on the festival schedule. A trivial matter by comparison, but it was something to say.

'Probably none. We can hardly cancel at this late date, and really, there's no reason to. It's as if…as if we had seen a frightful road smash, with someone killed. Dreadful, but…'

'Yes, of course.'

'And rehearsals won't be interrupted if we can get back at some reasonable time this afternoon, or even this evening,' he went on. 'Sir John may have to spend a bit of time tomorrow calming everyone down. Musicians don't have the most tranquil of personalities, and as I said, a good number of the singers are on this boat.'

'And you also said, or implied, that there are problems already.'

'Yes, but nothing I can put my finger on. There's a feeling. For one thing, the mezzo hasn't shown up yet, so we've had to juggle the schedule. Small disagreements flare up into tempers. No one has actually stomped out of a rehearsal or thrown anything, but there was a moment or two when I thought it might happen.' He made a frustrated gesture. 'It's probably just my imagination.'

At that point a small group of people strode down

the footpath that bordered the canal. They were in plain clothes, but were quite obviously official.

'I believe,' I said to nobody in particular, 'that Her Majesty's Constabulary have arrived.'

After that things proceeded in fairly good order, if slowly. Every passenger's name had to be taken, along with address and other contact information. Everyone was questioned briefly about the accident. No one knew anything of importance, except those in the group that had gathered so disastrously around the door. And from the little I overheard of their responses, they were so confused and garbled as to be virtually useless. Summarized, they amounted to: 'We were trying to get a good look/good picture, but everyone was pushing, and then...'

We were among the last to speak to the police. Alan discreetly pulled out his warrant card and introduced himself. 'I've been retired for quite some time, of course, and I'm here on holiday and entirely as a private citizen. But if I can be of any help, of course I'll do what I can.'

'Thank you, sir. We'll bear that in mind,' said the officer who seemed to be in charge. It was apparent from his tone of voice that he had no intention of calling on Alan for anything whatsoever. Alan smiled and bowed, and moved us away from the little knot of people who remained.

'Well, that's that. One aches for the poor victim, and the family, if any, but as Nigel says, it's nothing to do with us, after all. I understand they've laid on transport back to Llangollen. So we should get back in good time for you to get your beauty sleep, Nigel. There are several good restaurants in Llangollen, I believe. Shall we try one of them for a spot of dinner?'

Nigel was inclined, over dinner, to be apologetic. I

was not about to put up with that. 'My dear boy, you couldn't possibly have predicted a bizarre accident like that! And it was a lovely trip until then. I'll never forget the views of the mountains. And the river in Llangollen, with those lovely rapids...' I trailed off. I was suddenly reminded of Alan's comment about the rocks in the River Dee, not something I wanted to think about just then.

We finished our meal quietly, drove back to Tower, and went to bed early and with great relief.

'BUT HE WAS one of ours!' Nigel looked up in great dismay from the paper he was reading at the breakfast table. 'The man who fell yesterday. He was in the chorus for the opera scenes, or at least some of them. Remember that baritone I told you about? Daniel Green was his name, I remember now.'

'Oh, Nigel! And you said he was really good, with maybe a career in front of him. What a pity! What happened, does it say?'

Nigel scanned the item again. 'No. Just "police are investigating". That sounds suspicious, wouldn't you say?'

He addressed the last remark to Alan, who made a rocking motion with one hand. 'Perhaps. Most likely they either don't want to commit themselves at this stage, or have some ideas they weren't eager to release to the press.'

'It seems peculiar to me,' said Nigel stubbornly. 'I mean, if it was just an accident why don't they say so? And if it wasn't—'

'Sorry to interrupt, darling,' said Inga, 'but if we don't start in five minutes you're going to be late for rehearsal, and you know how much Sir John appreciates latecomers.'

'Oh, Lord, is it that late?' Nigel pushed his chair back. 'Just let me brush my teeth and get my music, and I'm right with you. Alan, Dorothy, you're welcome if you want to come along.'

I looked at Alan. 'We might as well,' he said. 'You'll find the castle interesting, and we've always liked to listen to a concert taking shape. We'll take our own car, so if we get bored we can find something else to do.'

In this unfamiliar part of the world I had no better suggestion, so Alan got the car and pulled it up to the door behind Inga, and when Nigel flew out the front door, his hair in disorder and his shirt untucked, we waited until he had thrown himself into their car, and then followed.

'Do you know where we're going?' I asked Alan tentatively. 'Just in case we lose them?' I had no idea what kind of a driver Inga was. Some are courteous when being followed, driving fairly slowly, signalling, and so forth. Some emphatically are not.

'I know where Flint Castle is, certainly.' Alan's voice was edging toward annoyed. Although he is a most even-tempered man, he tends, like most of the male sex, to be testy about the matter of asking directions.

I sat back to enjoy the scenery. It was worth seeing. North Wales, where it is not mountainous, is rolling country, beautiful in its variety. I thought I saw a stone circle, or something of the kind, but before I could ask Alan to stop so we could take a look, he said, 'Drat!'

'What?'

'That's Flint Castle, just up ahead. And Inga and Nigel are nowhere to be seen. I lost them several curves back, but they were ahead of us until then.'

'Maybe they stopped somewhere, for gas or something.'

'In this country it's petrol, and I doubt it. I think we're

in the wrong place. I don't see anyone carrying instruments or the like.'

Woops! He was definitely getting a bit snappish. He very, very seldom corrects my English.

'Oh, dear. I suppose they didn't actually say the rehearsal was at the castle, did they? We just assumed. But look, Alan, what does it matter? I've heard about Welsh castles all my life, and this looks like a marvellous one. I like this better, to tell the truth. We can wander around at leisure with no rehearsal going on. We'll hear all the music later, anyway.'

'Are you trying to chivvy me into a better mood, wench?'

I grinned at him. 'Worked, didn't it? Let's buy tickets and a guidebook.'

Signs posted at the entrance informed us that the castle would be closed to visitors the following week, because of 'The First Annual North Wales Music Festival'. I always think it's pushing one's luck to call something the 'First Annual', because who knows what the future will bring? I kept my thoughts to myself and silently wished them all the best of British luck.

I had never seen a castle—a real castle—before. I had visited ruins, quite incomplete, but this was so complete as to make it almost possible to visualize it in its glory days. It still had a moat, though now water lilies and swans prettied it up and made it possible for one to forget its defensive purpose. The portcullis was long gone, but the slit through which it descended was still there.

The guidebook explained the elaborate, multiple systems of defence. Outer bailey, inner bailey, walkways on the outer walls, towers, arrow slits…

'Good heavens!' I said when I had absorbed some of the basics. 'The remarkable thing is that the defences were ever breached. I would have thought this place would be safe from anything except aerial attack.'

'And siege. Don't forget siege. If no one could get in, neither could anyone get out if the place was surrounded. An attacking force could starve them out.'

'But if they were prepared for a siege, with food stored away and a source of water...' I studied the plan of the castle provided in the guidebook. 'And look! There was a well, right there.' I pointed.

'You're right, to a degree. But there were forms of aerial attack, you know. No aircraft, but a good catapult could fling a fair-sized boulder over the walls, and then there were flaming arrows and the like.'

I shuddered. 'The capacity of man to invent diabolical instruments of destruction hasn't changed much over the years, has it? The technology is different today, but the will to annihilate is the same. Let's talk about something else. Did people actually live in this place? Those stone walls couldn't have done much to keep out the cold and damp.'

'There were fireplaces,' said Alan. 'See those recesses in the walls, there, and there? And of course the lord of the castle would have had furnishings to make his household at least minimally comfortable. Cushions, hangings to keep out drafts, shutters for the windows and later even glass. We might not have found it ideal, but they didn't do so badly for themselves. Shall we wander on?'

'Sure. I want to see the chapel.'

There was an arrow pointing the way, up a steep and narrow stairway edging a wall. I was willing to bet it had not had a railing back when the castle was in daily use, and was profoundly grateful that it had one now, especially since it leaned noticeably outward.

It led us to a narrow interior passage lit mostly by widely spaced arrow slits. Oh, there was an occasional electric light, but not enough to make me happy. I fought to stave off claustrophobic terror. There was, I kept telling myself, nothing to be afraid of. Alan was here, the passage wasn't going to close in on me, there was plenty of air to breathe.

We couldn't walk abreast, but I stayed so close behind Alan that I was in danger of stepping on his heels. After several centuries the passage widened out into a well-lit space. I took a few deep breaths. 'The chapel?' I said hopefully, though it certainly didn't look like one.

'A latrine,' said Alan, pointing to a sign on the wall. 'Sorry. Are you all right?'

'No, but let's push on. We're bound to get there eventually.'

'Why don't you go first? Is it better when you can see a clear space in front of you?'

'Marginally.' I gritted my teeth and moved out of the light.

'Aaaahhh!'

FOUR

'WHAT? WHAT IS IT, love? Are you all right?' Alan asked frantically.

I flailed wildly at my face and neck. 'A spider! There was a web, and I ran into it, and this huge spider...oh, Alan, can you see it? Did it get into my hair?'

I was trembling and my heart was racing. Alan pulled me close to him and held me with one arm while with the other he patted me down like an efficient policeman.

'It's all right, love. No spider. It's all right. Easy, dear heart. Here, let's go on to where it's lighter.'

Murmuring encouragement, he pushed me ahead, and finally, finally, we were in the ancient chapel, a place of light and peace and calm. There was a bench in front of the simple wooden table that served as the altar. I sank down on it and tried to catch my breath.

Alan waited patiently, his hand warm on my shoulder.

'I'm sorry,' I said finally. 'I didn't mean to make a fool of myself. Maybe there never was a spider. But there was definitely a web. It brushed my face, and...well, I wasn't quite myself anyway.'

'Don't worry. No one else was around, and I'll never think you a fool. Look, love, these walls were painted once. See the remnants?'

I appreciated Alan's attempt at distraction and tried to respond. There were certainly tiny flakes of colour still adhering to the walls. 'What a shame it's all gone. Do you suppose there was once stained glass in the windows?' The tiny lancet windows were still attractive with their simple, clear diamond panes.

'Probably. And a much more elaborate altar. It's remarkable, though, that this much has been preserved.'

I sat and let the peace replace my irrational fears, until a small group of tourists appeared and we left to make way for them. The way out, fortunately, was far less convoluted than the way in, and we were back on the grass of the inner ward.

'This must be where they're going to hold the festival,' I said, looking around. 'That sort-of window over there would serve as a perfect balcony for an antiphonal choir, or trumpet fanfares. But goodness, there's no shelter at all. What on earth are they going to do if it rains?'

'Carry on, I expect. We are rather renowned for that approach, you know.'

'Keep calm and carry on, as the wartime posters said. I want one of those T-shirts. But seriously, wouldn't the singers worry about their throats and the players about their instruments?'

'Perhaps, but...'

'Dorothy Martin?'

The accent was Canadian, the voice familiar. I turned around. 'Penny? What a pleasant surprise! What are you doing here?' Penny Brannigan, an ex-pat like me, had moved from Canada to a small Welsh village some years ago. We met when I dropped into her salon one day to have my first-ever manicure, and again while Alan and I were doing some walking in the Cotswolds.

'The same as you, I imagine,' she replied. 'Touring Welsh castles. This is a terrific one, isn't it? Lots of atmosphere. I even imagined I heard a bloodcurdling scream a few minutes ago. A ghost in the dungeons, no doubt.'

'Oh, dear.' I could feel my face growing warm. 'That was me. I'm an absolute idiot about spiders, and I thought I saw one. I know for certain there was a web.'

'Ooh! I hate spiders! I was shut up in an old basement once when I was a child, and it was full of them.' She shuddered. 'And the webs are just as bad. When they brush against your face…'

Alan's mobile tootled just then. He glanced at it, then answered. 'Ah, Nigel. We were beginning to wonder what had become of you two.' Pause. 'Yes, we gathered as much. No, we're having a fine time exploring Flint Castle. Are you going to have time for lunch?' Pause. 'Right. Give me directions, and I'll repeat them to Dorothy so she can write them down.'

He dictated Nigel's directions to a pub not far away. 'Penny,' he said courteously, 'we're about to have lunch with some friends. Will you join us?'

'Thanks, but I'm meeting someone for lunch, too. Great to see you again!'

We waved and made our way to the car park. I left the castle somewhat reluctantly, spider and narrow passages notwithstanding. Now that we were out in the sunshine, I was once more fascinated with the labyrinthine design of this remarkable structure, with its spaces for living and working and sleeping and praying, its massive defences, and its ability to withstand its enemies, except for the final and inexorable one of time.

'Let's come back after lunch,' I urged Alan as he looked for the way out. 'I want lots of time to explore this place.'

'Excepting the inner passageways, I presume?'

'We can buy a flashlight somewhere. Light helps a lot.'

When we met up with Nigel and Inga, everyone was full of explanations and apologies.

'I thought I'd said where we were rehearsing,' said Nigel. 'No, no, this round's on me. What's everyone having?'

The day had become very warm, so I opted for cold lager, the rest jeering at my American tastes, 'wanting every drink to freeze one's teeth'. I ignored them. 'So where are they in fact rehearsing?' I asked Inga, while Nigel and Alan went to the bar to get the beer and order our food.

'Well, they couldn't very well keep the castle closed to the public for two whole weeks, not in high tourist season, so Sir John, or his secretary probably, found a nice big parish church nearby. The acoustics are quite different from an outdoor venue, of course, but there's plenty of space, and there'll be mikes and speakers at the castle, so Nigel thinks it should work out. That's not the problem.'

'So what is? Thank you, Nigel.' I raised my glass in salute.

'You tell them, Nigel.'

He nodded, but first buried his face in his pint. 'Ahh! That's better. Good beer in this place. So Inga's been telling you about our prima donna, has she?'

'No,' I said, 'she's left the story to you. Tell.'

He downed another healthy swallow of beer. 'Well, you know I told you the mezzo hadn't got here when she was supposed to? She lives in South America some-where—Brazil, I think—and there was some problem about flights. Weather or something. Anyway, she's here now, so we're doing the opera scenes, without the cho-rus, just the quartet. And I personally think she'd have done us a favour by staying away.'

'Oh, dear. Why? Can't she sing?'

'Oh, she can *sing*.' Nigel finished his beer. 'She's not perfect, but who is? Lots of power, lots of drama, and she'll make a fantastic Carmen. What that woman doesn't know about sex…'

'Right,' said Inga, addressing her own beer.

'I see,' I said, somewhat amused. 'So she's flirting with all the men in the festival and alienating all the women?'

'Yes, but it isn't just that. I mean, one almost expects that sort of thing from her type. It doesn't mean anything. But Gracie—'

'*Gracie*? You're not telling me someone who can sing Carmen and incidentally set the whole festival on its ear is named Gracie!'

'Her name,' said Inga, deadpan, 'is Graciosa de la Rosa. I'm told the word means "enchanting" in Portuguese.'

'Not her real name, then?' I asked the question in all seriousness, but Nigel howled.

'Everything about her is unreal, right down to her fingernails! I don't know where the woman's from, originally. She's certainly of some Latin background; you've only to look at her. And she speaks English with a sort of all-purpose Latin accent, but even that might be put on. I'd bet my last vocal cord that her name is a Latina equivalent of Jane Smith. At any rate, "Graciosa" is absurd. So we call her Gracie. She hates it.'

'Which must improve her temper mightily,' said Alan. 'You're implying that no one in the company can bear her. What has she actually done to set you all against her in one morning?'

'Let me count the ways! She's still using music for some of her arias, and what she has memorized, she gets wrong. She takes her own tempo, whether or not it's what Sir John wants, and very sweetly says she "feeeels it" her way. She upstages everyone, and manages to ruin our sightlines to Sir John, so we miss some of the subtleties. We're not working with the orchestra yet, and she's managed to infuriate the pianist already.'

'I take it the pianist is a woman,' I suggested.

'Of course,' Inga murmured.

'Why doesn't Sir John simply sack her?' asked Alan. 'Oh, thank you.'

Our food had arrived, a ploughman's lunch for everyone, with local cheese that looked extremely inviting. We dug in, and no one spoke for a bit.

'More beer, anyone?' Nigel asked when he'd taken the edge off his hunger.

We all turned him down, I because beer makes me sleepy after lunch, the others because they were driving.

'I won't, then. Well, you ask, Alan, what we've been asking ourselves since ten minutes into the rehearsal. Which was when Gracie condescended to show up, by the way. Sir John is wonderful to work for, as I've said, but he is demanding. None of us can understand why he puts up with this...er...witch.'

Nigel has always had a tendency to watch his language around me. I find it charming, even though my own language can get a trifle salty now and again. 'So what *has* he done about all her mistakes?' I asked.

'Damn all, really,' said Inga crisply. 'He stops rehearsal and takes it again. And again, and again. Sometimes he'll make a mild comment like, "*Pianissimo*, please, Madame de la Rosa." Which she pays no attention to, of course. Mostly he just does it over and over until either she gets it right or he gives up and goes on.'

'Which,' said Nigel gloomily, 'has got our rehearsal

schedule even more wildly out of whack than it already was. So I'd best get back. Inga, are you coming with me, or do you want to go with Dorothy and Alan?'

'We're going back to the castle,' I said firmly. 'I haven't seen nearly enough of it yet. But we could run you back to the Tower, if…'

'Of course I'd love to see the castle with you. I've not really toured it myself, and today's our last chance before the festival takes over.' She gave Nigel a peck on the cheek. 'Good luck, darling. Stiff upper lip and all that!'

WE HAD A wonderful time at the castle. I decided to give the interior passages a miss, but there was certainly enough to see outside. We walked along the tops of the walls, where sentries would have patrolled back when the castle was a living fortress.

'You were going to tell me something about Edward the First,' I said suddenly, apropos of nothing.

Alan got that lecturing gleam in his eye. 'Yes. He's the reason most of the Welsh castles exist.'

'The Welsh built them to defend themselves against Edward?'

'Quite the opposite. Edward was waging campaigns against the Welsh. This was in the late thirteenth century, and Llywelyn—you know about Llywelyn?'

'Vaguely. Prince, or princeling, of at least part of Wales. Go on.'

'Well, Llywelyn was causing Edward lots of trouble, rebelling and so on, and Edward decided to put a stop to it once and for all. He mounted a huge army and quelled the rebellion, killing Llywelyn in the process. Then, to maintain his hold over Wales, Edward built castles at a great rate, impressive castles meant to keep the Welsh under his eye.'

'Under his heel, Nigel would say,' murmured Inga.

'That too,' Alan admitted. 'But some of the castles were never finished, and others were used by the English for a relatively short time, because Edward turned his attention to the troubles he was having with the Scots, on his other border, and those occupied him the rest of his life. So there you have it. Potted history of Edward the First. Probably wildly inaccurate. My school days are a long way behind me.'

'Most of it's in the guidebook,' said Inga with an impish grin.

'Hush, child! I must preserve my image. Dorothy thinks I know everything.'

I laughed rudely at that, and we walked on to the grassy expanse that, according to the signs, was once the banqueting hall.

'Inga, there's nothing much in the way of a roof anywhere. What are they going to do if it rains for the festival?'

'Tents. Big pavilions for the audience are easy, and they've found someone who can rig canopies over some of the performing areas. Nigel tells me they're going to use almost the whole castle, using the passages and stairs as entrances and exits, and that bit over there—' she pointed to the window I had already noticed—'for antiphonal effects. It should be quite splendid, really. If only that idiotic woman doesn't spoil it!'

FIVE

WE CONTINUED THE discussion over dinner. We'd decided to dine in style at The Stables Bar, the restaurant at a luxury country house hotel called Soughton Hall. 'Some of the more affluent musicians are staying here,' Nigel confided, 'including Sir John and his family. Inga and I actually prefer Tower, though. It's not only cheaper, but we're very fond of Charles and Mairi.'

'They're delightful people,' I agreed. 'But I wondered where the dogs were.'

'They keep them out of the way of guests,' said Inga, 'and this morning Mairi told me Judy has young puppies, so she's a bit skittish.'

'But I want to see the puppies!' I exclaimed. 'If Judy will let me. Nigel, is Sir John here?'

He looked around the crowded room. 'In the corner, there, with the woman and the two small children.'

'Oh, but they're adorable!' I exclaimed. The children were dressed in pale blue, the little boy in shorts and a soft white shirt, the girl in the same shirt, with a blue skirt and a blue bow in her hair.

'They are, aren't they?' said Inga softly, and I knew she was thinking about Nigel Peter.

The twins had been so well behaved that I hadn't noticed their presence earlier, but it was late for such young children to be up, and the boy was beginning to fuss.

The two parents worked together like a smooth team.

The mother spoke gently to the little girl, pointing out something of interest in the room, while Sir John picked up the boy and hoisted him on to his shoulders. 'Shall we go for a ride?' I heard him say, and the two of them made for the door, while the woman and girl followed hand in hand.

They passed near our table, and I got a good look at Sir John. He looked infinitely weary, though when he turned to answer a remark from his son, he made an effort to smile.

Alan saw it, too. 'Did rehearsals go any better this afternoon?' he asked Nigel.

'Worse, if anything. All the soloists are demoralized. We missed our cues, forgot the words, and lost our tempers. Sir John was positively haggard by the time he finally turned us loose. We were an hour late, and that's going to cost the festival quite a lot, even though the instrumentalists weren't with us. Tomorrow we have dress rehearsals, with orchestra and chorus, and it's going to be bloody. Sorry, Dorothy, but I meant that almost in the literal sense as well.'

'He certainly looked haggard just now, and it surprised me. He seemed so happy a moment before, with those delightful kids. And you didn't tell me his wife was pregnant.'

'I didn't know. That's probably one reason why she's with him on this jaunt. She's fairly far along, isn't she? He probably didn't want to leave her. He's besotted with his family, or so the gossip has it. But he's definitely worried about the festival. If there isn't some sort of blow-up before it's all over, I'll be very much surprised.'

'Hmm,' said Alan thoughtfully. 'Has any security been arranged?'

Nigel looked startled. 'I hardly think so. This isn't a football match. One doesn't expect a scrum at a performance of *The Creation*!'

'Perhaps not,' said Alan, 'but I think Dorothy and I will take in the final rehearsals. They should be interesting, at the very least. Are you still in the church tomorrow, while they get the castle ready for you?'

'No, we really have to do these last ones at the castle, to get comfortable in the space and work out technical problems.'

'Not to mention personnel problems,' I muttered as our dinners arrived.

THE LOVELY WEATHER broke next day. Alan and I looked out our window and could see nothing of the hills, only the pond, dimpled with raindrops, and the trees, blowing madly in the wind. Nigel was depressed and silent at breakfast, so we let him alone, but I couldn't help wondering how much shelter tents and canopies would provide in a gale.

The castle, when we got there, was the scene of barely controlled chaos. The wind had indeed torn ropes from their moorings, and canvas flapped wildly as shouting crews attempted to subdue it. Electrical cables snaked everywhere, posing hazards for unwary walkers, and musicians wandered about looking lost while stagehands set up chairs and risers and music stands that kept falling over in the wind. Shouting, a good deal of swearing, and the scrapes and tootles of instrumentalists trying to tune and warm up competed with the howl of the wind and the crash of flying objects in an almost solid wall of noise.

'Nigel, this is impossible!' I shouted against the clamour. 'Nobody can rehearse in this!'

He simply nodded and went off in search of someone who might know what was happening.

Alan pointed the way under the main gate, which still had a roof and provided some shelter from the stinging rain. Of course a lot of the others had the same idea, and the space was crowded with disgruntled musicians. Above the other voices rose a powerful, rich complaint. 'I will not risk my voice in this weather. I will not rehearse here! It is r-r-ridiculous!'

If I had needed any clue to make assurance doubly sure, that extravagantly trilled *r* would have decided that matter. I raised an eyebrow to Inga, who nodded. Indeed, it was Madame Graciosa de la Rosa, holding forth.

'She's risking her voice all right, having a temper tantrum at that volume,' I said close to Inga's ear.

'One can only hope she'll lose it altogether,' was the reply.

Gracie couldn't possibly have heard the exchange. I had barely heard Inga myself. But the diva shot us a look so venomous that I clutched Alan's arm. Could the woman read minds? Or lips?

Alan covered my cold hand with his warm one and mouthed, 'Careful, love.' I noticed he turned his head away from la Graciosa when he did so.

Nigel reappeared and formed his hands into a megaphone. 'We're to go back to St Elian's,' he roared. 'BACK TO ST ELIAN'S. Half an hour. Pass it on!'

Amid grumblings, the crowd began to disperse, pulling jackets over their heads, or over their instruments, and moving towards the car park. Soon only the diva was left, drumming her fingers impatiently on the ancient stone wall as our small party left. 'Nigel!' she called imperiously.

'Ignore her,' said Inga, but Nigel turned, with reluctance.

'Find John and tell him I must ride with him to the church. My driver has left. Or I will go with you. Yes, that will be better.'

'Sorry, my car's full. I'll tell Sir John.' And Nigel pushed us out the doorway at what was very nearly a run.

Fortunately the conductor was approaching his car as we reached ours. Nigel hailed him. 'Sir! Madame de la Rosa is stranded without a driver. I'd give her a lift, but as you see…' He gestured to our small car and largish party.

'Oh. Oh, of course.' He managed a smile and waved us on.

'Nigel, what is wrong with that man?' I demanded when we had achieved the safety of the car and Nigel had cranked the heater up to its highest notch. 'It's more than just the stresses of the weather and an uncooperative mezzo. He looks absolutely ill.'

'I don't know.' Nigel sounded miserable. 'I've never seen him like this.'

'Darling, you've not seen him all that often in any condition, have you?' Inga put on her most practical, matter-of-fact voice. 'He's probably coming down with a cold, and some men are no good at being ill. You droop like a wounded heron whenever you have a sore little finger, you know.'

'I do not droop!' said Nigel, enraged. 'I am very careful to suffer in silence.'

'Loudly,' said Inga.

They bickered happily for the short drive to the church.

It was, of course, a good deal longer than half an hour before the rehearsal got under way. No sound or lighting equipment was needed here, but chairs had to be brought back from the castle, dried off, and set up. Risers had to be assembled for the chorus. Instruments had to be retuned. Then everyone had to wait for Sir John, who was, inexplicably, late.

And then the miracle happened. Maybe it was the critical nature of the situation. There was now less than one full day of rehearsal, in the wrong venue, before the festival opened. Crisis does sometimes draw people together, and does sometimes bring out the best in even the most difficult personalities. For whatever reason, even though Sir John still looked very ill indeed, the morning rehearsal went as smoothly as a bowl of cream. Voices blended. Violins soared, trumpets sounded clear and bright and joyous. The opera scenes brought tears to my eyes more than once.

Most miraculously of all, Gracie, the erstwhile blight of the festival, was all sweetness and light. She sang gloriously, cooperated with the other singers, followed the conductor flawlessly and, as Carmen singing the 'Habanera', won the applause of the other musicians, a rare accolade which she acknowledged with becoming modesty.

'Thank you, ladies and gentlemen,' said Sir John when the applause had died down. 'You have worked splendidly this morning, and I am most grateful. I am also happy to tell you that the weather has improved a great deal, and we will be able to continue our work this afternoon at the castle. We have very little time, as you know, so may I ask you, please, to hold very strictly to one hour for lunch. Sandwiches have been provided for those who do not wish to find a nearby eating place. We will begin again at one thirty. Thank you very much.'

'I, for one,' I said when we had settled ourselves in the car with some excellent sandwiches and bottles of water, 'would not have believed it. What happened to turn that surly mob into a well-oiled musical machine?'

'The music, of course!' Nigel waved his bottle of water in the air as though saluting St Cecilia, the patron of music. 'It hath charms to soothe the savage breast, as is well documented.'

'Hmm,' said Alan. 'I remain an agnostic on that point. Certainly it wasn't doing much charming yesterday, by your account.'

'Well…no. But Graciosa had just joined us. Sometimes it takes a little while to adapt to a group.'

Graciosa, I noticed. Not *Gracie*. Nigel had adapted quickly, it seemed. I shot a glance at Inga to see how she was taking this. Her face was unreadable. I changed the subject. 'You know, I thought I recognized Madame this morning. I'm sure I've never seen her perform, but there was something familiar about her, something… I can't put my finger on it.'

'The universal diva personality,' said Inga, her tone extremely dry. Nigel gave her a puzzled look and then applied himself to his sandwiches and a study of the music to be rehearsed in the afternoon.

'Clueless,' Inga murmured to me.

I nodded and shrugged. 'Men,' I murmured back.

I would just as soon have skipped the afternoon rehearsal. Though I am ashamed to admit it, an afternoon nap has become more and more appealing with my advancing years. But Alan pointed out that we had only one car, which would have meant delivering Nigel and Inga to the castle, delivering me to Tower, and then going back later to pick them up.

'You could take me home first,' I argued, 'and Nigel could get his own car.'

'I doubt there's time for that, if we're to get Nigel to the rehearsal on time. In any case,' he said, lowering his voice, 'I want to be there. There's thunder in the air.'

The other two had gone to dispose of our rubbish in a bin, so I was the only one to give him a questioning look. The sky had cleared to a benign June blue, with nary a cloud in sight, and the wind was now the merest zephyr.

Alan simply shook his head and started the car. 'Come, you two. Your carriage awaits.'

I had expected the castle to be as chaotic as before, but Sir John, or one of his minions, had accomplished yet another miracle. The crew had evidently got to work the moment the weather improved, and worked furiously ever since. The pavilion for the spectators had not yet been erected, but all the arrangements for the musicians were complete, right down to music stands that now stayed quietly where they belonged and cables that were decently placed out of traffic areas.

'It's a different world!' I exclaimed as Nigel went off to his assigned spot, Inga determinedly following him.

'But with the same inhabitants,' Alan replied.

I was annoyed. 'Why are you so determined to be gloomy? It's a beautiful day, everything is going well. Why borrow trouble?'

He shook his head. 'I don't know. You're well aware that I'm not subject to premonition, but a policeman learns to be attuned to atmosphere, and I just don't like the atmosphere around this festival. Nor do I have great faith in sudden conversions. I may be wrong. I hope I am. But when people I love could find themselves in trouble, I'd rather be there, to prevent if possible, to help if not.'

I gave his arm a squeeze, and we walked over to a convenient bit of wall where we could sit and watch.

This afternoon they were rehearsing some of the sacred music, a full rehearsal with all forces, soloists, chorus and orchestra. They began with the most complex work, the 'Lord Nelson Mass'. In a departure from the usual format, for that work the conductor had chosen to put the soloists in the part of the castle I'd called the balcony. As they assembled there, Inga, rejoining us, explained, 'Because of the acoustics of the place, Sir John thinks their voices will carry over the chorus and orchestra better from up there. We'll see, of course. It depends on how well the sound engineers have done their work.'

The usual preliminaries took less time than usual. The orchestra got itself tuned without an undue amount of the fifty-stomach-ache noise, the chorus settled into its sections, Sir John tapped his baton and captured everyone's eye, and they were off.

Those opening measures of the 'Lord Nelson', with their almost harsh military overtones, always send chills up my spine, and here, in what once had been a fortress and a garrison, I could almost hear the thunder of hoof beats as the enemy approached. Then the chorus came in with their demand—yes, demand!—for mercy, and I was caught up in the splendour of the music. The soprano soloist was excellent, soaring into difficult, high passages with apparent ease and total control, and the acoustics from the balcony seemed to me to be working exactly as intended.

I glanced at Alan. He appeared to be lost in the music. Or was his rapt concentration fixed rather on the musicians?

Sir John let the 'Kyrie' run through to its conclusion before stopping. He ran the first few bars of the chorus entrance again, insisting on perfectly clean articulation of the eighth-notes, and perfect, clipped diction. By the second repetition, he had what he wanted, and they went on to the 'Gloria'.

This was the first chance I'd had to hear Nigel, since the full quartet sings in this movement. I leaned forward to catch his full, rich tenor as he and the baritone sang together in a lovely and moving duet.

Then Madame de la Rosa joined them, and I could hear only her superb voice. Not that she overpowered the others. She was behaving impeccably, keeping her voice and her temperament under control. But my word, the strength of that voice! She made the others sound like amateurs, even Nigel, dearly as I loved him.

Now all four were singing together, and Graciosa raised her head as her voice soared to what must be the very top of her range…and then higher, and higher, into a terrified, terrifying scream. She dropped her music, clawed at her face and neck and hair, turned around, screamed again, backed up against the stone railing of the balcony…

And as the music faded disjointedly away, and in what seemed almost like slow motion, she was over the railing and pitching to the stone pavement twenty feet below.

SIX

ALAN WAS ON his feet running toward Graciosa before anyone else had much chance to react. I stayed where I was, but Inga, after a moment, followed Alan. Sir John got a slower start, but with less distance to cover he beat Alan by a nose. He started to kneel.

'Don't touch her, if you please, sir. I am a policeman, and must make sure that she is not disturbed until the local police arrive.'

'But she needs medical help! We have to get her to a doctor!'

Alan had laid his fingers lightly on her neck, the neck that was twisted in a very odd way. 'I'm afraid she is beyond any human help, sir.'

'No… You don't mean…'

'I'm afraid so. Now, Sir John, you can be a very great help if you will. Please ask the musicians, and the crew and so on, to stand clear, but to *stay on the premises*.' He already had his phone out and was punching in the familiar number. 'And someone—ah, Inga, my dear. Would you go up to the balcony—gallery—whatever the thing is called, and make sure no one disturbs anything up there.'

Inga looked horrified. 'Then you think…?'

'I don't think anything at the moment, but you know any sudden death must be investigated. Go, child!'

She went.

I very much wanted, needed, to talk to Alan, but now

was perhaps not the time. He had his hands full. I would wait until the official police arrived.

Meanwhile I tried to make myself useful. I thought I could perhaps assist Sir John, who seemed to have his hands very full of assorted musicians, all of whom were upset. He didn't seem to be doing too well himself, for that matter. There was sweat on his brow, and his hands were trembling.

'Sir John,' I said tentatively. He turned around and looked at me blankly.

'Do I know you?'

'No, but I'm a good friend of Nigel Evans.' Then, when he still looked blank, 'Nigel Evans. Your tenor.'

'Oh, yes, of course. Did you want to speak to him? Because I think he's still up…' He gestured towards the balcony, without looking at it.

'No, I don't need him. I think you need help, though, and I came to offer it. You'll forgive me for saying you don't look at all well. May I bring you some water?'

'No, no, I'm fine, really. Someone told me to…' He looked helplessly at the crowd of musicians, who were milling around and getting far too close to the pathetic body of Graciosa.

'That someone was my husband, and he wouldn't want you to overtax yourself. If you'll sit down, I'll find someone to bring you some water—and is there some medication you should be taking?' I didn't quite want to say so, but the poor man looked very much as if he might be having a heart attack.

'No, I… Very well. I do feel a bit odd. But it's nothing serious, madam, I do assure you.'

'Good.' I half pushed him into the chair recently occupied by the concertmaster, and snagged a wandering clarinettist. 'Go to the gift shop and buy this man some water,' I ordered her. 'Do you have money?'

She took a good look at Sir John, then nodded and set off at a brisk pace.

'But the musicians…'

'You leave the crowd control to me. I used to be good at it.'

I grabbed Sir John's microphone from its stand and bellowed into it. 'Ladies and gentlemen! Your attention, please! QUIET, please!' These were not the schoolchildren I used to be able to quell with my voice alone, but they responded gratifyingly. 'Thank you,' I said in a slightly more restrained tone. 'As you know, there has been a tragic accident. If you have not already realized it, I am sorry to tell you that Madame de la Rosa died in the fall.' A little ripple of shock and unease. 'The police will be here soon, but until they arrive, you are asked please to keep well away from the scene of the accident, but remain within the castle precincts. Thank you.'

'What will happen with the festival?' shouted one of the crowd.

There were murmurs of disapproval, and I was a little shocked myself, but it was a legitimate question.

'I don't know. I'm sure Sir John will work that out with the police, and you'll be informed as soon as possible.' I switched off the mike and put it back on its stand. The noise level picked up again as everyone began to buzz about the situation, but over it I heard, with great relief, the sound of sirens. The Force had arrived.

Then of course Alan was kept busy talking to the officer in charge, while another, his second-in-command, presumably, attended to Sir John. Still others began to separate the musicians into manageable groups for interviews. Eventually one of the lesser lights, a beefy, rather sour-looking man of about fifty, approached me.

'And you'd be Mrs Nesbitt?'

'Mrs Martin. But yes, Mr Nesbitt's wife.'

His expression told me what he thought of women with names different from their husbands'. 'Right,' he continued, making a note. 'And what can you tell me about all this?'

He wasn't Welsh, that was certain. There was none of that Welsh lilt, that softness of accent. Nor was there the courtesy of manner I had met with so far. What was he doing in the police on this side of the border, I wondered. Besides annoying the natives.

Those thoughts took only a portion of my brain, while I framed an answer to his question. 'I was in a good position to see her fall, better than most people here, because they were busy playing and singing, and I was merely observing. She was singing, and hit a high note, and then it went higher and higher and turned into a scream, and then she fell.'

'She screamed *before* she fell? Are you sure?'

'I can,' I said, very much on my dignity, 'tell the difference between singing and screaming. And yes, it was before she fell. And now I stop to think about it, she was also sort of flailing about, slapping at her hair and neck.'

'Hmm. A bee, maybe. And who was near her at the time?'

'The other three soloists.'

'Names?'

'I don't know all their names. The tenor is Nigel Evans.'

'A Welshman, then?'

'His father was. Nigel has lived in England since he was very young.'

'And how do you know so much about him?'

My irritation with this mannerless oaf was growing. 'He has been a good friend for many years,' I said frostily.

'I see.' He made another note. 'Know anything about the others?'

'Only that they sing like angels.'

'Yes, well, maybe one of them wasn't so angelic.' He slapped his notebook shut. 'That's all for now, Mrs Nesbitt.'

'One moment, young man.' I let him see my anger. 'For one thing, that is not my name. As you know perfectly well. For another, if you think that one of the other soloists pushed Madame de la Rosa to her death, you are quite mistaken. They were not near enough to her to trip her, their hands were occupied with their scores, and their minds and souls with the music. *Good* afternoon!'

I stalked off, seething.

'Problems, love?'

Alan had come up behind me. I turned to him. 'Not really, I suppose, except that I just had a close encounter of the idiot kind.'

'Ah, that would be Sergeant Blimp, I expect. I saw him arrive and pegged him as one of those coppers who's never done anything useful in his life, but has also never done anything quite stupid enough to get him sacked.'

'The name would be appropriate,' I agreed. 'I don't know what his real name is, as he didn't bother to introduce himself. He pretended not to know what my real name is, either. But the worst thing is that he didn't listen to a thing I told him. He's decided Nigel probably did it, because he has a Welsh name. He's English—Sergeant Blimp, I mean.'

Alan looked grave. 'If he were under my supervision, that sort of attitude would be just cause for a dressing-down, if not worse disciplinary action.'

'He wasn't overt about it, but his face, like mine, shows his thoughts only too clearly. But never mind him. I've been wanting to talk to you, because I finally remembered something important. You know I said I thought I recognized Graciosa?'

'You've remembered why?'

'Yes, and I think we ought to pass it along to the police. Alan, she was on that canal boat.'

'But she said she didn't even get to England until that night!'

WE WERE ON our way back to Tower. We were all exhausted. The police had questioned everyone at length, though they had not, to my relief and Sergeant Blimp's apparent consternation, questioned Nigel any more closely than anyone else. Apparently the inspector in charge, whose name was Owen, was aware of Blimp's bias against the Welsh and discounted it automatically.

The fate of the festival had still not been decided. The next day, Sunday, had always been scheduled as a day of rest for most of the participants before the gruelling week ahead. But Nigel was more interested, just now, in my insistence that Graciosa had been on board the canal boat when the unfortunate baritone fell overboard.

'You're sure?' he said for the fourth or fifth time.

'Nigel, I'm sure.' I tried to be patient. We were all upset. 'I didn't recognize her for certain this morning, but when she fell and I got a good look at her, something clicked, and I remembered. I'm terrible with names, as you probably know, but I remember faces. She was on board that boat.'

'Then why did she lie about it?' Nigel said, running his fingers through his hair so it stood up on end. 'When do you think she really did come into the country? Did she miss the early rehearsals on purpose? It's an extremely unprofessional thing to do.'

'You're not a professional singer,' I reminded him. 'Maybe she wasn't either.'

'But we're all being paid for this gig,' Nigel retorted. 'Not a lot, but we are receiving payment. That makes it a professional engagement. But she wasn't behaving like a professional, even after she turned up. I can't make any sense of it at all.'

'The police would like to know the answers to those questions, too,' said Alan soberly. 'It should be easy enough to find her passport and check the date of entry. After that, though, the waters become murkier. She was the only one who could have answered most of your questions.'

'And what I'd like to know, most of all,' I said, 'is the reason for her sudden reversal of personality. Fire-breathing dragon one moment, angel of sweet reason the next. Frankly, at the moment I can think of only one explanation for such a dramatic change.'

'Drugs,' said the other three in near-unison.

Alan smacked his knee. 'Dorothy, you may have hit on it! A drug reaction might also explain that odd sort of fit she went into just before she fell. It looked to me almost like a severe allergic reaction. I need to mention this to the inspector.' He looked for a place to pull off the road, and found none.

'I did tell Sergeant Blimp about her peculiar behaviour,' I said. 'It actually looked to me more like an attack of hysteria, but I suppose drugs could cause that. Maybe a hallucinogenic? Anyway, he wasn't impressed.

He barely listened, in fact, because he'd decided you pushed her, Nigel.'

He chuckled. 'Yes, I picked up on that. I tried hard to summon up a Welsh accent to make him even happier with me, but as I've never lived in Wales nor learned the language, I couldn't do it. I'm not worried about him. That type is all froth and no beer.'

'And Inspector Owen has the measure of him, I think,' said Alan. 'I'd like to phone him, but there doesn't seem to be a pullout. It will just have to wait until we get back to Tower.'

We were only a few minutes away, but we drove on into Mold to pick up some provisions for supper. None of us felt like going out. While Inga and Nigel and I did a little quick shopping, Alan made his phone call.

'He was polite about it, but I rather got the impression he thought I was meddling,' he reported when we got back to the car with our bags. 'Apparently the medical examiner found no outward signs of drugs use. They routinely check, of course. But I think he will now order drugs tests with the autopsy. He wasn't happy about it.'

'Expense, delay?' I queried.

'Not to mention interference from a superannuated retiree. And an Englishman, to boot.'

We ate our suppers sitting in a pleasant gazebo at Tower, but the picnic spirit was notably lacking.

SEVEN

I WAS WIPED out by bedtime, and had intended to sleep late the next morning. But with its usual perversity, my brain started functioning at sunrise, which is very, very early in June in Wales. I got up, went to the bathroom, and then tried to get back to sleep, but every time I edged over into a nice fuzzy state I would see and hear Graciosa, screaming and then falling, falling, and my eyes would pop open again. I finally gave up, got up and dressed as quietly as I could, and made myself a cup of instant coffee, which I loathe but drank anyway for the caffeine. Then I let myself out of the room, closed the door softly behind me, and walked downstairs. It still wasn't six o'clock, but to my great relief, Charles was already up, attending to the dogs.

'You're up early, Dorothy,' he said, raising his eyebrows. 'I thought Mairi told me late breakfast for you today.'

'That's what I thought, too,' I said ruefully. 'I couldn't sleep. I'm not hungry, though, Charles. I wonder if you could disarm the alarm on the front door, so I could go for a walk. When are the others having breakfast?'

'The alarm is shut off. I leave a rope across the staircase until I do that, so don't worry. And the others have booked breakfast at nine. You won't want to wait that long, I'm sure. Just come to the kitchen when you're ready, and give a shout if we're not in sight.'

I wandered for a while around the extensive grounds,

admiring the gorgeous old oak trees, their leaves so much smaller than the ones at home, their shade welcome against the sun that, even at that hour, was hot on my skin. I tried hard to think about nothing but grass and trees and birds and flowers, but every now and then a strain of music in my head would turn into the 'Lord Nelson', and then of course I was back again, watching her fall...

I wondered about Alan's explanation of her behaviour just before she fell. She had acted a lot like someone trying to scratch everything at once, as perhaps in an allergy attack. I tried mimicking her movements, as best I could remember them.

She had started screaming. Or rather her singing had turned to screams. That was, I was reasonably sure, before she began flailing about, although it had all happened so fast. She had pawed at her face, neck and hair, had turned around, facing away from the balcony opening, had screamed even louder and backed up...

'What on earth?'

I screamed myself, or squeaked, at least. 'Nigel! Don't you ever do that again! You scared me out of seven years' growth!'

'Sorry! One doesn't make much noise, walking on grass. I came out to tell you we all got up early, and breakfast will be ready in about fifteen minutes. But what were you doing just now with that St Vitus dance routine? I thought you'd gone mad.'

'Well, I didn't mean to have an audience!' I turned back to the house with him. 'I was trying to work out what Graciosa was doing just before she fell. You were there, right next to her. What was your impression?'

'I don't know that I have one. I was watching Sir John

and the score, because I had an entrance just a few bars later, and was sort of caught up in the music, you know?'

'So was everyone else, I suspect. It really was glorious. I do hope…oh, it sounds terribly heartless, but I do hope the festival can continue. Are there any understudies for the soloists?'

'I don't think so. I don't have one, I know. At least, if I do, Sir John hasn't told me.'

I sighed. 'It does seem a great pity, when everyone's gone to such a lot of work, to have it end like this. And if that's a selfish thought, well, I'm sorry. But I didn't know the woman, and what I learned of her personality, until yesterday, made me profoundly glad I *wasn't* in her acquaintance.'

'She could sing, though.' Nigel shook his head sadly at the death of an artist.

We all tried to be cheerful over breakfast. Charles and Mairi knew, of course, what had happened, and had tried to raise our spirits with a breakfast even more splendid than usual. There was a compote of fresh pineapple, strawberries, and kiwi, with thick cream to pour over it, along with the usual eggs and bacon and sausage and mushrooms and tomato and toast and Charles's incomparable marmalade. But we were edgy, waiting for news. News of the festival, news of the investigation.

Alan's phone rang, and we all jumped. He doesn't usually bring it to the table, but today was different. He excused himself, and when he came back, he looked discouraged.

'There were no signs of drugs in Madame de la Rosa's system,' he told us, 'and Inspector Owen was remarkably crisp about that report.'

'Oh, dear.' I sounded as guilty as I felt. I had been the one to hint at the possibility of drugs, and wasting police time and money isn't a joke. 'It was nice of him to tell you, though. Did he say anything else?'

'They've found her passport. She entered this country in early February—'

'February!' said Nigel, enraged.

'—from New York,' Alan finished. 'She carried an American passport.'

We sat, stunned. Everything Graciosa had said was a lie. There were too many questions even to put words to them.

'Well,' I said finally. 'Well. I don't suppose they've managed to trace her family.'

'They don't even know her real name at this point. Plainly she used a stage name, but that's the way her passport reads, too. They'll try to trace a next-of-kin, but I don't imagine they'll try too hard. They've really done more than they needed to already, for an accidental death.'

And then Nigel got the phone call that told him that another mezzo had been found, that the festival was continuing, and that special rehearsals had been called for the soloists that afternoon.

Epitaph for Graciosa, I thought. The queen is dead; long live the queen.

WE ALL DROVE into Mold for church at St Mary's, where, as Charles had told us, memorials to his ancestors were numerous. Afterwards we found ourselves some lunch, and then Alan and I decided to attend rehearsals with Nigel and Inga. They were to be held in the same parish church as the earlier rehearsals, not in the castle. Apparently there was considerable debate about whether to use the castle for the performances.

'In the nature of a jinx, is that the thought?' asked

Alan as we drove through a pastoral landscape that would have made Constable drool.

Nigel laughed. 'I suppose that may be part of it. But musicians, though they may be temperamental, are a practical lot, you know. I imagine Sir John is mostly concerned about the logistics of a change and the effect on the box office.'

And again I thought what a pity it was that no one seemed saddened by Graciosa's death. Upset by the circumstances, yes, and worried over the fate of the festival, but not grief-stricken.

When we got to St Elian's, I wondered if I was going to have to change my mind. Sir John seemed to have aged several years since yesterday. A person's hair doesn't turn grey overnight, no matter what the writers of romantic fiction would have us believe. But a face can take on a drawn, grey look when its owner is ill or sleep-deprived, or troubled almost beyond endurance. The poor man, who couldn't have been much over forty, looked like a grandfather. A decrepit grandfather.

Surely musical and administrative problems wouldn't cause distress that acute. Could he really be missing his extremely difficult mezzo?

Inga noticed it, too. 'What's wrong with Sir John?' she whispered. 'He's coming apart at the seams.'

I nodded. 'Maybe he has a lot of money invested in this project, and he's afraid it's going to fail.'

'Maybe,' she said, but she sounded sceptical.

The rehearsal was going badly. The new mezzo hadn't anything like the power and drama of Graciosa (who had?), but she was better than adequate, and note-perfect. It wasn't that. Even I, who know music only as an avid listener, could see that the problem lay behind the baton.

Sir John failed to cue entrances. He turned over two pages of the score at once and got hopelessly lost. He was sweating profusely, though the church, like most medieval churches, was extremely chilly.

After an hour he laid down his baton and cleared his throat. 'Forgive me, ladies and gentlemen. I am wasting your time. You are well-prepared; I am not. I apologize, and I promise not to let you down tomorrow.' He cleared his throat again. 'Taking all circumstances into consideration, I have decided that we will stay at the castle as planned. We'll simply have to keep our fingers crossed about acoustics and moving from place to place. Please be there by noon, so that we will have a little time to review before we begin. Thank you.' He closed his score with a shaking hand and walked over to the pianist.

The singers stood there for a moment, nonplussed. Then, with shrugs all round, they gathered up their personal belongings and walked into the nave.

Alan, Inga and I went to meet Nigel. He was looking stunned.

'I never would have believed it,' he began. 'Sir John Warner unprepared for a rehearsal! I'd sooner have expected the Queen to appear in public without a hat.'

He opened his mouth to say more, but I put a hand on his shoulder. Sir John was approaching.

Nigel turned quickly, but the conductor addressed Alan. 'Am I right, sir, in believing that you are a retired policeman?'

'Quite right,' said Alan, a trifle startled. 'Long retired. I was the chief constable of Belleshire for some years.'

'Then may I speak to you for a moment?'

Alan gave me a what-on-earth-is-this-about look and went with Sir John to a quiet corner. At least it might

have been a quiet corner, but for the acoustic proper-
ties of an ancient stone church. As it was, the three of
us clearly heard Sir John's whispered colloquy with my
husband.

It was brief. 'You see, sir, I'm not sure what to do,
and I thought I'd like to speak with you before I go to
the local police. I have some information they may need
to know.' He paused. His back was to us, but I heard
him swallow. Hard. 'It's…the thing is… Graciosa de la
Rosa was my wife.'

PART TWO

EIGHT

'THE POOR CHAP didn't know where to turn, so he came to me.' Alan took a fairly hefty swig of bourbon. 'What he needs is a solicitor, of course, but he's quite frantic about not letting Lady Cynthia find out, at least not until the time comes, if it comes, when he must. It wouldn't be very good for her in her condition, I shouldn't think.'

We were sitting in the lounge at Tower trying to make sense of the latest development, Alan and I with our bourbon, Inga and Nigel with wine. Charles and Mairi, after providing us with glasses, and plates for our cheese and biscuits, had left us discreetly alone, although I knew they were dying to find out what was going on.

I must have gasped back at the church, or made some noise, anyway, when I heard what Sir John had to say, because Alan had bundled him off to the vestry or some-place where they could talk in genuine privacy. He had obtained Sir John's permission, however, to tell the three of us his story, if we promised not to let it go any further.

'You remember, of course,' Alan began, 'the story about the shipwreck years ago.' We nodded. It had been a spectacular news story. More than a hundred lives had been lost, and many more were presumed dead, their bodies resting somewhere in the Mediterranean. 'Mrs Warner was reported missing. Mr Warner, as he was then, hadn't seen her since the first hint of trouble, when they were separated. He tried to look for her, but the crew insisted that he must board a lifeboat immediately. Then something happened. He still doesn't remember what, but evidently something must have fallen on his head. It was a pretty chaotic scene, I gather.' He paused for another sip of his drink.

'At any rate, he lost consciousness, and the next thing he knew was waking up in hospital in Athens several days later with only the vaguest memories of the whole affair. He says the doctors told him he was lucky to have survived, for he'd had a severe concussion, with subdural bleeding, the lot. When he began to sit up and take notice, the first thing he wanted to know, naturally, was Delia's whereabouts. That was her name then—Delia Lopez Warner. Sir John is reasonably certain it was her real name.

'The hospital authorities couldn't, or wouldn't, tell him anything about her, so when they finally turned him loose he hounded everyone he could think of—the Greek police, the shipping company, any other passengers he could find. He made no headway at all. In the end, of course, he had to go back to England and carry on.

'Reading between the lines, I gathered the marriage had not been a success. He was grieved at her loss. Back then, I mean. I could feel that as he spoke of it. But I could also sense that he was not devastated. He went on with his career, which even then was promising. He was constantly meeting other musicians, naturally, and eventually he met a charming pianist and fell in love with her.'

'Lady Cynthia,' said Nigel.

'Yes, but it was just plain Cynthia Hailes then. Well, it had been nearly seven years since the shipwreck, and Warner had heard nothing from or about Delia. He and Cynthia wanted to marry, so Warner began proceedings to have her declared legally dead. There was no trouble about it, and when the formalities were accomplished Warner and his Cynthia were married and started a family.'

'And then Delia shows up, with a new name and, I'm guessing, malice in her heart.' I groaned and looked at my empty glass. Alan held up the bottle, but I shook my head. A headache in the morning wouldn't help anything. 'But does it make any real difference? Legally, I mean.'

'That's what I don't know.' Alan ran a hand down the back of his head in a familiar gesture of frustration. 'Personally, I doubt that it would. He went through all the proper legal steps, and it would seem apparent that she knew where he was and chose to remain apart from him. She obviously kept in contact with the world of music and could hardly have helped knowing. He could probably have sought a divorce on the grounds of desertion. But of course he didn't, because he thought she was dead.'

'But you're not a lawyer,' Inga pointed out. 'You could be wrong. He could still be legally married to her. I mean he could have been, only that now she's dead.'

'Exactly,' said Alan, and there was a melancholy little silence.

'Did he tell you what happened when he gave her the ride from the castle to the church? Good grief, only two days ago! Seems like forever.' I shook my head at the elastic nature of time.

'He did.' Alan seemed reluctant to go on.

'Let me guess. A nice little spot of blackmail, right? She offered not to spill the beans if he would—do what? Fork over some cash? Use his influence to get her roles?'

'That's what it amounted to, but cash, not musical

pull. Apparently she realized even he couldn't force anyone to hire her.'

'And did the poor man agree to her terms?'

'If we are to believe him, he did. With extreme reluctance, but he felt he had no choice. In their brief marriage, he'd learned how rapacious she could be, and how single-minded in pursuit of her ends. He didn't quite say that. I'm reading between the lines.'

'I'd wager he's telling you the truth,' said Inga. 'About promising to give her what she demanded, I mean. In the morning, she was exactly like a cat who'd been out in the rain: spitting and furious. And yet an hour or so later she was licking her lips over cream. Oh, yes, she'd got what she wanted.'

'Pity she had so little time to enjoy it,' said Alan, and there was an undertone in his voice I didn't quite understand.

'What?' I asked.

'It's only that…if Sir John was in any doubt about the legal ramifications of Delia's reappearance, he had to consider his wife and family. Three excellent reasons to…well, to want her to disappear again.'

We all protested. Nigel was the loudest. 'It's impossible! He's a truly good person. Everyone who's ever had anything to do with him knows that. He wouldn't even think of it.'

'And Alan!' I broke in. 'Even if he were capable of such a thing, in theory, he was nowhere near her when she fell. Something like two hundred people can testify to that!'

'Yes, of course. I'm only… Ignore me.'

'What I want to know,' I persisted, 'is why Sir John hired her. Yes, she was an excellent singer, but there are lots of excellent singers in the world. I know the auditions were blind, and ten years is a long time, but wouldn't he have recognized her voice, anyway? He'd been married to her, for Pete's sake. Why did he bring her here?'

'I have no idea,' said Alan. He stood. 'I'm past the point of thinking logically, in any case. And you, Nigel, have a good deal of singing to do tomorrow. We'd all best get to bed.'

THE FIRST OF the concerts, the Opera Scenes, was scheduled for two in the afternoon. Nigel, however, disappeared immediately after breakfast. 'I don't know if we're ready for this,' he had kept saying nervously as he toyed with his breakfast. 'We've been through this only once with what's-her-name, and the chorus hasn't worked with her at all. Some of the entrances are tricky...'

'Nigel,' said Inga calmly. 'You know every note by heart, and so do the others. It'll be splendid. Calm down.'

'I'm going over early,' he said, not having heard a word she said. 'I don't care if the others are there or not. I just want to... I don't know what I want to do, but I can't simply sit and wait.'

'Is Nigel thinking about taking up music professionally?' I asked Inga after he'd left for the castle. We were sitting with Alan in the lounge, and I was trying, not very successfully, to knit a scarf. 'He's being very intense about this.'

'Heavens, no! He's more realistic than that. The world of professional music is as cut-throat as they come, and he wants no part of it, not to mention the insecurity of music as a career. He makes a good living as a techie, and he quite enjoys what he does, so he'd never give it up, even if it weren't for his responsibilities.'

'You and Nigel Peter,' I said, nodding. 'How is the imp today?'

'Splendid, I gather, but oh, I do miss him.' She sighed and returned to the subject of Nigel and music. 'It's just that…oh, well, he's a perfectionist, and he puts his heart and soul into his music, just as he does with everything else. As you see. This is his first important set of concerts since he left King's, and he wants it to be perfect.' She sighed. 'Poor darling. I do hope it comes off well, for his sake.'

I shot a glance at Alan, who was apparently absorbed in a book about medieval architecture. 'And for Sir John's sake,' I said quietly. 'I wonder if he feels better now that he's bared his soul to Alan, or worse.'

Inga shrugged. 'Will Alan tell the police the whole story, do you think?'

'There doesn't seem to be much point, does there? If the official police decide Delia's death was an accident, that's the end of it, and if they decide otherwise, there's no way Sir John can have been involved. He was nowhere near her, not to mention that he was conducting a complex piece of music and had no attention to spare for anything else.'

'But they'll want to know her real identity, won't they?'

'Well, yes, there is that. Oh, dear, what do you suppose I've done now? The pattern isn't coming out right.'

Inga, who was an expert knitter, leaned over my chair to inspect my work. 'I think,' she said tactfully, 'you dropped a stitch or two several rows back. I could try to pick them up for you, but it would be better if you just ripped it out to there and started again.'

I sighed. 'I'm hopeless at ripping out. At least I'm very good at ripping out, because I have to do it so often, but I'm no good at picking up the stitches afterwards. Would you mind?'

I handed the whole mess to her, the trailing yarn brushing against my face as I reached up. 'Ugh! I hate things touching my face like that. Gives me the shivers.'

Rapidly, expertly, Inga repaired my mistakes while I pondered. 'I wonder if there's a way to let the police know about her real name without telling the whole story? Well, no,' I answered myself, 'of course there isn't, because her last name was Warner, and they're bound to make the connection. Oh, why couldn't the miserable woman just stay lost?'

'I imagine,' said Alan, 'that Sir John is having precisely those thoughts.'

'I thought you were immersed in that book!'

'I was. Using my eyes and mind does not shut my ears. And yes, my dear, of course I'll have to tell the police. Or rather, I shall ask Sir John to do so.'

'After today's concert!' Inga and I said in unison.

'Of course. The matter is of no great urgency, after all. The woman died an accidental death.'

I looked at him sharply. His face was absolutely bland. I know that expression. It means that behind it, he is 'given furiously to think', as Hercule Poirot used to say. But I had no idea what he was thinking.

NINE

WE TOOK INGA out for a pub lunch, but none of us ate much. Nigel's nerves, and the whole upsetting situation, had taken away our appetites, and for me, that takes some doing. We got to the castle far too early for the concert, but there was already a good crowd waiting to get in.

'I wonder how many of them are music-lovers, and how many sensation-seekers?' I asked, *sotto voce*.

Alan made that waggling motion with his hand that meant something like 'six of one, half-a-dozen of the other'.

'I think you're giving them the benefit of the doubt,' I said cynically.

'I think you should have eaten a better lunch,' said Alan, with his usual infuriating assumption that my spirits are dependent upon my stomach. Infuriating, because he's so often right.

'Alan Nesbitt, if you offer me a chocolate bar, I swear I'll...'

'Eat it?' he suggested while I struggled for the right word.

My only reply was a dignified silence. I thought I heard Inga giggle, but when I looked at her, her face was completely sober.

Well, I thought with an inner sigh, if I'd relieved her nerves a bit, my little snit had done some good.

The gates were opened at last, and the queue began

to move. Our comp tickets allowed us admission to the choice seating, not in the front rows, where the sun was slanting in under the tent, but a few rows back, in the shade and, Inga explained, in the area where the acoustics worked best.

Whatever the other omens for the day, the weather was at least cooperating magnificently. The sky held those little puffy white clouds that make the blue even bluer by contrast—what my father used to call 'fair weather clouds'. The air was balmy, with just enough breeze to make sitting in the shade perfectly comfortable. We found our seats, and I began to relax, though I kept my eyes firmly away from the balcony.

Nigel had told us that for this concert, since the soloists were the focus of almost every piece, the balcony wouldn't be used. A stage had been erected, a couple of feet above ground level, with a podium at the front for Sir John, mikes for the soloists, and risers at the back for the chorus. The orchestra's chairs ranged around the stage on a tarp that had been laid on the stones of the courtyard. The audience, besides those under the tent, were seated wherever there was room—in the anterooms off the forecourt, in any room that had a window giving on the action, and even on the walkway atop the walls. I shuddered at the sight of those fearless souls and hoped, first, that they had a good sense of balance and no acrophobia, and second, that they'd brought lots of sunscreen. My American friends laugh at the idea of getting a sunburn on this island of mists and rain, but it's just as possible here as in, say, southern California. It simply takes a little longer.

Glancing down at the programme, I found that the *Carmen* scenes had been omitted. Poor Delia. The 'Habanera' had been her showpiece, her great triumph at the rehearsal. Or at least Graciosa's triumph. I had, I realized, no idea whether young Delia had been a singer, back before she was lost at sea and became Graciosa and…and what? Where had she been all those years? What had she been doing? Studying music somewhere, one assumed. A voice like hers didn't develop all by itself. She'd had training, had acquired experience, had learned roles. Where? In America, where she'd apparently acquired citizenship? But how on earth had she ended up there? Why had she made no attempt to be reunited with her husband?

I was so absorbed in my thoughts that I didn't notice Sir John's entrance until Alan nudged me to applaud. Sir John bowed, and then turned to the microphone.

'Thank you, ladies and gentlemen. I'm delighted to welcome you to the first concert of what we hope will be the first annual Music Festival in Wales. I am aware that bringing choral and vocal music to Wales is in the nature of bringing coals to Newcastle.' Laughter from both audience and musicians. 'I'm therefore especially gratified by your large attendance this afternoon.

'As you know, the proceeds of this festival will go to the Royal National Lifeboat Institution, a cause that you may know is dear to my heart, as I nearly lost my life in a shipwreck some years ago.'

I held my breath, but, apart from a pause to clear his throat, he went ahead smoothly.

'I hope that, in addition to your contribution in the form of your attendance, you will be generous with your donations to the collection jars set about the castle. Thank you. And now, ladies and gentlemen, let us welcome our soloists.'

The soloists filed on, to more applause, and the magic began.

They started off with several scenes from *Barber of Seville*, that perennial comic favourite, and went on from there to *Madama Butterfly*, for me the best of them all. Puccini just wrote one matchless tune after another. Sir John had chosen the gorgeous love duet between Butterfly and Pinkerton, the famous 'Un bel dì', and the hauntingly lovely, infinitely sad Humming Chorus. I got tears in my eyes, and even Alan found he had to blow his nose.

'Pinkerton is such a rat!' said Inga, when they had finished the set. 'I wanted to slap him silly, and then I remembered that's Nigel up there.'

'He's a different person when he's singing, isn't he? He's really, really good, Inga.'

I would have said more, but Sir John gave the downbeat, and the orchestra struck up the aptly named Grand March from *Aïda* to give the first half of the concert a rousing finish.

The audience was appreciative in that restrained, well-mannered way I have come to learn is typical of Britain. No roars of 'bravo', no standing ovation such as one might have expected in Milan—or, for that matter, New York.

'They're really enjoying themselves, aren't they?' said Inga, a sparkle in her eyes as she looked around at the concert-goers standing, stretching, chatting. 'It's going frightfully well.'

Ah, well, if I found the audience response a bit tepid, obviously that was my faulty perception. 'I, personally, thought it was glorious. But I do need to find something in the way of a loo. I hope they've laid on extra ones.'

They had. I'm not fond of portaloos, but I'll use them in case of dire necessity. These weren't too bad, as such things go, and I emerged feeling much better. Inga found me. 'Do you want to go back and talk to Nigel?'

'No, I don't want to break the spell. Anyway, that isn't Nigel just now. It's Count Almaviva, and Pinkerton, and next Alfredo and Edgar. I don't want to distract any of them!'

So we took our seats and chatted until Sir John re-entered and began with the overture to *The Marriage of Figaro*, which he had substituted for the *Carmen* scenes. It was a brilliant piece of programming. Lively, a tie-in to *Barber* in the first half, and something most of the orchestra could probably play in their sleep, with no rehearsal. The audience loved it. Then the chorus sang the 'Va pensiero', the Chorus of the Hebrew Slaves, and sang it so beautifully that the audience, now getting into the spirit of the thing, insisted it be repeated.

Then on to *Traviata* and more tears, and finally *Lucia,* culminating in the renowned Sextet, with two of the singers from the chorus taking the other two parts. The audience demanded an encore of that, too, and applauded for more. Sir John finally had to go to a microphone.

'Ladies and gentlemen, we are gratified that you enjoyed this performance so much. Forgive us for ending such a pleasant afternoon, but remember that we have a great deal more music to perform this week. We hope to see you back here tomorrow afternoon. Thank you!' And he dismissed the orchestra and singers with a nod, and the audience began to come down from their euphoria and drag themselves back to everyday life.

I didn't want to do that. I'd been quite literally 'carried away' by the music. Not physically, of course, but my mind and soul had been, not in a castle where I had watched a young woman die, but in another world, a world where tragedy was cloaked in melody and where, in any case, everyone would be alive again once the curtain came down.

I became aware that Alan was watching me. 'Earth to Dorothy,' he said with a grin. 'Ready for your tea, love, or are you still "out there" somewhere?'

I gave a deep sigh. 'Returning, I guess, but oh so slowly and reluctantly. As for tea, what I actually want is nectar. Ambrosia. Whatever one drinks in the Elysian Fields. But I suppose tea will do.'

I found my handbag and got myself organized, and Nigel strolled over to meet us.

'Well?' he said. He stood in the standard opera 'heroic' pose, shoulders back, head erect, and the cocky Welshman was all on top.

'Very nice, Nigel,' I said in a saccharine nanny voice. 'You all really did quite well, and I'm sure it'll go better tomorrow.' And then at the expression on his face, 'Gotcha! You were looking so smug, I couldn't resist. You know perfectly well it was splendid. Alan, shall we... Alan?'

My husband, at my side only moments before, had vanished.

'I think,' said Inga quietly, 'he's gone to talk to Sir John.'

Well, that, as the English used to say a couple of generations ago, rather took the gilt off the gingerbread.

'I'd forgotten, for a while,' I admitted. 'I suppose it's terrible. A woman died, only a few days ago and a few feet away, and for a time I forgot all about her. The music...'

'It isn't terrible,' said Inga firmly. 'None of us really knew the woman, and from all accounts, she wasn't very nice to know anyway. It's silly to think you should grieve for her just because you witnessed her death.'

Any man's death diminishes me, I thought, but Inga was right. I couldn't drum up any real grief for Delia, only a kind of pity, sorrow for the waste of a life that could have been so rich. 'Are they going to give her any sort of tribute during the festival?'

'That's still under discussion. I think Sir John is of two minds about it, and a few of the musicians are dead set against it.'

'But why? It would seem to be the decent thing to do.'

Nigel squirmed a bit. 'A few guys in the orchestra used to know her, and I think maybe one or two in the chorus. The world of really excellent musicians is a small one, you know, and she's…she wasn't exactly popular. One gathers she didn't mind who she trampled on, if they got in the way of her career. And you have to remember…' Nigel looked around and lowered his voice. 'Nobody else knows who she was. That she was married to Sir John back when, I mean.'

'Well, I still think… Oh, Alan. All right?'

'Sir John is feeling a good deal better about it today,' said Alan as we made our way with the crowd out of the castle precinct. 'A wildly successful concert has something to do with it, I suspect. He's also talked to his solicitor, who thinks, I gather, that the whole thing is a tempest in a teapot. He's going to speak to the police, but I doubt they'll take it any further. Now, where shall we have tea?'

TEN

WE ENDED UP opting for beer instead. The afternoon was hot, and the selection of pubs nearby seemed better than the selection of cafés. Nigel was in tearing high spirits. The music, which had lulled me into almost a dream state, had energized him like a drug. He was full of stories. The baritone had suffered a bad attack of hiccups just before going on, and Nigel was hilarious about the various remedies that had been pressed on the poor man. 'Somebody tried scaring him with a grass snake they found somewhere, but it only succeeded in causing hysterics among some of the women in the chorus. Then they wanted to make him breathe into a paper bag, but they could only find a plastic carrier bag...'

'But that's dangerous!' I said, eyes wide. 'They could have...'

'And very nearly did,' Nigel agreed. 'I'm sure he saw his life flash before his eyes. Probably the fright was what actually cured him.

'Then there was,' he went on, 'the panic when one of the altos in the chorus couldn't find her music, and the percussionist lost the rabbit's foot he always carried for luck, and one of the violinists broke a string and didn't have a spare.'

'Goodness,' I said, fascinated at this glimpse backstage. 'I never thought about how many things could go wrong at a concert. It looks so flawless and easy from out front. And I never thought of musicians as being superstitious.'

'Oh, Dorothy!' said Inga, rolling her eyes. 'You have *no* idea! And the higher they climb in the ranks, the worse they are. Nigel's not professional, so he's escaped most of the idiocies, but…'

'We're nothing like as bad as actors!' Nigel protested. 'They've made a religion of their fetishes.'

'I've heard about some of the *Macbeth* ones,' I said. 'Is it true some actors won't even speak the name of the play?'

'Not in a theatre, they won't. It's supposed to be the most frightfully bad luck. And heaven forbid you should quote from it, especially in a dressing room.'

'"Double, double, toil and trouble",' Inga and I recited in unison.

Nigel held up his hands in mock horror. 'Cease your incantation!' he cried dramatically.

'No, really though, how on earth do they manage ever to put on a production of the play? I mean, one has to speak the lines.'

'Don't ask me. I'm not an actor.' Nigel addressed himself to his pint, and Inga added, 'Thank God.'

Our pub crawl turned eventually into an early dinner, which became ever more hilarious as several other musicians drifted in, saw us, and joined the party.

They were an extraordinarily diverse group. They all spoke English, but a lot of other languages were mixing in as well, and accents I couldn't even begin to identify.

A few I was certain of, though. Or at least almost certain.

'Are you two American or Canadian?' I asked a young couple. 'After living over here for several years,

I can't tell any more, and people can get annoyed if I get it wrong.'

'American,' they answered with a grin. 'And which are you? Actually, you sound English, but you said...'

Alan and I both laughed at that. 'You think I sound English. The English think I sound American. I sometimes think I'm the man without a country.'

They looked blank at that, and I chuckled again. 'Sorry. An old story. Very old, come to think about it. Anyway, I was born in southern Indiana, but I've lived in England for quite a while now. You sound more or less midwest—am I right?'

'Right on the nail-head. Springfield, Illinois, but we went to the IU School of Music, so we were almost your neighbours for a while.'

'Well, I'm impressed! The School of Music turns out some fine musicians. Are you singers or instrumentalists?'

'Oh, I'm so glad you didn't say "singers or musicians",' said the young woman. 'We've had a lot of battles about that over the years, because we're one of each. I play the violin, and my brother's a singer, a bass.'

'That's *basso profundo*, kid,' said the young man. 'I'm Larry Andrews,' he added, putting out a hand, 'and this is my twin, Laurie. This is the first chance we've had to work together since college.'

The four of us introduced ourselves. 'So what have you been doing since college?' I asked.

'Oh, you know, the usual,' said Larry. 'We both auditioned all over the place, and we got lucky. I'm with the San Francisco Opera chorus, and Laurie, our virtuoso, plays with the CSO.'

'The Chicago Symphony?' said Alan, with something like awe in his voice.

'I'm only a ringer,' Laurie hastened to explain. 'They're on tour right now and didn't need me, and when Larry told me the SFO didn't need him for a month either, we decided to try out for this, and we got lucky again!'

'I don't imagine,' said Alan, 'luck had a great deal to do with it.'

'Oh, but some of the people here are really good. Nigel, you were fantastic in the opera scenes today.'

'Thanks,' said Nigel, trying with little success to look modest, 'but the chorus and orchestra really tied it together.'

'Well, I very nearly came untied, I can tell you,' said Laurie.

'Or unstrung,' put in her brother.

'Oh, you're the one with the broken e-string!' said Nigel.

'And no replacement, like an idiot,' said Larry casually.

She punched him on the arm. 'I did too have replacements. I always carry them. I told you! Somebody swiped them, not just the e-string, but the whole kit and caboodle. And they were good ones, too, and they don't come cheap!'

'Hey, admit it, kid, they just fell out someplace. Nobody'd steal 'em.'

Laurie was getting annoyed. I stepped in hastily. 'Well, the orchestra sounded wonderful, so you must have managed. With a borrowed string, I suppose?'

'Yes, and now I have to find another set someplace so I can replace the one I used. And I don't know my way around over here well enough to have any idea where…'

Her voice was rising, and Larry draped a casual arm around her shoulders. 'Relax, kid. It ain't the end of the world. You did a great job, with a string that wasn't what you're used to, and not even broken in or anything. We'll find you some strings someplace. You probably won't even have to use them.'

Laurie leaned back against her brother. 'Sorry. Didn't mean to fall apart. It's just…with everything happening…'

'What you need is another drink,' said Larry. 'And just you listen to big brother. Yeah, I'm sorry the woman died that way. But mostly because she made trouble even by dying. I can't pretend I'm sorry she's gone, and this festival's going to work one whole hell of a lot better without her, so buck up.' He stood. 'Who else wants another beer?'

Laurie rolled her eyes at his departing back. 'He loves to play the big brother and boss me around, just because he's twenty minutes older.'

'There was certainly no love lost between him and Delia!' I said.

'Who?' Laurie looked puzzled, and Alan shot me a warning look.

'Sorry. Grace—the woman who died, whatever her name was. I'm bad at names.'

'Graciosa. That wasn't her real name, though. I don't know what her real name was, but she was a real pain. Larry was a little out of line just now, but he was right about one thing. Nobody liked her very much.'

'Nobody here at the festival, you mean?'

'Nobody in the known world of music,' said Larry, returning. 'Or at least opera. I only met her once before, in San Francisco, and she nearly killed the production. She's famous—well, she was famous—for causing trouble wherever she went.'

'She had a beautiful voice,' I said tentatively.

'There are lots of beautiful voices out there,' said Laurie, with a little of the instrumentalist's arrogance she didn't know she had. 'It's nice when they're attached to decent human beings.'

'But what did she *do*, to make everyone hate her so? I mean, Nigel here told us she was pretty unprofessional in rehearsal, and that's certainly enough to get everyone miffed. And I saw her…well, I guess you'd call it "temperament" that morning at the castle, when the weather was so awful. But I wouldn't call any of that "causing trouble", exactly.'

'Oh, no,' said Larry. 'That sort of thing was just her warm-up routine. The main act was destroying other people's careers.'

Larry had maybe had one beer too many, or else his singer's voice was easily audible by nature and training. At any rate, he'd been getting louder and louder, and we'd gathered a small crowd of the other musicians.

Now one of them joined in. 'You've got it in one, lad,' he said. 'She tried it with me. Nearly pulled it off, too.'

That started the chorus. The first man who spoke was a singer who'd been trashed by Gracie's antics in quartet auditions for an opera production in Prague. 'She'd give me the wrong cue, or come in a half-beat too soon, so my entrance sounded late. And when I lost my temper, she screamed in the middle of my tirade and claimed I'd hit her. She actually gave her own arm a nasty pinch to leave a bruise. Where it didn't show, of course.'

I had no chance to express indignation, for the cellist was eager to tell about the time Gracie broke her bow. 'I was playing in a pick-up orchestra in Strasbourg, and I said something about her to the conductor while we were taking a rehearsal break. Well, he didn't like her either, and he laughed, and Gracie heard us. She just

happened to be standing next to my desk, and she...
I'm not quite sure what she did, but somehow my bow
ended up on the floor in pieces.'

'But that's—'

'Fortunately it wasn't my good bow. I was using a
cheap one, because the best one was being re-haired
and the music wasn't all that demanding. But I had to
rent another one, which cost just about what I was being
paid for the concert.'

Some of the stories involved people who weren't
there. And the reason they weren't there was always the
same: Gracie had managed not just to damage their careers, but to put an end to them entirely. She had spread
rumours, had given misinformation about audition dates
and places, had in at least one case caused physical in-
jury to keep someone out of a performance. 'My wife,'
said the man telling that story. 'She used a throat spray,
and Gracie, who was the understudy, substituted sham-
poo. She just wanted to make Sue sick, but there was an
allergic reaction, and she'll never sing again.'

That one quieted the crowd enough that Alan could
ask, 'But why did no one ever sue her, or charge her with
criminal conduct? These stories are appalling!'

'Because she was clever,' said the woman with the
cello story. 'She managed things so nothing could ever
be proved. And she slept with enough of the conductors
and managers that they'd take her side. At least temporarily. Then if they started to get fed up, she'd threaten
to tell their wives and/or girlfriends.'

'Yeah, we couldn't figure out why Sir John was
putting up with her.' That was Laurie again. 'It's well
known that he's incorruptible. He married sort of late,
and he's absolutely crazy about his wife and kids.'

I wanted to divert that speculation, and besides I was

bursting with my own question. 'But *why* did she do all those awful things?' I was horrified by the stories, but what seemed to be missing was any compelling reason for such atrocious behaviour. 'The woman could sing. Why did she have to resort to the whole bag of dirty tricks?'

'Because she had to get to the very top, and she wasn't good enough to do that on the strength of her voice alone. She had an ego the size of Siberia, and a heart the same temperature.' Larry had taken the floor again. 'She could have had a very nice career in the third rank of opera. Small roles, regional companies, summer opera. But she wasn't interested in that sort of thing. In fact, we were all surprised to see her here, because this is a great festival, but let's face it, it's not exactly Glyndebourne. And she wanted nothing but the best. She wanted to be Renée Fleming, Deborah Voigt, and Anna Netrebko rolled into one, and the only way she could get to where she wanted to be was by climbing on other people's corpses.'

It was a chilling epitaph. By common consent, we quietly finished our drinks and went home.

ELEVEN

SOMEHOW, WHEN WE got back to Tower, we weren't in the mood for bed. Instead I brewed tea for all of us and we sat around in the lounge, pondering.

'I almost let the cat out of the bag, didn't I?' I said, handing Alan his cup.

'You let it entirely out, my dear. Fortunately everybody'd had a bit to drink, so I think they didn't notice, particularly.'

'Such a silly name, Graciosa.' I yawned.

'Actually it's quite pretty,' said Inga. 'It was just so wildly inappropriate. Heavens, I knew she was unpleasant, but whole new vistas opened up tonight.'

'And not very scenic ones, either,' said Alan. 'Nigel, how is it that you'd never heard any of these stories?'

'I'm not a real musician.'

'Indeed you are!' said Inga warmly.

'All right, I'm not professional, if you prefer that term. I mix with geeks and nerds and students, not singers and violinists and that crowd. I do take in *Opera*—the magazine, I mean—so I follow the gossip about the big names, but as you heard, our nasty little piece of work wasn't quite there yet.'

'I wish I could think it was a pity that she never will be, but I'm afraid I'm not that nice.' I yawned again. 'Sorry.'

'The interesting thing about tonight's little therapy

session,' said Alan, 'is the discovery of how many people are delighted that Delia's gone.'

Nigel started to hum a tune I couldn't quite recognize until he put words to it. 'Delia's gone, one more round, Delia's gone.'

I sat up straighter. 'Good heavens! That's a very old song! I heard it first when I was in college, which was long, long before you were born. Harry Belafonte sang it.'

'And Johnny Cash, and a lot of other people,' said Nigel. 'My mum liked that sort of thing when she was a kid, and collected it, and played it when I was a kid. I liked it too, and I remember quite a lot of it. Do you know the story behind it?'

'I didn't know there was one.'

'There was a real murder. Delia was almost a child, I think, and someone shot and killed her. Not much romance there, one would think, but years later they wrote a beautiful ballad about it.'

'Well, if there's one thing we know for sure,' I said, standing and beginning to collect cups, 'it's that this Delia wasn't murdered. Even though a lot of people may have wanted to do the deed. I've had it, folks. See you in the morning.'

'BUT, ALAN!' I sat up suddenly in bed a few hours later. 'I think she *was* murdered! And I think I know how they did it!'

'Lovely, darling. You're quite right.'

I looked at Alan suspiciously. His eyes were tightly closed.

Our window faced east. The sky was that milky colour that comes just before sunrise on a fine June day, which meant it wasn't yet five in the morning. I suppose

Alan had a perfect right to be sound asleep, but I was absolutely awake and, I knew from bitter experience, was not going to be able to get back to sleep. I sighed loudly.

Alan didn't stir.

Very well. I had to try this theory out on someone. Would either of the Wynne-Eytons be up at this hour? Probably not.

I got up, used the bathroom, and made myself a cup of tea, hoping that perhaps the hideous scream of the kettle might wake Alan. I let it sound for only a second, though. In the calm of early morning it sounded loud enough to wake the whole house, and quite possibly rouse Delia at the morgue, or wherever she was.

When there was still no response from Alan I realized I was on my own, unless I woke him forcibly, and for various reasons I didn't want to do that. Not least that I wanted him in a good mood when he did finally come to.

I drank my tea and thought about my idea. The more I considered it the more sense it made. I would have to check it out, of course. Did I know someone who could provide me with the evidence I needed?

The trouble was, I didn't really know anyone much around here. Back in Sherebury there were any number of people I could ask, but here? Alan and Nigel and Inga. And our hosts, of course, but I didn't really know them well. Maybe tomorrow morning—well, this morning, actually—I could go into Mold and see if there was a shopkeeper who could help. I tried to remember the shops I'd seen in Mold. Clothing stores, a charity shop, pubs, a library, a police station. A butcher, a baker, a candlestick maker...

'Having a nice snooze, love?'

I started awake at Alan's touch. The sun was shining in the window brilliantly, and I had a terribly stiff neck.

'Was I snoring, or thrashing about, or something?' Alan went on.

'Oh. No. No, I woke up really early with something important to tell you, but you were still asleep, so I got up to wait until I could decently wake you, and I must have nodded off.'

'And now we're both awake, so are you going to tell me how Delia was murdered?'

'You heard me! You were awake! And you made me wait all this time!'

'I was asleep. Some things one remembers even if one heard them while sleeping. So…?'

I contemplated remaining in my snit, but only briefly. I was too eager to hear Alan's reaction to my idea.

'Well, it started with a dream, or a nightmare, really. I was back in that awful passageway in the castle, and there were spiders everywhere, and I was trying to brush them away.'

'I remember that, too. At least I remember you crying out in your sleep.'

'Yes. In my dream you said something soothing. Or was that real?'

Alan shook his head. 'Reflex on my part, perhaps. Go on.'

'Then I was seeing Delia fall again, and again, and again. And each time, before she fell, she was trying to brush spiders away.'

Alan got the point at once. 'Those motions she made. Yes, you could be right. But are you suggesting that someone salted that balcony with spiders, or planted a fake one?'

'No, something much simpler than that. Actually, it was something Penny said that brought it to mind. Not spiders. Spider webs.'

'That disgusting spray people use at Halloween? The singers would have seen it immediately. We'd have seen it from the audience, come to that.'

'No. Something much more subtle. Violin strings.'

Alan looked at me and waited.

'They're thin and lightweight and neutral in colour. If they were hung from the roof of the balcony, dangling just far enough to blow in Delia's face or hair, I don't think she or anyone else would have noticed them until she felt them.'

'Hmm. And that girl Laurie says her spare set went missing.'

'Exactly.'

'But the question is, when? Nigel told us about the problem as part of the pre-concert madness yesterday. Delia died on Saturday, two days before.'

'Well, I thought of that, of course. The thing is, Laurie's e-string didn't break until just before the concert, so she didn't need a new one till then. Would she have noticed that the spares were gone?'

'I hope you don't plan to ask her,' said Alan.

'Why not? How else will I know?'

'Think, dear heart! Either she is telling the truth, and someone stole her strings—how absurd that sounds! Wasn't there a ridiculous song some years back about someone stealing someone's heartstrings? Whatever they might be.'

'Probably. But go on.'

'Very well. Either she's telling the truth, or she is not. If she is, and you start her thinking about when the strings vanished, she may start wondering why you want to know, and that may lead to her questioning others. Then, if your theory has any validity—'

'She could be in danger. Yes, I do see. And of course,

if she's lying, if she laid a booby-trap herself with her own strings—you're right, it does sound odd—then I've alerted her, and she could run away or…'

'Or decide that you, or we, pose a danger to her. Don't speak to her about it, Dorothy.'

He stalked into the bathroom, and I sat, somewhat deflated, trying to work the crick out of my neck. He was right, of course. Now that I had what I was perfectly certain was a sound theory about a way Delia could have been murdered, I couldn't see any way of taking it further. Any questioning of anyone concerned with the festival could raise suspicions in the mind of whoever was guilty.

Well, perhaps I could find a music store somewhere and at least take a look at violin strings. I realized I actually had little idea what they looked like off the instrument. And surely I could find some way to examine that balcony. If someone had hung something from its ceiling, there ought to be some trace.

The strings might even still be there! If the castle had been locked up since the rehearsal…if no one had been up there… And then I was deflated again. The police had been up there. They had presumably investigated thoroughly. If there had been anything hanging from the ceiling, they would have noticed.

But wait. Delia had been pawing at her face and hair. Suppose she had torn them down. Would they have been clasped in her hands as she fell?

Slowly I shook my head. If she had felt something in her hands, she would have thought it was part of a spider web, and would have been frantic to get rid of it. I knew that for a certainty. My arachnophobia isn't as severe as my claustrophobia, but it's bad enough that I knew exactly what Delia would have done.

And in that case…

Alan came back into the room, freshly showered and shaved. 'You have an "aha" look about you, woman,' he commented.

'My famous un-poker face again, eh? I'll tell you all about it after I've cleaned up.'

So, fifteen minutes later, while I was combing the tangles out of my wet hair, I told him where my train of thought had led me.

'You're quite sure she wouldn't have grasped them?'

'Quite sure.' The mere thought made me shudder.

'What *is* it about women and spiders?' Alan inquired, shaking his head a little.

'I don't know. I have no idea. Some of them are poisonous, of course, but not many, certainly not most. It's no more rational than any other phobia. I know spiders are very useful creatures that eat things like flies. I know they're amazing engineers, that their webs are admirable structures and often very beautiful. I also know that when I see a spider, or especially when I brush up against a web, my skin starts to crawl and I have to get away.' I shuddered again. 'I'd rather not talk about it, if you don't mind.'

Alan accepted that, though still obviously wondering how an otherwise intelligent and fairly sensible women could so fear a harmless creature perhaps a millionth her size. 'So what do you think happened to your hypothetical violin strings?'

'I think she pulled them down. Now that I come to think of it, that could have been what made her fall. They caught in her fingers, and they offered some resistance. That is, if they were taped or glued to the ceiling. She wouldn't have expected that and—oh, Alan, that would have made it much, much worse! It would have been as if the spider was pulling back—quite irrational, but dreadful. She would have fought all the harder, and when the strings suddenly gave way, her momentum...'

'You have too good an imagination, love. You're looking quite distraught. What you need is some breakfast to take away the nightmares. Get into some clothes, and let's see what Charles and Mairi have for us this morning.'

I was happy enough to drop the subject of spiders, but on the way downstairs I said, 'After breakfast, I want to find a music shop and look at some violin strings.'

TWELVE

NIGEL AND INGA were just finishing their last pieces of toast when we walked into the breakfast room. 'Morning, sleepy-heads,' Nigel greeted us.

'Ah, youth,' I declaimed. 'Up with the birds, full of energy. Actually, I was up before any of you. Only I fell asleep again.'

'Ah, age!' said Nigel wickedly. 'The privilege of sleeping late, dreaming away one's days, basking in the golden years.'

'A little respect for your elders, boy,' said Alan. 'And since you're astir so early, what are your plans for the morning? The concert's not until three, if I remember correctly.'

'Yes, and I don't have much to do today. It's song cycles—well, you've read the program—and there are only two for tenor. And I've sung them before, so I don't have to practice. Inga and I thought we might drive in to Chester, spend the morning there and have a bit of lunch. I've oceans of time.'

That suited my purposes splendidly. Chester's a good-sized cathedral city, and a big tourist destination because of the cathedral, the Roman wall and other ancient remains, and most of all its unusual shopping area, the Rows. Beautiful half-timbered buildings, some authentically Elizabethan, others lovely Victorian copies, hold shops of every kind. That in itself would be enough to attract visitors, but Chester is, I believe, unique in that the shops are on two levels. Above the street level, arcaded walkways lead to a second set of shops above the first. Some are simply the second storeys of large establishments, but most are separate entities, often small, quirky, and entirely delightful. There was bound to be at least one music shop among them.

'Oh, Nigel, what a lovely idea! Alan and I would love to go with you. At least I would. Shopping isn't always his thing.' I questioned him with a glance.

He, of course, knew perfectly well what I was thinking. He grinned and said, 'I think I'll go for a stroll instead, if nobody minds. There's some lovely countryside around here, and I haven't stretched my legs in days.'

Well, that suited me. I could combine my search for intelligence with a bit of real shopping, and I truly do love Chester. The taste Alan and I had had of it on our way to Tower had only whetted my appetite. 'Right,' I said. 'Oh, Mairi, good morning. I think I'll just have cereal and toast this morning. I've been eating far too much, and I'm keeping Nigel and Inga waiting.'

I hurried through my breakfast, with some regret at the thought of the lovely bacon I was missing, and brushed my teeth in record time. I'd floss tonight, I assured my mirror, a promise I make with regrettable frequency and too often forget to keep.

The day was another picture-perfect one. 'How long can this last?' I wondered as we sped toward Chester, just the other side of the Welsh-English border.

'Until the festival's over, I devoutly hope,' said Nigel. 'A storm like the one on Saturday would be a disaster.'

'Couldn't you move the whole operation into the church?'

'Not easily, and I'd imagine not without paying a whacking great fee for the privilege. Of course I don't have anything to do with the business end, but a small festival like this one doesn't take in a lot, and then there's the RNLI to think about. Extra expenses are a constant worry.'

'Sir John has pots of money,' said Inga comfortably. 'He could come up with the cash if necessary.'

He might not have had so much if he'd had to pay Delia what she was demanding.

For an awful moment I was afraid I'd spoken the thought aloud, but as there was no response from the other two, I realized I hadn't. They were very quiet, though, and I wondered if they might be thinking much the same thing.

Delia's death had been awfully convenient for a lot of people.

Most of the shops weren't open yet when we got to Chester, so we wandered about in the cathedral for a while. It's smallish, as cathedrals go, but then most cathedrals look small compared to Sherebury's. Chester's has some lovely details, including the most magnificent bishop's throne, or 'cathedra', that I've ever seen. As the good cathedrals almost always are, it was teeming with visitors.

'Too bad more of them don't make it to church on Sundays,' I murmured. For England, these days, is not a nation of church-goers, more's the pity. Even if I had no concern for English souls, I hate to think about the beautiful medieval churches all over the United Kingdom being closed for lack of attendance, and going into disrepair for lack of funds.

When we left the cathedral, blinking in the sunshine, we headed straight for the Rows. I had forgotten how festive the shops could look on a brilliantly sunny June day. I could let my eyes unfocus and almost believe I was watching a medieval market day, for the area was closed to almost all vehicular traffic, and people were everywhere. Flowers decked many shops, flags and banners hung from others, and the noise was terrific.

'All right, I have some shopping to do, and I'm sure you two have your own plans. So before we separate, where shall we meet for lunch, and when?'

'The Coach House?' suggested Inga. 'They do a lovely ploughman's, with local cheese.'

'A good pub,' I agreed. 'Twelve thirty? One?'

'We'd better make it twelve thirty, because I need to be at the castle a bit before three. And the first one there orders beer for three, right?'

On that happy note we separated and I headed straight for the Tourist Information Office to ask them to help me find a music shop.

I got lost a couple of times, but finally found the shop, and… Oh, dear!

I suppose I should have expected such hordes. There was a big music festival in town, after all, or if not exactly in town, then not very far away. Musicians need musical supplies. Duh.

And of course the first people I ran into were the twins, Larry and Laurie.

'Hello!' said Laurie. 'I'm sorry, I can't remember your name, but we met at the pub last night. I didn't know you were a musician.'

'Dorothy Martin. And I'm not. A musician, I mean.' I looked around, frantically hoping to see something that would give me an excuse for being there. Instruments. Instrument cases. Printed music. Music stands. Stand lights. The hundreds of other small items that musicians require. 'I think, actually, I may be in the wrong place. I was hoping to find some CDs of the music being performed this week, but it looks as though this place stocks only items for making music, not for listening to it.'

Weak, but they were Americans, too, and unfamiliar with British shops. They might buy it.

'I suppose you're here for new violin strings,' I went on brightly. 'Such a shame about yours going missing.'

'Yeah, and if I ever catch whoever took them, I'll wring his neck. I don't suppose you have any idea how hard it is to play a whole concert on a brand-new string.'

'Well, no, I actually don't. Why does a new string make it harder?'

'Well, for one thing, it wasn't the kind I usually use. I prefer gut strings, and the one I bummed is steel. There's a lot of difference in sound. But the big thing is, strings stretch as they're played. Once you've got your strings played in, they're pretty good at maintaining pitch. But a new one, besides sounding crude, stretches out of tune really fast, so you have to keep retuning. It's a big pain.'

'I can see it might be. But I thought all violin strings were made of cat gut. Though as a cat lover I find the idea somewhat repellent. Aren't steel strings for guitars?'

'Come on.' She took me by the hand and led me through the crowded shop. 'You need an education.'

I wasn't sure I actually did need exhaustive knowledge about violin strings, but I certainly needed to take a good look at some, and Laurie was giving me a wonderful opportunity to ask questions without raising suspicion.

'Here we are.' We had arrived at the back of the shop. 'Now look. See all the different brands? They really are different, too, and some are a *lot* more expensive than others.' She pulled one packet off its display hook and showed me the price tag.

'*Seventy pounds?*' I was in shock. 'For a few feet of… whatever they're made of?'

'I told you. These are the very best. They're gut at the core—sheep gut, by the way, it never was cat— wound with silver and gold, and they have the most gorgeous sound. They break in fast, they're really stable once they've stretched; they're ideal, really. But that's… what…well, over a hundred dollars, anyway. I buy these at home; I can't afford them here, not with maybe having to pay duty when I get back to the States. And of course I also have to buy a replacement set for Jessie, the guy who gave me his.'

'Now I understand why you were so upset at losing yours. So what are you going to do?'

'I'll get these for myself.' She replaced the first packet with care amounting almost to reverence, and pulled another off a hook a few displays down. 'These are perfectly adequate, at about half the price. I don't like the sound much, but they break in relatively fast. If I replace the e-string right away and play like mad until tomorrow, it'll do well enough. Better than Jessie's, anyway.'

'Tomorrow? Not today?'

'Today's just art songs. Larry's singing a couple of them, but they're accompanied by piano. So I've got the day off, or I would have if I didn't have to spend it fiddling. And I'll get these.' She pulled off another packet. 'They're the kind Jessie uses. I can't stand them, but to each his own. And it was really nice of him to let me use his. I was panicked.' She pulled a wallet out of the colourful canvas carryall she was using for a handbag and surveyed its contents ruefully. 'Looks like cheese and crackers for the rest of the trip! Now if I can shove through to the checkout…'

'Look, Laurie.' I planted myself in front of her. 'We

don't really know each other, but we're fellow Americans. And I'd hate for you to leave this country remembering a theft as your most important experience. I'd like to pay the difference between those,' I pointed to one of the packets, 'and the strings you really want. It's not so much, really, and I'm not on the kind of budget you are. And then I'd like to take you to lunch. I'm meeting Nigel Evans and his wife at a delightful pub not far from here. How about it?'

'Oh, I couldn't let you do that, really. I'm sorry I griped so much about it. Honestly, these will be fine.'

'They won't, and you know it perfectly well. Besides, it's silly to spend your money on something you'll never use again after this week. Laurie, I'd like to do this, for you and for the sake of music.'

I could see her hesitating. 'My dear, I'm nearly seventy. I don't have all that many more years to listen to music, even if I keep my hearing to the end, and to tell you the truth it's getting a little dodgy. And I don't have children of my own to give presents to. And my husband and I aren't exactly rich, but our money will certainly last us to the end of our days. So please?'

She gave in, with a broad smile and hug. 'We'll make it a loan, okay? As soon as I get home and start earning some money, I can pay you back.'

'If you think you must. Now let's buy those things, and then would you like to come shopping with me? I need a new summer hat.'

Laurie, who had probably never worn a hat in her life, was greatly bemused by my efforts to find one I liked. 'But where do you wear them?' she asked.

'Anywhere I like. I know almost no one else does any more. I don't care. I like hats and I look nice in them, and I'll tell you a little secret. Men love hats. I've had more compliments than I can count from perfect strangers. Makes Alan quite jealous.'

'Really?' was all she said, but she tried on a hat or two, all the same. When I finally found one I loved, I caught her in front of a mirror with a modest straw boater on the back of her head. She burst into giggles when she saw my reflection looming in the mirror.

'I look like an idiot!'

'Well…' I took the hat off her head. 'That's a nice hat for you, but this is the way to wear it.' I put it well forward on her head and tilted it over one eye. 'There. Now you look like an old-fashioned French schoolgirl.'

She did, too. Laurie had shoulder-length blonde hair. Last night she'd had it pulled back in one of those scrunchy things, but today she'd held it in place with a huge barrette, the kind that always reminds me of a heavy-duty paper clip. She'd removed it to try on the hat, and her hair rippled down, clean and shiny. With the hat, she looked exactly like Leslie Caron in *Gigi*, if Gigi had been a blonde.

'You don't think I look silly?'

'Do you think you do?'

'Well…actually I think I look sort of nice.' She took the hat off with some reluctance. 'But I can't afford it, and anyway I'd never wear it.'

'I'll accept the poverty excuse. Been there, done that. But never be afraid to do something because you think you'll look foolish. The secret to enjoying life is not to mind making a fool of yourself. Now, let's go find Nigel and Inga and some lunch.'

I wore my new hat out of the store. It was a broad-brimmed pink affair with a single, huge pink rose, and it didn't go at all with my jeans and T-shirt. Never mind. I liked it, and on the way to the pub two men told me how nice they thought it was. I winked at Laurie.

Nigel and Inga were, of course, used to my eccentricities, and didn't turn a hair at my appearance. 'New one?' asked Inga.

'Just bought it. What do you think?'

'It suits you,' said Nigel. 'I've ordered you a pint and a ploughman's. I hope that was all right. I'd have ordered something for you, Laurie, but we didn't know you were coming.'

'I didn't know myself. We ran into each other, and Mrs Martin invited me to come along.'

She looked over the menu and settled on a ploughman's lunch, also. 'Not that I really know what that is, but if you all say it's good, it's okay with me.'

Inga noticed Laurie's parcel. 'Did you find something exciting?'

'Just new strings. I got two sets, one for me, one for Jessie, the guy who let me use his.' She opened her mouth to say something more, with a glance at me, but I gave a tiny shake of my head. My small contribution to the deal was our secret.

'May I see?' asked Inga. 'I don't think I've ever seen them except on a violin.'

I breathed a sigh of relief that I'd said nothing of my suspicions to anyone except Alan. Inga was perfectly natural in her request, and had played nicely into my hands.

Laurie obligingly took out the expensive packet of superior strings. 'They don't really look like much.' She opened the packet and let the strings slide out on to the table, making sure first that it was clean. 'Amazing that something so ordinary-looking can make such beautiful sounds, isn't it?'

THIRTEEN

I LOOKED AT THEM, and my heart sank. They were loosely coiled, and even without touching them I could see that they could never be mistaken for spider silk. They weren't anything like fine enough, and they looked springy. Still… 'How long are they?' I asked. Inane question. They would obviously be long enough to stretch from one end of a violin to the other. But Laurie obligingly stretched one out for me. And when she let go of one end, it immediately snapped back into its coil.

So much for a lovely theory.

Still, there had to be some reason for someone to have taken Laurie's strings. I spent the rest of our lunch trying to think of one and forgetting to drink my beer.

'Sorry to break this up,' said Nigel, popping the last fragment of cheese and bread into his mouth, 'but I have to get to the castle. Laurie, can we drop you somewhere, or did you drive?'

'Me? Drive in this country? On the wrong side of the road? You've got to be kidding. I took the bus from Flint. The service isn't bad at all.'

'But a car is a lot quicker,' said Nigel. 'I'll bring the car round, and you can tell me on the way where you're staying, Laurie.'

'You went awfully quiet, Dorothy,' said Inga softly to me while we waited for Nigel. 'Are you not feeling well?'

'I'm fine, just a bit perturbed. I'll tell you later,' I said, with a sideways glance at Laurie.

Laurie, it turned out, was staying with her brother in a B & B in Flint, so Nigel dropped Inga and me off at Tower, while he and Laurie headed on towards Flint.

'Right,' said Inga after we'd waved them on their way. 'What's going on?'

'Oh, nothing really, except that I had a silly idea, and it was just proven wrong. Let's get Alan, and we'll have some tea and I'll tell you.'

Alan was napping, but he woke readily enough and accompanied me downstairs to the lounge.

I told them the whole thing. 'And it turns out violin strings aren't a bit the way I thought they were. Not to mention the fact that the new ones come all curled up. You couldn't get them to hang straight down unless you weighted them. Which would sort of defeat the purpose.'

Alan was inclined to be philosophical about it. 'Ah, well, it was a good theory. Pity it didn't work out.'

'Yes,' said Inga slowly, thoughtfully. 'But then why *did* someone steal Laurie's strings? It seems a pointless thing to do.'

'They wanted a better set for themselves,' said Alan. 'You said, Dorothy, that the ones she prefers are very expensive.'

'But that doesn't make sense, either. At least from what I gathered from Laurie, no musician would deliberately switch strings just before a performance. Laurie's doing it with the one string, because she hates her borrowed one. And of course when a string breaks, the player has no choice. But to steal a whole set of strings just before a concert—that seems to me highly unlikely.'

'I remind you,' said Alan with his infuriating logic, 'that we don't know when those strings were stolen. *If* they were stolen. We only know when Laurie says she missed them.'

One of Alan's chief constable moments. I find them infuriating, especially because he's always right.

'Well, then, let's ask her,' said Inga. 'We don't have to say anything about Delia. Or Gracie, rather. I keep forgetting! We can just say we're disturbed about the theft and would like to catch the rat who did it.'

Alan shrugged. 'And if Laurie tells you the truth, which is not certain, where will that lead you?'

'I trust her, Alan,' I said, a trifle huffily. 'Now that I know her a little better, I like and trust her. She'll tell the truth. As to where it will lead us, who knows until we find out?'

But the fact was, I was stuck and I knew it. I was utterly convinced that Delia had been murdered, but I had absolutely no idea how. It seemed to be an impossible crime worthy of John Dickson Carr.

Alan and I decided to skip the art songs, as neither of us is very fond of them. Inga, of course, was duty-bound to show up, so we dropped her off at the castle and tried to think of something to do with the afternoon.

'Are there any other good castles around?' I asked. 'I've developed a bit of a taste for them.'

'You ask that in Wales?' said my husband with a tolerant grin. 'This small country has more castles than anywhere else in Europe. The very best, in my opinion, is only a few miles west. You'll like the town, too.'

So we found ourselves in Conwy, which fitted exactly my idea of what a medieval town should be. Small, crowded, surrounded by its ancient wall, and loomed over by its fairytale castle.

'Oh, that's the castle of my dreams!' I said at my first sight of it. 'It's perfect!'

It had everything. Lots of towers, battlements, arrow slits. Lots of rooms inside, though none of them, of course, had a roof. It had no moat, but it had not, when first built, needed one, for it was then protected on three sides by the River Conwy and on the fourth by a steep hill. Although I didn't take time to read the guidebook carefully, it looked to me as though the defences had held throughout its history. Certainly it didn't look as though anything short of a bomb could touch it now.

And there were no dark interior passages, thank heaven!

After we'd wandered a bit and got a feel for the place, we went in search of tea and found a pleasant little tea room in one of the steep, narrow streets. 'It's a good thing we parked down there on the bridge,' I commented, looking out the window at the drivers trying to navigate a street that was plainly too narrow for vehicular traffic. 'Driving in this place must be a nightmare.'

'Walking is pleasant, though. How about a turn on the town walls after tea? They're nearly complete, I believe, and have some magnificent views.'

Long ago, before I ever visited England, if someone mentioned walking on walls, I pictured a hazardous activity, teetering along, reminiscent of a cat on a back fence. It isn't like that at all, of course. The wall surrounding a medieval town is really two walls, set five or six feet apart, with the space in between filled with rubble or something. Whatever it is, it's quite solid, because it's paved over at the top, and one can walk quite easily from one guard tower to the next.

Well, I say quite easily. In Conwy it's a bit of a challenge, actually, because of the terrain of the town. The wall had to follow the shape of the hills, of course, and though they smoothed it out a bit with the wall higher in some places than in others, there are still some steep grades on the top, and in some cases a flight of steps up to the tower, and another coming down. Add in the hard round cobblestones underfoot in some sections, and I was quite glad when we came to a place where steps led back down to the street.

'I'm glad we did that,' I said to Alan when I got my breath back. 'Most interesting, and you were right about the views. Do those mountains have a name?'

'That's Snowdonia,' said Alan. 'The highest mountains in Britain, outside of the Scottish Highlands.'

'I've heard of Mount Snowdon. Is it one of those we saw?'

'It's a bit too misty today to see it. I'll show you before we go home, if the weather keeps fine.'

'I keep wondering how I've managed to reach my advanced age and yet stay so ignorant about most of the world. Here's all this beauty been within my reach for years now, and I never even knew about it.'

'You're just going to have to live a good deal longer, the better to see more.'

We walked back to the car in companionable silence, but I thought about what Alan had said.

'Delia didn't get to see as much as she should,' I said in the middle of a long silence.

'You're really worried about her, aren't you, love?'

'You know, I am. I think it's sad that nobody liked her. Imagine going through life making enemies. It sounds as though she travelled a lot, but I'll bet she never even saw the beauty wherever she went. I've heard Prague is one of the most beautiful cities in Europe, but all Delia wanted to do there was claw her way to a winning audition. She must have been a very unhappy person.'

'She certainly made a lot of other people unhappy,' said Alan. 'I'm not sure she deserves your sympathy.'

'Oh, but that's just it, don't you see? She *didn't* deserve sympathy. She didn't deserve love. But that's an awful way to go through life. I would hate to think of people being glad when I die. And Alan, that's why I'm determined to find out who killed her.'

'You really believe she was murdered.'

'Don't you?'

He didn't reply for a beat or two. Finally he said, 'I suppose I do. I don't want to. There's absolutely no evidence to sustain the notion. But I don't like coincidence. Never have. And it seems too great a coincidence that she was here surrounded by people who had good reason to hate her, and she died in what looked like an accident. No, I agree with you. She was murdered. But I haven't an idea how, much less how we're going to prove it.'

FOURTEEN

INGA AND NIGEL were back at Tower when we got there. We told them about our afternoon, and Nigel came over all Welsh again, taking as much pride in Snowdonia as if he'd invented the mountains himself.

'So how did the concert go?' I asked when I thought he'd gone on about it long enough.

He shrugged. 'Well enough. We had a good audience, but somehow none of us were really "on". I never thought I'd say it, but we missed Gracie.'

'Goodness! Why?'

'Well, you wouldn't have thought art songs were her thing. Not dramatic enough. But she did a really good job in rehearsal—the only thing she did right until the Habañera—and somehow it energized us all. Without her, today, it was all sort of flat.'

'Could it have been the conductor?'

'No conductor.' Nigel gave me a sideways grin. 'You really don't know much about art songs, do you?'

'They've never been my favourites,' I admitted.

'They're accompanied by piano, and they're really duets between the singer and the piano. No conductor. Sir John sat in the audience the whole time.'

'Oh. Stupid of me; I should have realized that. I only asked because a conductor's mood can have such an influence on a performance.'

'You're right, of course. But this afternoon it was the singers. There was... I don't know, an uneasiness.

Maybe it was what's-her-name—Pat—who set everyone off.'

'Who's Pat?' Inga asked.

'Oh, didn't I tell you? It was a bit sad, actually. Did
I tell you that some of the singers today were from the
chorus? There are some really good voices there, solo
voices, but as there's only a quartet for most things, only
four of us are officially soloists. But for this afternoon
Sir John really spread the wealth around, so to speak.
So some of the extras got to talking about Dan Green,
that baritone—the one who fell off the boat, remember?'

I was shocked to realize that I had almost forgotten.
'Oh, dear. I suppose he had friends in the group?'

'Worse than that. His fiancée.'

'Oh, dear heaven! One of the singers?'

'She had been in the chorus. She dropped out when he
died, as you'd expect. But she came round today to say
goodbye. She's going back home, but she should have
known better than to show up just before a concert. It
upset the singers.'

'Nigel, think what you're saying!' I took his hand.
'She wanted to talk to people who'd known her dead
lover, who might sympathize or at least offer her some
support. She wasn't thinking about a performance. Did
she have any particular friends among the other singers, do you know?'

'I don't, actually. You understand I didn't really know
either of them. There are eighty people in the full chorus, though they don't all sing everything, and I've met
only one or two.'

'Well, if the poor child didn't have any close friends
here, or any family—where's home, do you know?'

'No idea.'

'I'd like to find out. I feel guilty that I'd forgotten

about the man until you reminded me. I'd like to at least send the girl a card, or some flowers, or something.'

'The world lost a fine mother when God didn't give you children,' said Alan, with that warm note in his voice that always makes me melt.

'Well, I suppose I've been making up for it ever since. Nigel, do you think you could get her address for me? I'd really like to make sure she's going to be all right.'

'I suppose the festival secretary would have contact information for all the performers. I could check with her.'

'Do, please. But not,' I added firmly, 'until tomorrow. This evening we need to go out for a nice dinner and try to forget about everything but good food and good wine and good friends.'

Next morning, though, Alan and I barely let Nigel finish his breakfast before reminding him of our request. 'Just a phone number, Nigel, if that's all you can get. But an address would be useful, too.'

'And what excuse am I going to give to the secretary?'

'The truth is usually the easiest,' said Alan. 'Say you learned yesterday that Pat was a good friend of the man who died, and your friend wanted to express her condolences.'

Nigel repaired to the front drive to make his call (the walls of the house being too thick for good mobile reception), but was back in less than a minute.

'She said the policy is to release no personal information about any of the performers. She suggested I could give her a card, and she'd send it along to Pat.'

'Oh, but I'd much rather see her, talk to her, if she lives anywhere near here…'

'Well, then,' said Alan, rising from the breakfast

table. 'Perhaps we can convince Sir John to give you what you want, Dorothy. And the impulse does you credit, love. Is there a rehearsal this morning, Nigel?'

There was. This afternoon's programme was the Haydn oratorio *The Creation*, and as the new mezzo had had no opportunity to rehearse it with the orchestra and chorus, they were going to run through bits of it this morning.

'Good. When does it begin?'

'We're called for nine thirty,' said Nigel, looking at his watch. 'I've plenty of time.'

'Ah, but I'd like to chat with Sir John before you get started. Do you want to come with me in, say, fifteen minutes, or would you rather leave a bit later?'

Nigel elected to relax for a little longer, so I rushed to get teeth brushed and hair combed, while Alan did everything but jingle his car keys. His impatience made it easier for me to skip flossing once more. 'My teeth are going to fall out one of these days,' I complained as I fastened my seat belt.

'What's that in aid of?' he asked, heading up the drive.

'You keep on hustling me out of the house before I have time to floss. My dentist says it's so important.'

'Hmph. You never have been very faithful about it, that I recall.'

'True. But what's the hurry, anyway?'

'I'm not sure. I just feel finding this Pat person might be important. Don't ask me to explain why. I don't know.'

I'm usually the one with the illogical hunches. Alan has been known to tease me about them unmercifully. I opened my mouth, took a look at his intent face, and decided it was wiser to keep still.

Sir John had just arrived at the castle when we got there. We found him conferring with the festival secretary in a small room they had set up as an office. The snaking electrical cables, the laptop and printer and boxes of programmes looked very odd juxtaposed against the ancient stone walls. The sun beat down, warm even at nine in the morning. I tried not to imagine what effect rain would have on the electronics, in a roofless room.

'Mr Nesbitt!' said the conductor, looking up in evident surprise. 'What brings you here at this hour?'

'I'm afraid I need to ask a favour. There was a young woman here yesterday, Nigel tells me, a Pat something, who was a member of the chorus but dropped out. I'd like to speak to her, but your excellent secretary didn't think she should give Nigel her phone number. I thought perhaps you might reconsider.'

'Of course. Sheila, do you know the girl's last name?'

Sheila did. She was very efficient, and like functionaries everywhere, somewhat protective of her territory. She found the information, wrote it on a slip of paper, and gave it to Alan without speaking a word. We walked out of the office.

'How did the police react to the news about Gracie's real identity?' Alan asked Sir John in an undertone.

'They seemed grateful, since it meant they could trace her movements somewhat more easily. If they decide to do that. I got the impression they had more or less decided to write off the incident as an accidental death.'

'There will have to be an inquest, though,' said Alan, frowning.

'Yes, they told me that. But they've kindly put it off until the festival is over. This is Wales, after all, and apparently several of the men in the force sing in local choirs. Anything that interferes with music is more or less heretical.'

'And how right they are!' I said. 'I'm glad they didn't give you any trouble about it. And, Sir John, I'm so sorry about all this. It must be very difficult for you.'

'Not so much as you might think,' he said. 'It was a terrible shock to see her again, and then to have her die that way…but I lost Delia years ago, and Cynthia and the twins are my world now.'

'And music.'

'And music, of course. I would die without music.'

He said it without emotion, a simple statement of fact. I found it extremely moving, and would have made some comment, but Alan was so eager to be off, and trying so hard to conceal it, that I forbore.

The minute we were out of the castle precincts, Alan phoned the number he had been given for Pat Stevens. He tried it twice, in case he'd punched in the wrong number the first time.

'Voicemail. Let's go.'

He handed me an OS map and the paper he'd been given. There were two addresses, one a B & B in 'Northop, nr. Flint', the other in Manchester.

'But Alan,' I pointed out, 'she won't still be at her B & B, will she? She took that just for the festival. Nigel said she was going home.'

'We'll try the B & B first,' he said.

I said no more. Obviously 'first' meant that if we didn't find her there, Alan planned to go all the way to Manchester. I hadn't the least desire to do so today. It wasn't all that far away, really, but it's a huge and largely modernized city, and the chances of getting lost in it were great. If she really had left for home, I'd content myself with a card, and try to phone her later. And I wanted to be back for the afternoon concert. But Alan had a bee in his bonnet. I kept my opinions to myself and my eyes on the map.

We found the B & B with no trouble. It was a small-ish stone cottage set in an attractive garden, not actually in the village of Northop but on the outskirts. The young woman pulling weeds from around the roses was pleasant, and fortunately not terribly inquisitive. Yes, Pat Stevens was staying there, she told us in a marked Welsh accent. No, she hadn't yet left, though she was planning to do so later today. There was nobody at her home, her hostess thought, but with the terrible thing that had happened—we knew about that? Well, one could understand that she found it too hard to stay near the festival. No, the hostess wasn't planning to attend any of the concerts. She loved a good men's choir singing Welsh songs, but this other sort of music wasn't her cup of tea. And would we in fact like…?

'Thank you, no. We'd like to talk to Miss Stevens. Is she in?'

In, but still in bed, the hostess thought. She hadn't even got up for breakfast, though as to that, she hadn't been eating well, or sleeping well, either. She, the hostess, had heard her pacing the floor last night till all hours.

Alan and I looked at each other. He glanced at his watch. It was nearly ten.

'Would you mind if I just went up and knocked on her door?' he asked. 'My name is Alan Nesbitt, and I've come from the festival with a message for her. I was told to deliver it personally. Perhaps she's up but not ready to come down.'

'Happy to meet you. I'm Bronwen Thomas.' The hostess looked slightly dubious. 'I don't like to disturb my guests, but I suppose… Oh, well, come up, then.'

Mrs Thomas brushed the dirt off her hands and knees and led the way up a narrow staircase to a minute landing with two doors. She tapped on the closed one. 'Pat, *fach*,' she said softly.

I raised my eyebrows at Alan.

'Small, I think, literally,' he whispered. 'I believe it's also used as an affectionate term.' His eyes were on the door.

'Pat, there are some people here to see you,' said Mrs Thomas, a little more loudly.

'Allow me,' said Alan, and although his voice wasn't loud, it was commanding. The woman ceded her place without question.

'Miss Stevens, I'm here from the festival. Open the door, please.' He rapped on it.

No response.

He put a hand on the knob. It turned readily. Mrs Thomas made a little noise of protest.

The room was empty. The bed had been neatly stripped, sheets and blankets folded and piled on the mattress. Wardrobe doors gaped open.

Pat was gone.

FIFTEEN

THERE WAS AN envelope on the bedside table. Mrs Thomas picked it up, opened it, and pulled out a folded piece of paper and some banknotes. She read the message, tears starting in her eyes. 'She's gone. Here, if you're her friends you'll want to read it.'

She handed the note to me. Aware that I was not really Pat's friend, privy to her correspondence, I nevertheless read:

Dear Bronwen,
You've been kind and I knew I'd cry if I had to say goodbye, so I'm just leaving. I don't know quite where I'll go from here. I can't go back to Manchester just yet. It wouldn't be the same without Dan. There's no one else. I hope this is enough to pay for my stay. If I've left anything behind just keep it, or toss it.
Pat.

'Dan was her young man,' said Bronwen sadly. 'And that fond of each other! They lit up a room with the looks they gave one another. Ah, it's a great pity!'

I got teary, too. 'That poor girl! Alan, I must write to her. Maybe when the festival's over we could go see her on the way home. Oh, I know Manchester isn't on the way home, but you know what I mean.'

'Hmmm,' was all Alan said. He's fond of those ambiguous noises, and I've become quite good at interpreting them. This time, though, I couldn't catch his thoughts. He thanked Mrs Thomas and we went on our way.

We came to a crossroads and Alan hesitated. 'I've half a mind...' he muttered.

That I *could* interpret. 'No, Alan. We don't have time to go to Manchester and get back in time for the concert. And anyway she wasn't going there yet, so we don't know where she might be. Not to mention the little matter of lunch. And I want to hear *Creation*. I've never heard it, only a couple of bits. And there's not all that much hurry to see Pat.'

'You're right. Yes, of course you're right. It's only... Dorothy, did you ever consider that Daniel Green might have been pushed out of that boat?'

I opened my mouth for an automatic reply, and closed it again. After some thought, I said, 'At the time I didn't even give it a thought. Now, with everything else that's been happening, I don't know. What gave you the idea?'

He ran a hand down the back of his neck. 'Just that, I suppose. You know I don't like coincidence, and I get suspicious of a string of "accidents".' His tone put clear quotation marks around the word. 'When several odd things happen within a given group of people, and one of them is acknowledged to be a trouble-maker, I begin to wonder.'

'But the troublemaker is dead herself—and, we think, murdered.'

'She was on that boat, though. You saw her. What if someone was aiming for her and missed?'

'What a dreadful thought!' I shuddered. 'Someone would have had to really hate her. So far all we've learned is that a lot of people had grudges against her. A grudge is scarcely enough to lead to murder.'

'It is if you live and move and have your being in the world of grand opera. A grudge murder is almost a cliché plot device in a tragic opera. And from everything we've seen and heard, that was the way Delia operated. Her emotions were all on top, and precious little restraint did she exercise over them. What if someone else had that same outlook on the world? It's my opinion that a person with that mindset, given the opportunity, would have given Delia a push without the slightest qualm.'

I thought about that for a mile or two. 'I suppose someone might have done such a thing,' I said finally. 'But surely, when he realized his mistake, he wouldn't have tried again.'

Alan shrugged. 'The mistaken-identity thread runs through a lot of opera, too. If we're talking about a complete egoist, he isn't quite sane. Anyone who gets in his way can be brushed aside like a bothersome fly. As easy to brush away two flies as one.'

I shuddered. 'That's a truly terrifying idea. The thing is, the only person in this entourage who fits that description—the complete egoist—is Delia. And Delia was the victim.'

'Delia was the only one who displayed that personality openly. There are nearly two hundred people involved in this festival, one way and another, including the support staff. Are we in a position to say that none among them harbours that kind of overweening pride and arrogance?'

'No, of course not. It's just—it's awful to think about someone so eaten up with hatred. And I still can't imagine a motive strong enough…' I trailed off, suddenly appalled at where our thoughts had led.

'He wasn't on the boat, Dorothy. He was rehearsing with the orchestra that day. Remember?'

'Thank God. I couldn't bear the thought—and he's just not that sort of person.'

'He's a musician, Dorothy, and a damn good one. He's bound to have a fair-sized ego. But I agree, he seems a decent sort of man. And in any case he's completely out of the picture, for either death.'

'All right, here's another thought. Where was Pat while all this was going on? Alan, I remember that scene. I wish I could forget it. There was a general out-cry when Dan fell, but no single outpouring of grief. No one seemed to care very much, in fact. Which was rather callous, I suppose, but certainly human nature.'

'Plainly, Pat wasn't there, for whatever reason. But Delia was. I keep coming back to that. Could she have suspected that the push was meant for her? How would one have expected Delia to react? How did she, in fact?'

I racked my brains. 'The only thing I remember, or think I remember, is her complaint about the delay. At least someone with a loud voice and a foreign accent complained. It could have been Delia.'

'Or almost any other woman.' Alan sounded dispir-ited as we turned into the car park of a promising-look-ing pub.

'The trouble is,' I said as I made my careful way over the gravel, 'that we don't know enough.'

'And of course, as usual, we haven't the slightest ex-cuse for asking questions. After you, my dear.' He ush-ered me into the pub with a gallant gesture.

We continued to discuss it over lunch. 'We could go to the police,' I offered with little enthusiasm. 'The of-ficial police, I mean. Inspector What's-his-name.'

'Owen. As Welsh a name as you'll find anywhere. And exactly what would we tell him? That we have a great many unsupported suspicions?'

'You think too much like a policeman. Our ideas may not have a lot of evidence behind them, but they're not exactly unsupported. We have experience of crime and criminals, you over a lifetime, and me for a good few years now. And we have experience of life, and the way people behave, and misbehave. When we form opinions, they're worth considering.'

Alan smiled at me. 'I'm not the one you need to convince. I agree with every word you say—as an individual. But as the policeman I once was—'

'And still are and always will be,' I interrupted.

'As a policeman I have to look at evidence. And we have none, not one jot or tittle, that either Daniel Green or Delia Warner was murdered.'

'Then we'll just have to get some, won't we?'

'And how do you propose to do that?'

'First of all, by talking to Pat as soon as we can reach her. Why don't you try her phone again?'

But again there was no answer, and it was time we headed to the afternoon concert.

THE MUSIC TOOK my mind off everything else for a blissful afternoon. Sir John had chosen to use the English translation of the oratorio, and the setting of those familiar words was glorious. I could hardly believe that in a lifetime of enjoying great music I had never heard this before. The critics would later speak of the performance in awed terms, calling it perhaps the best *Creation* ever performed with semi-professional musicians. They didn't put it quite that way, of course, but that was what they meant. I only knew that I was transported, transformed.

When it was over, the audience simply sat in silence for a long moment before breaking into wild applause.

I clapped until my hands hurt, and Inga and Alan right along with me.

When Nigel joined us, flushed with the thrill of performance, he brought the American twins with him. Amid a spate of mutual congratulations, Laurie turned to me. 'Hey, I owe you a lot, Mrs Martin. That new string made all the difference! Could you hear it?'

I smiled and shook my head. 'Not with all the other glorious noise going on! I don't have that good an ear. But the whole thing was splendid, orchestra, chorus, soloists and all. Look, if you two don't have any plans right now, how about going with us for a magnificent tea, or a drink if that suits your American tastes better?'

'Hey, I don't have anything against tea,' said Larry. 'And by "a tea" they mean a meal over here, don't they?'

'They do indeed. And I'll bet that hotel—what's its name, Nigel, where we had dinner that one night?'

'Soughton Hall. They don't do teas in the normal run, but Inga and I found a place that does, called Bodysgallen Hall. It's a hotel in a seventeenth-century manor house, near Llandudno. I think you'll like it.'

'Well, then,' said Alan, beaming, 'we'll go to your unpronounceable hotel and celebrate with a fine feast of carbohydrates. Nigel, if you'll lead the way, and take Inga and Larry, I think we can fit Laurie and her violin into our car.'

On the way the conversation was all about the concert, revelling in one glorious moment after another. 'It's funny. You know how they say the onlooker sees most of the game? Well, in a concert, the orchestra doesn't usually hear much of the music. We're too close to it. I can hear the violins, and sometimes the other strings, and everyone can hear the brass!'

'I imagine sometimes you wish you couldn't,' I put in.

'Well, they do get loud! But everything's different in an outdoor setting. The acoustics don't work at all the same way as in a concert hall. And this afternoon—oh, it was almost as if I were in the audience, only better. I could hear everything, and how it all blended together, and yet I was a part of it, helping make that fantastic music! It was… I can't even describe it!'

'You really love what you do, don't you, Laurie?'

'When it's like today, more than anything in the world.' She thought about that for a little, and then giggled. 'Well—there's a guy back home…'

And we all laughed. 'But,' I said, 'if you had to choose between him and music…'

'Well, I guess I did that this summer, didn't I?' she said, after a moment. 'He wanted me to stay home and party with him. He's got a lake cottage in Michigan somewhere, with a sailboat, and it would have been fun. But I couldn't pass this up!'

'Does your brother have a girl in the States?' asked Alan.

'No one serious. It's all about music with him, too. He's even more intense about it than I am. He'll never settle down, I don't think, unless it's with another musician. And that doesn't always work out so well, if either of them tours at all.'

'I've always thought,' I said, 'that a musician's life wasn't an easy one. Unless you're in the very top rank, there's always financial insecurity. And as you say, schedules can really complicate family life.'

'No, it isn't easy, not unless you get a good teaching position in a university someplace. But that can be maddening, trying to teach kids who have no talent, or no ambition. Maybe it was better back in the days when musicians were hired by kings and people like that, and worked in the court.'

'Like Haydn's musicians. A friend of mine wrote a book about Haydn once, and I read bits of it. He'd managed to find rosters of the court musicians of the time, even including what they were paid! It would have been a lot more interesting if he'd been able to figure out what that equalled in present-day dollars, but even without knowing that, it obviously amounted to a handsome chunk of money for the Austrian princes to shell out.'

And we went on talking about Haydn and the Viennese court until we got to the hotel.

They were able to provide us with as lavish a spread as anyone could have asked for. 'Good grief, I'll gain five pounds just looking at all this,' I groaned, while loading my plate with three sandwiches, a scone, and a slice of bara brith, the Welsh fruit bread. 'Tomorrow I've got to take a long walk. I've been sitting too much.'

Alan very wisely said nothing at all.

When my appetite was at last sated, I refilled my teacup and raised it in a toast. 'Here's to a host of fine musicians, making beautiful music!'

'Hear, hear!' said Alan.

I had come down somewhat from my Haydn-high and thought it might be time to ask a few searching questions. 'And speaking of musicians, did any of you get to know Pat Stevens? She was the singer whose fiancé fell off the canal boat.'

'Oh, that's right, you were going to talk to her today,' said Nigel. 'Is she coping?'

'She had already left when we got to her B & B.' Alan stepped smoothly into the conversation. 'She left a note for her hostess, saying she wasn't going home yet a while. Would any of you know where she might have gone, instead?'

The three musicians looked blank. 'I suppose I knew her a little,' said Larry slowly, 'but she wasn't an easy person to know. She and Dan were so wrapped up in each other, there wasn't much left for anyone else.'

'We'd very much like to find her,' said Alan. 'Did you happen to overhear anything about her family or friends?'

Larry's face changed. 'Say, what is all this, anyway? You're sounding like a cop. Why do you want to know so much about Pat? She didn't do anything!'

I sighed. 'Oh, dear. The thing is, kids, Alan *was* a cop. He's been retired quite a while, but he was a chief constable for years, if you know what that is.'

'I think I do,' said Laurie. 'I've read a few Agatha Christies. Sort of like a fancy sheriff, isn't it?'

'Sort of. Anyway, he can't help sounding like a policeman sometimes.'

'But to answer your question, Larry,' said Alan, 'no, there's no question of Pat having "done anything", as you put it. We'd just like to talk to her because, frankly, we think there might be some question about how Dan met his death.'

'You're not saying she had anything to do with it!' Larry was getting upset.

'Look, we seem to have got off on the wrong foot somehow,' I said in a placating tone. 'Nobody thinks Pat did anything wrong. It's just that we got to thinking, Alan and I, that it was a little odd, Dan falling off the boat that way. We don't think Pat was even with him on that little trip.'

'No, she wasn't,' said Larry, snapping his fingers. 'I remember now. She wasn't feeling so good that day. She thought she might be coming down with a sore throat, and that's serious for a singer. So she decided to rest that day, but she wouldn't let Dan stay with her. Seems he was crazy about boats, and she didn't want him to miss it. A shame she didn't keep him away, as it turned out.'

'We didn't go, either,' said Laurie. 'I...well, I hate to admit it, but I'm scared of heights. And Larry wanted to work on a couple of passages in the "Lord Nelson" that he wasn't real sure of.'

'And what my baby sister isn't saying is that we were both just a little homesick. I mean, there's lots of interesting things about this country, but it's not much like home. So we just holed up in our B & B with some beer and potato chips and wished there were some baseball on TV.'

'Ah, well.' Alan raised his hands in resignation. 'There was always some hope one of you had heard something, but plainly it's not going to be that easy.'

'Why don't you just call her?' asked Laurie. 'Or doesn't she have a cell phone? We didn't bring ours because we didn't think they'd work over here, but she's a Brit.'

'She has a mobile,' said Alan. 'She's not answering.'

'You don't think...' Larry bit his lip. 'She couldn't be in any sort of trouble, could she? I mean, if you're right, and her boyfriend *was* pushed off the boat, and she knew something about it...'

Well, I wasn't going to touch that one. I didn't see any possible answer that wouldn't reveal our ideas about the murderer having achieved his goal, and I was sure we weren't ready to do that yet.

'We have no reason to believe Pat is in any danger,' said Alan smoothly. 'I'm inclined, myself, to think she has simply gone off by herself to try to put her life back together. But we'd like to find her, all the same. Too many peculiar things have been happening of late, and we, Dorothy and I at least, would like to make some sense of them.'

'So,' said Nigel slowly, 'you think De—Gracie was murdered, too?'

That one I could deal with. 'I would like be sure that she was not. Wouldn't you?'

Nigel shook his head. 'Dorothy, it's just not possible. You forget—I was there. There on that balcony with her. No one pushed her. She just started screaming and backed up too far, and fell. It happened too fast for any of us to try to save her. It was an accident!'

Laurie shook her head in turn. 'No, Nigel, that's not good enough. We know she wasn't pushed off that balcony. But *why* did she scream? What frightened her? And why did she wave her arms around like that? It was almost… I saw an old movie once about someone who was on some drug, a hallucinogenic, and this person had the most terrible visions. A "bad trip", they called it.'

I exchanged an amused look with Alan. This young innocent was describing as history what had been very much a part of our own youth, although I'd never indulged in LSD and I very much doubted that Alan had.

'Anyway, I didn't think about it at the time, but do you suppose something like that could have happened to Gracie?'

It was, of course, a perfectly reasonable theory, only most of us knew it wasn't true. I let Alan field that one again. 'The police often test for drugs in cases of unexplained death. The only drug in Madame de la Rosa's system was a trace of acetaminophen. One assumes she'd had a headache.'

'She *was* a headache,' muttered Larry. 'And I'm

sorry, but she's giving me one now. I hate to break up the party, but I need to get back to the B & B.'

'Oh, Larry, I'm sorry,' I said. 'This was supposed to be a celebration and I turned it into a wake.'

'Don't worry. It's just reaction. Laurie'll tell you I get like this after performances. I'll be fine after a nap. And anyway, now I know what a real English tea is.'

'Welsh,' said a chorus of voices.

SIXTEEN

'WELL, THAT DIDN'T get us anywhere,' I said when we were back at Tower. I had kicked off my shoes and stretched out on the bed.

'No,' said Alan, taking off his own shoes. 'Not very far. We confirmed that Pat wasn't on the boat. If you nap now, you won't be able to get to sleep tonight.'

'We already knew she wasn't on the boat. Or at least we deduced it. I'm not going to nap. I just wanted to put my feet up.'

Alan chuckled, and that was the last thing I heard for a couple of hours.

'Well, I didn't *intend* to fall asleep,' I said when I finally roused.

'It's all those carbs. Lays you out flat, every time. Are you ready for some dinner?'

'After "all those carbs"? You must be kidding! I never want to eat again.'

'There are not a lot of other options for evening entertainment in these parts. We could always go for a walk. It won't be dark for at least another three hours.'

'I don't feel like a walk.'

I was feeling, in fact, contrary. It was a predictable result of an afternoon spent on an emotional roller-coaster, with a big meal and an unwise nap. Knowing that didn't make me feel any less prickly.

'Well, it's that, or television, or a pub. Or I could

borrow a spade from Charles and dig a hole you could crawl into.'

'It doesn't sound like a bad idea. Oh, I suppose we could go to a pub. I'm not in the mood for a raucous one, though. And I'd just as soon not run into any of the musicians.'

'Shall we ask Nigel if he knows of a quiet spot nearby? Or does he count as a musician?'

'No, he's more like a grandson, even if he does sing. I won't hold his voice against him.'

Nigel and Inga were amenable, and Nigel was amused at my request that he name a pub. 'Just because I'm half Welsh,' he said mildly, 'you expect me to know all about Wales. I'd never been here before we came to rehearse. And though my mother had learned a little Welsh from my father, I've forgotten everything she tried to teach me about the language, except how to pronounce it— after a fashion. But I do know how to use a computer.' He fired up his laptop, quickly searched the Internet, and found two or three pubs that looked suitable. One was quite nearby and proved to be, as promised, quiet, if unremarkable.

'Beer?' Alan asked all of us.

I still felt contrary. 'Wine for me. A good burgundy, if they have it.'

Somewhat surprisingly, they did. It was in fact good enough that my mood actually mellowed after a few sips. I even began to feel some pangs of hunger.

'Nigel, do they do food, do you know?'

'Aha!' said Alan. 'This is the lady who, about an hour ago, was never going to be hungry again.'

'A lady,' said Inga firmly, 'is entitled to change her mind. I'm hungry, too, though I wouldn't have believed I could be.'

'I think they only do bar snacks,' said Nigel doubtfully, looking around. 'I don't see a menu anywhere. I could ask.'

Perhaps it was Nigel's winning ways, but some sandwiches soon appeared, crusty bread with lovely warm bacon and some sort of delectable cheese melting softly into the bread. By the time I'd worked my way through mine, I was feeling civil again.

My expressive face must have shown my improved mood, because Nigel, somewhat tentatively, brought up the afternoon's subject again.

'Do you know, I've been thinking about Dan Green, and I remembered that there was someone who might help you find Pat. He's in the chorus, a tenor, and he was by way of being a mate of Dan's. I think someone said they went to school together, and then Dan did a bit of travelling around Europe before he settled in Manchester. And this chap was with him part of the time. Or something like that. I wasn't paying a lot of attention, and I've probably got it all wrong.'

'I thought he didn't have any friends here. Didn't Larry say something like that?'

'Well, it was all sort of awkward. I gathered the two of them had rather gone about together for years, and Pat...'

'I see.' I nodded. 'Pat was jealous. Understandable, but unwise of her to show it.'

'Yes, well, Dan sort of had to go behind Pat's back to talk to this chap. I can't recall his name, but I can point him out to you tomorrow, if you want to talk to him.'

'We very much want to talk to him,' said Alan. 'He'll be singing tomorrow, will he?'

'Oh, yes, in fact he has a solo. Tomorrow's Gilbert and Sullivan, you remember, and Sir John passed the wealth around. So this fellow gets to sing "A Maiden Fair to See", from *Pinafore*.'

'Lucky boy! That's a great piece,' I said. 'Well, we won't bother him before the concert, but afterwards, maybe we could take him out for a drink or something and pick his brains. Thanks, Nigel!'

WE ENDED UP staying at the pub for another couple of rounds, and as a result I slept much better than Alan had predicted, and much later. I woke up the next morning with the feeling that we were on the way to some solid information at last. The day was gorgeous, and I was in a good mood.

It was after ten before we finished a leisurely break-fast. We did nothing much for the rest of the morning, and skipped lunch. Nigel and Inga wanted to drive into Mold for a little shopping, so we agreed to meet at the castle in time for the concert.

We got there early, before the audience was officially admitted, but we walked in through the performers' entrance and found ourselves in a scene of confusion. Sir John was nearer to a temper tantrum than I had guessed he could approach, and the singers, chorus and soloists alike, were all talking at once.

'Silence!' thundered the conductor, and silence fell immediately.

'Now. Does anyone know where to find James O'Hara?'

The silence continued. Sir John smouldered. 'Sheila. You have tried his mobile again?'

'Every five minutes, sir. Voicemail, every time.'

'Sir.' It was Nigel's voice.

'Yes?' Sir John's acknowledgement was not cordial.

'I know the Rackstraw role, sir. I could sing it if you like. If no one else would prefer to do it.'

It took all of two seconds for the conductor to agree. 'Very well. Mind you watch the stick. You haven't rehearsed with the chorus, but we have no time for that. Thank you, Nigel.'

It was as if the castle itself heaved a sigh of relief. Another crisis averted.

I was not so happy. 'Alan…'

'Yes. Yet another missing person. And unless I'm mistaken, it's the one who knew Dan Green.'

'Well, it's the one who was singing the bit from *HMS Pinafore*, and that's the one Nigel mentioned, so…'

'So.'

We looked at each other.

I heaved a great sigh. 'Alan, the fates are against us. I'm not giving up on this mess, because I feel strongly about justice. You know that. I want justice for Dan, and even for Delia. She was a nuisance, but she didn't deserve to be executed for annoying people. But I'm for shunting it all aside until we can see a clearer way ahead. I could sit here and stew all afternoon, and it wouldn't accomplish a thing except making me miss some music I really enjoy. Agreed?'

'Agreed.'

I kept my vow. Actually, it wasn't hard. If there is music more rollicking and infectious and just plain fun than Gilbert and Sullivan, I don't know what it is. They did the familiar selections from all my favourite operettas, *Pinafore* of course, *Pirates*, *Mikado*, *Yeomen*, and some I didn't know at all, *Patience*, *Iolanthe*, *Sorcerer*. It was all good fun, and all performed splendidly. Nigel and the chorus worked together perfectly smoothly as he sang Ralph Rackstraw's lament about his star-crossed love; if I hadn't known he'd stepped in at the very last minute, I'd never have guessed.

The audience loved it. After several days of serious music, we were all ready to come down from the Olympian heights and have a little fun. This time there was no breathless hush at the end of the performance, but an outburst of applause, cheers, and laughter.

'That,' said Inga with deep satisfaction as we made our way to the exit, 'was great fun.'

'It was. Those two wrote the most inspired nonsense... Hmm?' For Alan had gestured for me to be quiet.

Sir John was standing at our side. 'I'm sorry to interrupt you, and I'm so happy you enjoyed the concert, but may I speak to you for a moment? All three of you?'

One does not ignore a royal summons. We followed him through the crowd, stopping with him while he graciously acknowledged comments from the audience, until we reached the relative quiet of the festival office.

He gestured me to the wooden folding chair, the only one available. 'Please. I'm sorry there isn't seating for all of you.'

I firmly refused. 'Sir John, we've been sitting through an entire performance. You've been working. Rest.'

With a sigh, he capitulated and collapsed on to the hard chair as if it were deep plush.

'Mr Nesbitt, this can't go on.'

Alan looked at him with a perfectly impassive face.

'You're thinking I'm concerned about the success of the festival. I am, of course. I have to be. But I am more concerned about the fate of my musicians. Two of them are now dead. Another two are missing. I can no longer ignore the fact that there is a...a malevolence hovering around this festival and these people. How many more?

How many more splendid young singers, and possibly instrumentalists as well, are threatened? Am I in danger? Are my wife and children? Cynthia has become quite worried about it, and that's not at all good for her just now.' He stood and began to pace the small room. 'It has to stop. I have to know what's behind all this. The authorities don't seem interested. They seem content to regard both deaths as accidental. That's the easy solution, but I can no longer accept it.'

'Nor can I,' said Alan. 'I never have been comfortable with the notion, and now with this most recent disappearance, I feel quite certain that there is, as you put it, a malevolence at work. My wife feels the same way, and so, I believe, do our young friends.' He gestured to Inga. 'The question is, what's to be done about it?'

SEVENTEEN

'YOU HAVE ALREADY been looking into the matter.' Sir John's tone made it a statement, not a question, but Alan and I nodded in confirmation. 'I would like you to continue to do so. I have no right so to infringe upon your time and energy, but—'

Alan held up a hand. 'Please. Dorothy and I are not only upset about the recent events, but I think I may say that we are personally outraged, not only by the crimes against Delia and Dan, and now possibly James, but by the crimes against music itself. That may sound grandiose, but we have loved music all our lives. It has enriched us. Listening to great music is for us almost a religious experience.'

'Not almost,' I said. 'It *is*. And how much more so must it be to make great music. I'm with Alan all the way on this, Sir John. You've held up astonishingly well in the face of everything that's happened, but you're quite right. It can't go on. We're eager to do anything we can to stop it. Of course we have no official standing, so we're a bit limited in what we can do.'

'I may be able to help with that problem. I've thought about it, of course. Dear heaven, I've thought about nothing else for the past week! Of course I'll put the full resources of the festival staff at your disposal. And then, I'm not without influence in certain circles. I think I can assure you that the police will at least not interfere with your investigations. And of course with the musicians…' He made a deprecating gesture.

'Your wish is our command,' said Nigel. His tone was light, but he meant every word.

'Well, at any rate, I shall ask everyone to cooperate with you to the fullest extent, and I think they will. They're a fine group of musicians, and a fine group of people.'

'Except for one of them, Sir John,' said Alan a trifle grimly. 'Except for one.'

'AND THEREIN,' I said later, 'lies the rub. It's the same old problem. We can talk to the musicians and ask them questions till we're blue in the face, and we may get truth from most of them, but all we'll do with the guilty one is warn him, or scare him away.'

'The trouble is, there are so many of them!' said Nigel. 'If there were some way to eliminate the impossible ones, I should think it would make things a bit easier.'

Nigel and Inga were sitting with us in our huge bedroom at Tower, trying to come up with a plan of action. They had entered enthusiastically into the spirit of things. 'You know,' said Inga, 'I do rather fancy myself as a detective. I learned a bit about people, all those years serving in the pub.'

'Perhaps,' said Alan, 'the first thing is to determine for certain who was on the canal boat. That would eliminate a great many people, for a start, at least for the murder of Dan Green.'

'Wait a minute! Are you saying that the same person didn't murder Delia?'

'I think, my dear, that we had best remember to call her Graciosa, or Madam de la Rosa, or even Gracie.

Anything but Delia. And to answer your question, I'm not saying anything of the kind. I'm saying only that we don't know enough to assume that the same person is responsible for both deaths.'

'Two murderers! In a group of peaceful musicians! It's hardly credible.' Nigel shook his head, some of his enthusiasm dampened.

'Let's not get ahead of ourselves,' I pleaded. I dug out of my handbag a pen and the little notebook I always carry, and began to make a list. 'First thing, find out who was on the canal boat. Shall we do that by talking to the musicians or to the boat people? Did they take names when you booked us for the trip, Nigel?'

'Yes, but do you think they'd tell us?'

'They might,' said Alan, 'with Sir John's name behind our request. The Welsh love and respect musicians, even English musicians. But I think we'd also learn a good deal by questioning the members of the chorus. You did say, didn't you, Nigel, that the orchestra was rehearsing that afternoon?'

'All day, actually. Well, I suppose they took a lunch break.'

'But they couldn't have got aboard the boat in that time. Dorothy, make a note for me to ask Sir John if anyone missed that rehearsal.'

I wrote it down. 'Okay, what else?'

'Once we know who was on the boat, shouldn't we ask them what they saw and heard?'

'The police will have done that,' I objected.

'Yes, but we'd be asking different questions,' said Inga. 'Not just about Dan, but about De—Gracie. Because, we might as well say it, you're thinking someone intended to push her and got Dan by mistake.'

'It makes a horrid kind of sense,' said Nigel. 'Given the complete unlikelihood of the whole scenario.'

'But don't you see?' I leaned forward. 'That's exactly what it is—a scenario. Alan saw that a little while ago. We're talking about operatic passions, the kind of passions we think Gracie lived with. We saw the way she acted, the aura of high drama she carried with her. Emotions like that are contagious. They infected the people around her. And someone carried the drama to the ultimate conclusion.'

But Inga wasn't paying attention. 'Dorothy, you've given me an idea! Passions, you said. She lived in the world of passions. Why have we never given any thought to her lover?'

'Lover?' said the other three of us.

'Surely she had one. At least one. Can you imagine a woman like that living celibate for the past ten years?'

Well, no. Now that Inga had said it, I could not imagine any such thing. She was the sort of woman who attracted men like flies, and who would want a man dancing attendance on her at every moment. She exuded sex appeal as a pine tree exudes sap.

Alan shook his head. 'Don't know how I missed that. I'm getting old. Do we have any idea who the current man was?'

'No, but I'll bet I can find out,' said Inga. 'Girl talk, you know? There will have been gossip. If there's a woman in the festival who didn't hate her on sight, I'll get me to a nunnery.'

'Not if I have anything to say about it,' said Nigel warmly.

'No fear. I'll get them to talk, and they won't be charitable.'

I wrote that down. 'That's brilliant, Inga. Well done!

And when we find out who he was, then we talk to him. He might be the murderer, don't you think?'

'Far stranger things have happened,' said Alan. 'It's a very good possibility. But we can't afford to neglect any other notions we might have.'

'Then we need to find Pat. And who was the guy who was friends with Dan?'

'James O'Hara,' said Nigel.

'Do you think they might be together?'

'It's possible, I suppose,' Nigel replied. 'But they resented each other a good deal. Or at least it was obvious that James resented Pat. Speaking of grand opera emotions! The Irish have this way of smouldering, d'you know? I didn't get to know James well; in fact I rather avoided him, because one felt he might erupt at any moment. I have no idea how Pat felt about him, but it's hard to believe either of them would seek out the other.'

'And if both are ignoring their mobiles, we have only the addresses they gave the festival organizers,' said Alan with a sigh. I knew he was thinking about driving to Manchester.

'And anything we can glean from the other musicians, don't forget.' I was determined to find some bright spots somewhere.

'It seems to me we're going to be holding a good many conversations with musicians,' said Alan. He sounded distinctly glum about it.

'But you like musicians!'

'I like to listen to them making music. I don't know that I like to ask them questions and expect sensible answers. Present company excepted,' he added, nodding to Nigel, who grinned.

'The real ones can get a trifle scattered, I agree. Especially in a situation like this, when we're all performing nearly every day, and doing demanding music. I think they can be sensible enough when the topic is something other than music.'

'All right, then. Here's our list. Find out who was on the canal boat. I think Alan had better do that, if everyone agrees.' Nods all around. 'And he can ask Sir John, or more probably his secretary, if anyone missed the orchestral rehearsal that afternoon. Then, we want to try to get information about De—Gracie's lover. Darn, I've got to stop doing that! Inga, you're going to take that on, right?'

'And enjoy every moment!'

'Indeed. You are revealing a spiteful streak I never would have suspected, young woman!'

She gave me a wicked smile.

'That leaves the hardest bit so far, finding Pat and James, apart or together, and that's probably going to involve a lot of those conversations you're dreading, Alan. Suppose Nigel and I get started on those, and then if we learn anything promising, we can get you involved. You do know how to conduct a proper interview, which we don't.'

'And where do you propose to do all this talking?' asked Alan. 'Because if you're taking the entire festival contingent out for drinks, I'll need to talk to my bank manager.'

Nigel guffawed and I chuckled. 'I imagine Sir John would bear the expense. But actually I was thinking of a more formal approach. For Nigel and me, that is. I think Inga has her own plans to infiltrate the women's gossip network, but for us, if Sir John would call everyone in, say, half an hour early for the next performance…'

But Nigel frowned and shook his head. 'No. Not before a performance. It would rattle some of them too much, and we have an early call tomorrow anyway, for a pick-up rehearsal. He can tell them they have to stay half an hour afterwards.'

'Won't they rebel?'

'It means extra pay for the orchestra and soloists. They won't object. I don't know that the chorus will be paid more, and some of them may try to leave, but there's an advantage to the castle venue. There's really only one way out. If Sir John stations himself at the barbican, no one will be able to sneak away.'

'So you're going to question them in a group?' Alan sounded dubious.

'Two groups, don't you think, Nigel? Orchestra and soloists in one room, chorus in another. And I think it might not be a bad idea if we asked Sir John to speak to them first, make sure they understand that he wants this business cleared up. They respect him.'

'More than respect. They—we—revere him as a musician and like him as a person. For me, doing a festival like this under his direction is the dream of a lifetime. Most of the others are professionals, so it isn't quite the same, but it's a feather in their cap, all the same. The performances have been spectacular, and the reviewers have lauded them, so everyone's CV will look that much more impressive. The group will listen to him and do as he says, I can guarantee.'

I swallowed. 'Then all I have to do is figure out what to ask them.'

Alan stood. 'You'll think better with some food inside you. Let's go find a meal.'

We didn't linger over dinner. We all had a lot to think about and plan. I was getting extremely nervous. The idea of a group interrogation was daunting. I do better talking to people one on one, but with something like a hundred musicians to question, it obviously had to be done en masse, at least to start. Only, what if everyone claimed to know nothing, to have nothing to say?

I went to bed early and dreamed I was in front of a classroom again, a classroom full of children who were not just quiet but silent, refusing to respond even to their names.

We all woke early, although I would have liked to stay in bed till a later hour. A long morning stretched in front of us, with little to do except fret. I'm very good at fretting, although a long life ought to have taught me that the exercise is unproductive of anything except an upset stomach.

I dressed quickly, leaving Alan in the shower, and went downstairs to find Inga in the hall, wide awake and restless.

'Dorothy, let's go for a ramble this morning. How are your knees faring?'

'Once I'm out of bed and moving, they're splendid. I can almost forget they're not original equipment.'

'And did you bring your walking stick?'

'I did, and boots as well.'

'Then I've a mind to roam the hills. The men can fend for themselves. I want lots of fresh air and sheep and sky.'

'It's the best offer I've had all week. Let me get my boots on, and tell Alan where I'm going, and I'll be with you in ten minutes.'

When I came back downstairs Inga had cajoled Mairi into some sandwiches and fruit to take with us. 'We can stay out all morning if we like, or if we get too tired, we can come back and eat our sandwiches here.'

It was a perfect day for a ramble, as Inga put it, and she was the ideal companion. She kept to a moderate pace, suitable to my age and condition, and didn't talk at all until we were well away from the house.

We had climbed a rise so gentle it had hardly hastened my breath, but now we were at the top and could see the rolling valley below. Sheep, with their half-grown lambs, grazed placidly in meadows full of soft green grass dotted with wildflowers. The sky was a soft, spring blue, not the hard, bright blue of full summer, and the clouds were as soft and fluffy as the sheep. Here and there a road, or a lane, led to a farmhouse with its outbuildings.

'You know,' I said dreamily, 'except for the occasional car or tractor, this could be the Wales of Brother Cadfael.' I'd recently been re-reading the marvellous Ellis Peters series about the twelfth-century Benedictine monk from Shrewsbury, who managed to stray into his native Wales much more often than the Rule would ordinarily allow.

'The houses would be different, though.' Inga liked the books, too, and the television series based on them. 'Timber-framed, most of them, not brick or stone. And there would be lots more horses and mules about.'

'The sheep would be exactly the same, though. Soft and silly. And I'll swear the hills and the sky haven't changed in those nine hundred years.'

Inga silently pointed to a jet trail high over distant hills, and we both collapsed into laughter.

'All right, all right. I'm a hopeless romantic. So sue me. But even you, my dear daughter of practicality, have to admit that this is an idyllic spot, whatever century we're in.'

'You're right. It is. That's why I wanted to come up here, for the peace.' She began to hum, softly, a melody that sounded vaguely familiar.

'That's lovely. Rather haunting. What is it?'

'Brother Cadfael would have known, or would have known the words, anyway. I'm not sure when someone came up with the music. It's a chant, the *Dies Irae*. Nigel taught it to me. The words are a bit depressing, but I think the tune is quite nice.' She hummed a little more of it.

'Now I know why it rang faint bells in my mind. It's one of the themes in the *Symphonie Fantastique*, isn't it?'

'I think so. I don't know the *Symphonie* that well. Nigel told me it's the requiem chant they used for solemn funerals and the like, long ago. The words are all about the Day of Judgement.'

'Hardly appropriate, then, for this gorgeous day.'

'We-ell…but if you were a Benedictine monk hundreds of years ago, and you thought mostly about death and heaven and hell and that sort of thing, maybe even a beautiful day might remind you of how few of them you had left, and how you'd better mend your soul in preparation.'

'But I'm not a Benedictine monk, and neither are you. How did you get started on this train of thought, anyway?'

But we both knew. Inga turned her head away from her contemplation of the sky. 'We can't get away from it, can we? I'd thought to leave it all behind for a few hours, but…'

'There's no leaving it behind. There never is, no matter what "it" is. You have to work it through, unravel the knot.' We walked on.

'But there are such a lot of knots to unravel,' said Inga after a time, in a small voice.

'Don't you think they may, in the end, all be part

of the same tangle?' I sat down on a convenient stile. 'I remember once rummaging through an old knitting bag and finding the most awful mess of yarn. I had no memory of why I'd left it like that, or even what I'd used it for, but it was a pretty colour of pink, so I decided to sort through it and see if some of the pieces were long enough to make bows for Christmas presents, or cat toys, or something.

'My dear, I couldn't even find an end, at first. There seemed to be no beginning and no end, which was so obviously impossible that I tried shaking and shaking the thing. It got itself into an even worse snarl, but eventually an end poked out, and I started following it through. It took days! I'd free a few inches, maybe a couple of feet, and then get so fed up I'd stop and do something else and let my fingers rest. Arthritic hands don't cope with snarled yarn easily. But I'm stubborn. I persisted, and eventually I had a lovely neat ball of yarn that looked like a full skein. And then I poked around the attic and found the rest of the yarn, the dozen or so skeins I'd put away years ago when I made such a mess of the first one.'

'And I suppose you knitted something beautiful out of it.'

'No, in the intervening years I'd discovered I really wasn't a very good knitter, nothing like good enough to make the sweater I'd planned. As you observed the other night. So I gave it away to a friend, who did make something beautiful. But the point I was trying to make is that even the most appalling tangle can often be worked out, given enough time and patience.'

'But time is just what we don't have! Dorothy, tomorrow is the last day of the festival. After the concert's over, everyone will go back to wherever they came from,

and you know some of them are from very far away indeed. Different countries, with different laws—it would
be next to impossible even to track down the murderer,
much less bring him or her to justice! It has to be over
before the last chord tomorrow!'

'Well, then,' I said, rising with a creak, 'we'd better
get moving, hadn't we?'

EIGHTEEN

NIGEL HAD ALREADY left for the castle when we got back to Tower, so Alan, Inga and I sat in the lounge and ate an early lunch of Mairi's sandwiches and fruit. I had called a strategy conference.

'Look, I've had an idea,' I said, with some hesitation. 'I don't know if it's any good, but we have to do something drastic. Inga reminded me that we have very little time to get to the bottom of the troubles. So I thought… but I don't know if Sir John will agree…or even if it's worthwhile…'

'Suppose you tell us what it is,' said Alan patiently, 'and perhaps we can offer an opinion.'

'Well, there's not a lot of time to plan it, but I thought, what if we have a party for the festival tonight? Or late this afternoon, I mean, just after the concert. Because we want everyone to stay around, so we can talk to them. And I thought about herding them into rooms and standing up in front of them and asking questions, and the more I thought about it, the less likely it seemed to be productive. So I thought, if we threw a party for them, they'd be relaxed and pleased, and we could mingle and talk, and maybe learn something important.'

'When you say "we", I assume you mean Sir John.' Alan's voice was flat and expressionless.

'Well, yes. That's why I don't know if he'll do it. It would cost a lot of money.'

'And you were planning to hold this party where? In the castle?'

'It would have to be, wouldn't it? If it were anywhere else, some people wouldn't come. And there'd be no way to make them come. But at the castle, as a surprise right after the concert…we could ask Sir John to invite them all, as a personal favour to him, so he could express his appreciation for all their hard work. Something like that. Only there's almost no time, and the logistics…' I ran down.

There was silence while the other two considered the scheme.

'The problems are obvious,' said Alan at last, 'but I don't have a better idea. You're right. At this point we must make the most efficient possible use of what time we have, and an informal gathering of the whole boiling of them might be what we need.'

'Or what will appear to be an informal gathering,' said Inga. 'I like it, Dorothy. It's the perfect setting for my gossip-mongering, at any rate.'

Alan looked at his watch. 'It's just on twelve thirty. The concert starts at two. It'll be over at—what, four?'

'No later than that,' said Inga.

'Then we need to get cracking right now. You two change into whatever you're wearing to the concert. I'll find Mairi and ask her about a caterer who can feed a couple of hundred people at short notice, and then I'll phone Sir John.'

'He'll be in the middle of rehearsal!' said Inga, scandalized.

'Then he'll just have to be called away.' Alan headed for the kitchen and Inga and I for our bedrooms.

I hadn't finished dressing when Alan called upstairs.

'Dorothy! I've found a caterer. She wants to talk to you about the menu.'

'But I don't even know if Sir John is willing to do this!' I hurried down the stairs, shoeless. 'Or whether there's a room at the castle we can use, or anything!'

'She needs to know now, this minute. In for a penny, in for a pound. We'll worry about the finances of it later.' He handed me the phone.

I found it hard to take Alan's attitude. We're not hurting for money, but we're not made of it, either. An impressive bash for two hundred people would make a hole in our bank balance big enough to drive a Rolls Royce through. Alan had been teasing about a pub bill for all those people, and this would be much, much worse. However, the caterer was waiting. I gulped and took the phone.

A menu was quickly settled. Four o'clock was tea time, so we'd have finger foods, but substantial ones, like bara brith and a new Welsh speciality I'd encountered at a village bake shop, called lamb oggies. A bit like pasties, little meat-filled pies, they can be delicious, and they're certainly filling. The caterer suggested other treats, saying firmly, 'I haven't time to bake anything, but I've these things on hand, frozen, and they'll do nicely. And tea?'

'Tea, yes, but also beer and wine. I'll leave the varieties up to you, but I want plenty. These people are going to be thirsty, especially the singers.' And it won't hurt a thing if they're well lubricated, I added mentally. We may have to arrange for some of them to be taken home.

I'd leave that up to Alan.

We settled details of tables and chairs, plates and glasses and napkins, and got down to the bottom line. I took a deep breath and asked.

It was fortunate for my peace of mind that Alan came up just then, mobile in hand. He simply smiled and nodded as I passed along the awesome total. 'You'll only be charged for the drinks that are consumed, of course,' she assured me.

'It's not a problem. Sir John Warner, the music director of the festival, will be paying the bill. Will you require a deposit?'

We settled that, too, and I punched the phone off and stood, weak-kneed. 'You came along in the nick of time. I think I might have had a seizure. I hope Sir John knows what he's getting into.'

'He said not to worry about the cost. He wants this matter settled and is willing to do whatever it takes. He thought it a brilliant idea, by the way.'

'And he wasn't upset about being interrupted in rehearsal?'

Alan chuckled. 'He wasn't. His secretary was. I had to do quite a lot of convincing before she'd let me talk to him, but he seemed unperturbed.'

'You can be very persuasive in full chief-constable mode.'

Inga came down the stairs, dressed rather more quietly than usual. Not that she's ever a flashy dresser, but she likes bright colours, and they set off her exquisitely fair colouring, inherited from her German mother. This time, though, she was dressed in monochrome, shades of black, white, and grey. The individual pieces of her ensemble were quite attractive, but they didn't go together. She looked a trifle dowdy, in fact.

Alan was somewhat taken aback, but I grinned. 'The harmless gossip, interested in the glamorous lives of others.'

'Got it in one.' She grinned back. 'Lead on, Macduff.'

'Yes, the sooner we get there, the better.' I was having a serious attack of nerves. 'I think I understand a little of how Eisenhower must have felt just before D-Day. And don't you laugh at me, Alan Nesbitt!'

He composed his face, with an effort, and led the way to the car.

The concert was over an hour away and the musicians were still rehearsing when we got to the castle. It was surprising how little of the sound escaped the thick walls. We could hear only isolated high notes from the car park, where we were nearly the first to arrive, the musicians all having strict instructions to park elsewhere.

I headed straight into the castle, without waiting for Alan and Inga. My first job as general of this operation was to find a place for the party. I had forgotten to bring my guidebook to the castle, with its convenient map, so I snatched one from the gift shop display rack as I went past. 'I'll pay later,' I called to the outraged clerk, and sailed into the castle proper.

The entire inner ward was occupied by the festival, both performers and, soon, audience. The anterooms along the way were also in use, for the office, storage, and the like. But the outer ward, some little distance away, had great possibilities. It was floored in nice soft grass, and one end of it was the right shape for a long table or two, to hold the food. There was also plenty of room for chairs, not in rows, but set about informally, the better for people to talk. They'd have to juggle their drinks, but party-goers everywhere have to learn to do that.

Yes, this would do. And it was, I judged, far enough away from the inner ward, with lots of nice thick walls between, that the caterers wouldn't disturb the concert as they set up. There was even, thanks to a wall that had crumbled centuries ago, access to the area that didn't lead right through what I now thought of as the concert hall.

Now, if only the caterers would get here with the tables and chairs and other paraphernalia before most of the audience began to arrive… And here, if I wasn't mistaken, they were.

At least, a woman in a white jacket was approaching me with a businesslike air. 'I'm looking for the person in charge,' she said briskly. 'No one in the gift shop seemed to know.'

'You must be Mrs Williams.' I held out my hand. 'I'm Dorothy Martin. I talked to you earlier.'

'Yes. Wanted the impossible, you did, and here am I to make it happen. You have a cheque for me?'

'Sir John does.' At least I sincerely hoped he did. 'They should be finished in a few minutes—or do I hear them breaking up now?'

The music had ceased, and we could hear Sir John's voice, carrying more clearly than the music had a moment before. 'Ladies and gentlemen, thank you for an admirable rehearsal. I am greatly privileged to work with such a fine group of dedicated musicians, both professional and amateur.' He pronounced the word the French way, with its implication of lover, devotee. A nice touch, I thought. 'I have what I hope will be a pleasant surprise for you after the concert. Because I've had to call you in early for this rehearsal, many of you will have had to do without your lunch. Therefore, I've arranged a party after the concert. This has been organized in some haste, so I'm not quite sure in which part of the castle it will be held; I'll let you know before the end of the concert. I've been assured that there will be plenty of food for all.' He paused artistically. 'And plenty of drink!'

That brought a roar of approval. Mrs Williams smiled.

'Two requests, then,' Sir John went on. 'I would like to ask you all to stay for the party, at least briefly, as I will have some important announcements to make. Second, please be discreet about mentioning it to any of the audience, as the festival can't quite afford to feed all of North Wales.'

And with that he dismissed them on a wave of laughter, and Mrs Williams and I could approach him about that little matter of money.

With that settled, Mrs Williams went efficiently about her business, directing the men bringing in the tables and chairs and beginning to unload coolers full, presumably, of food. I was sorely tempted to filch some of it; lunch had been awfully skimpy. But I refrained. There were much more important things to worry about than my stomach.

Inga had, I felt, the easiest assignment. She had only to encourage gossip, never the hardest thing to do in a group of people, especially when the beer and wine were flowing.

Alan was seeking some specific information, about who was on the canal boat on that fateful day. That might be hard for me, but he was trained to conduct interviews, and was very good at it.

Nigel and I, on the other hand, had no training at all. Nigel at least knew some of these people, having worked with them for two or three weeks. I had an acquaintance with the twins, Larry and Laurie, and less than that with the people who'd joined us at the pub a few nights before. What possible excuse could I make to justify my questions about Pat and James?

With my head empty of anything except forebodings, I found Alan and Inga and we took our seats for the next-to-last concert of the series.

NINETEEN

I'D BEEN LOOKING forward to this particular concert for a long time. The programme featured sacred music, mostly choral, mostly short and familiar. The first piece, and the last, were Alleluias by Randall Thompson and Mozart, respectively. In between were selections by composers as diverse as Bach and John Rutter. Every now and then an especially lovely passage would catch my attention, but then I went back to worrying about what was to come.

This was crunch time. By suppertime tomorrow, all these people would have dispersed, scattered to the four winds. If we hadn't found our murderer by then, it would be too late. The official police were not inclined to treat either death as murder and would have no interest at all in pursuing someone to another country, if that was the way our investigation pointed.

If it pointed in any direction at all. I faced the terrible possibility that we would never come to any conclusion—that these murders, if such they were, would never be solved, and that Dan Green and Delia Warner would never be granted the justice that was surely their due.

That was one of the times when the music broke in to my distracted consciousness. They were singing 'The Lord Is My Light', the old anthem I remembered from my youth in Indiana. It's always been one of my favourites, with its stirring music and its message of reassurance from Psalm 27. 'Whom then shall I fear?' And for a little while my fears were stilled, only to return when Sir John launched his forces into something I didn't know.

All too soon the final brilliant 'Alleluia' sounded, followed by thunderous applause that went on and on. I agreed with the sentiment, but wished they would stop and go home, so I could tackle my uncertain duty.

Sir John held out his hands to still them. 'Ladies and gentlemen, if you would like one more—'

He wasn't allowed to finish. The crowd roared their approval.

'Then we'll play and sing something I suspect you all know, and you'd be very welcome to sing along with us. In English or Welsh, as you choose.'

The orchestra played the last few bars of the great Welsh hymn that Nigel had led us in singing on the canal boat. Then Sir John turned around and gave the audience their cue.

They sang lustily. The words were incomprehensible, because even the English words had several variations, and with the Welsh mixed in, all that could be heard was the blending of voices and the strong goodwill that rose like a visible cloud from the hundreds of singers.

I tried to sing along, but I couldn't utter a sound. Alan took my hand and squeezed it, and of course that made things worse. When they had finished, to another round of applause, I had to find a tissue and dab away the tears.

'Okay?' Alan murmured in my ear.

'Okay. It was just…'

'I know. You can't listen to that sort of music impassively, can you?'

It was more than that, of course. Yes, I choke up when music touches me deeply, but I was also remembering the last time I'd heard this hymn, on the boat with the strong young voices singing in perfect harmony. And two of those voices were silenced forever.

It didn't do to dwell on that now. I had a job to do. Alan gathered Inga and me with a glance, and together we moved into the fray.

It wasn't yet four in the afternoon, not my usual hour for libations, but I felt an abstemious glass of wine would ease my nerves.

'Best have some food to go with it,' said Alan at my elbow. 'Find a place to sit down, and I'll bring you a plate.'

'But I need to circulate, mingle.'

'After you have some sustenance, love.'

I obeyed, the more meekly as I hadn't an idea what else to do. I looked around for any familiar face and spotted the twins sitting together with a small group. They had got their food and drink and were talking with animation. As I hesitated, Laurie looked up and saw me, and waved.

With dragging feet and a phoney smile, I walked over to join the group.

And the very first remark nearly undid me. 'Nigel tells me this party was your idea!' Laurie said brightly.

'Well,' I said, trying to give myself time to think, 'it was everyone's, really. Alan's and Inga's and mine, I mean. We thought it would be nice, after all your hard work, and so we suggested it to Sir John, and he agreed. So...' I waved my hand around. 'Everyone seems to be having a good time, don't you think?' I wished I had that wine in front of me. Teetering on the brink between truth and perjury is a nerve-wracking exercise.

'Brilliant,' said one of the other musicians, English by her voice. 'And we really did need it, especially after the encore.' There were nods and murmurs of agreement.

'He sprang that on us with no warning, and I don't mind saying it was hard to sing, after...'

She trailed off, and one of the young men finished for her. 'We sang it on the canal boat, you see. Nigel started it, and we all sang along. Dan sang with us, and then...'

Well, there was my opening. Would Alan never bring me my food and wine? I licked dry lips and said, 'Yes, I know. Alan and I were on the boat, too. In fact I've been trying to reach Pat—his fiancée?'

They nodded.

'I'm worried about her. She seems to have gone off into the blue, and I'm not sure she should be alone just now. I suppose I'm being an old mother hen, but...'

'She lives in Manchester, didn't she say?' someone said, and there were murmurs of agreement.

'We've tried to ring her mobile, and there's no answer. I suppose she could have forgotten to turn it on, or charge it, or something.'

'Or she's just ignoring it,' said Laurie. 'She might not feel like talking to anybody at this point.'

'She was talking to O'Hara,' said one of the men. 'When she came to say goodbye. Day before yesterday? I've lost track.'

'Day before that. Tuesday, it was. She came round because she was going back home. Didn't want to carry on with the festival. Which was understandable.'

'Yes, but she wasn't going home. I heard her say so. Too lonely without Dan, she said.'

I leaned forward toward the young woman who had contributed this bit of information. 'Did she say where she was going?' I asked, trying to display only mild interest.

The group exchanged glances, but no one seemed to have heard Pat say anything definite about her plans.

'Gone off with O'Hara, hasn't she?' said one rather loud young man. 'Off with the old, on with the new.'

'She's not a bit like that!' said a young woman indignantly. 'She was really in love with Daniel. They were planning to be married in October.' She dashed tears from her eyes. 'And James was Dan's best mate. They went off to mourn him together. That's all!'

'But *where* have they gone?' The mildly interested pose was getting harder to maintain.

General shrugs. 'Really, you mustn't worry about Pat,' said the earnest young woman. 'She'll be quite all right with James.'

If Alan hadn't turned up just then with food and drink, I think I might have screamed with frustration. I could only hope that Inga and Alan had better luck with their missions. I had made absolutely no headway at all.

But I despaired too soon. The party began to wind down, and the musicians were looking around for Sir John and his promised announcements, so that they could leave. I picked up my empty plate and glass, heading for a rubbish bin. Laurie stood at my side.

'Dorothy, I have to talk to you,' she said in a near whisper. 'Can we go someplace away from all this?'

It was important. I knew that after one quick glance. I took her arm. 'Here. Up this stairway. Quick.'

I was counting on the musicians' lack of interest in narrow, poorly lit passages. The fact that I wasn't any too fond of them myself was irrelevant at this point.

We made our way along to one of the wider places where there was a window. There wasn't another soul around. I turned to face Laurie. 'We won't be interrupted here. Tell me.'

She took a deep breath. 'I think Larry knows something about Pat and James.'

'Larry? But why hasn't he said anything? He knows we're all trying to find them.'

'I don't know! He won't even talk to me about it, and we've never hidden anything from each other!' She was nearly in tears. 'It's a twin thing, you know? I mean, we fight like crazy over all sorts of things, but we don't lie to each other, and we don't keep secrets from each other. When we were kids,' she went on, speaking from the great distance of her twenty-some years, 'we told each other everything, even the things we'd have died rather than tell our parents. I knew all about his first joint, and he knew about my first serious love affair—and calmed me down when it was over. It was nothing at all like what my girlfriends went through with their brothers. Larry's…well, it sounds sort of dumb, but he's my best friend. And I thought I was his. And now he's gone all quiet and moody, and that's not like him at all. And when I tried to talk to him about Pat and Dan and James and the whole situation, he just walked away.'

The tears were rolling down her cheeks now, and I put an arm around her shoulders and just held her for a few minutes.

This was a most unexpected development, and I wasn't quite sure what to do about it. If I tried to talk to Larry myself, and if by chance he'd seen us go off together, he'd think Laurie had betrayed him. As, in a way, she had.

On the other hand, if Alan were to question him, Alan who was trained for such things and had the benefit of a sort of semi-official status—well, not really, not any more, but would a young American know about the finer points…?

It might be worth a try. Alan would be able to make it

seem as if he was asking everybody the same questions—
as indeed he probably was.

'Look here, Laurie.' She had control of herself now
and was fishing in her handbag for a tissue. I pulled one
out of my pocket and handed it to her. 'Crumpled, but
clean. Now what I propose to do is this. I don't want to
talk to Larry myself.'

'Oh, no, you can't!' she wailed. 'He'd think—'

'Exactly. But what if I tell Alan what you've told
me—privately, of course—and he asks Larry some
questions? No, wait till I've finished. You'll remember
we told you Alan used to be a policeman.'

She looked instantly apprehensive.

I gave her arm a little shake. 'Stop being so scared!
He has no official standing any more, and anyway this
is Wales, not England. I'm a little hazy about the laws
here, and the differences, but the point is he couldn't clap
handcuffs on anyone any more than I could, or you, for
that matter. What he can do, though, is ask questions,
and he's very good at that. And I promise you, Larry
won't have any idea you've said a word to anyone. Will
you let me drop Alan a hint?'

She sniffed and blew her nose. 'This trip was supposed to be fun. Music, travel, the chance to go places
we'd always wanted to see. Now all I want to do is go
home.'

'May I talk to Alan?'

She gave me a dreary little nod. 'Everything's awful
anyway. I don't suppose it could get worse.'

Probably fortunately, I had a lot more experience than
she of just how much worse things could get. This wasn't
the time to tell her so.

'Go wash your face, then. Or no, wait.' I rummaged
in my large handbag and found a packet of moist tow-

elettes. 'Here, use these. The loos will be jammed, and you don't want to run into anyone looking like you've been crying. But you'd better hurry, because you mustn't miss whatever Sir John wants to say to you all.'

I gave her a pat to shoo her on her way. Then I took a deep breath and went to look for Alan.

I found him standing at the back of the assemblage of musicians, who had gathered, somewhat impatiently, to hear what Sir John had to say to them. I touched him on the shoulder. He turned, and I opened my mouth, but just then Sir John began to speak, and Alan put a finger to my lips.

'Wait,' he mouthed.

I shook my head and pulled him away. 'It can't wait,' I murmured. 'Come around the corner.'

He raised his eyebrows and followed me behind one of the stone buttresses that, though crumbling, still blocked a good deal of sound.

'You need to talk to Larry,' I said rapidly. 'Before he leaves here, if you can. I've just had a talk with his sister, though you mustn't tell Larry that. She's quite sure he knows something important about this whole situation. He might know where Pat and James are.'

'Got it,' he said, fading into the crowd that was now beginning to move toward the exit.

Bless the man for not asking questions!

I wondered, as I mingled with the musicians trying to find Nigel and Inga, what excuse Sir John had come up with to keep the musicians around for the extra hour. I was soon to know.

'I keep on losing everyone,' said Nigel, coming up from behind me.

'Oh, you startled me! I was looking for you, too. Where's Inga?'

'Still collecting gossip, I suppose. I've not seen her since the end of the concert. I thought she might have come round when Sir John dismissed us, but…' He gave a little 'who knows' shrug.

'What did he say to you, anyway? I was talking to Alan. I hope he made it sound important enough to keep you all here another hour.'

'Actually, it was important. He's added a piece to tomorrow's programme. An "In Memoriam" sort of thing, the Webber '*Pié Jesu'*. Do you know it?'

'I certainly do! It's beautiful. Who's doing the solo?'

Nigel looked at his feet. 'Well…'

'Nigel! Congratulations! I'll bet what's-her-name, the soprano, is ready to strangle you with her bare hands.' I deeply regretted the phrase the moment it was out of my mouth.

'Yes…well…of course it ought really to be a treble, but Sir John didn't want to try to find one at the last minute, so…'

'I'm sure you'll be wonderful. Sorry I was stupid about it.'

He made the kind of ambiguous gesture that can mean anything at all, and we stood in an awkward silence until Inga appeared out of the rapidly thinning group of musicians.

'You look like two strange cats. Your fur is bristling. Have you had a row?'

I shook my head. 'No, it was something I said, so stupid I won't even repeat it.'

'You're tired,' said Inga with a sigh. 'We all are. The afternoon has not been wasted, though. I would a tale relate, but I want to wait until we're all together. I saw Alan just now, deep in conversation with that American singer Larry. He, Alan I mean, said to tell you to come home with Nigel and me, and he'll follow.'

So we plodded off to Nigel's car, quiet and more than a little subdued. I realized that Inga was absolutely right. I was more than tired. I was discouraged, frustrated, and angry.

Angry? That one stopped me in my tracks. Surely not angry!

But yes. My mind, sorting out my emotions, had hit on the right combination. This lovely holiday in Wales, centred around the music we all loved, and in that most romantic of settings, a medieval castle, had become a nightmare not only for my small party, but for almost all the musicians involved. And poor Sir John! It must be worst of all for him. This labour of love had turned into a calendar of horrors.

He was quite right. It had to stop.

But how were we to accomplish that?

INTERLUDE

'BUT WHAT'S BEING done about it, darling?'

Lady Cynthia's voice was calm and controlled, but her hand shook a little as she poured a measure of whisky for her husband. The twins, asleep in the next room, had put up a struggle about bedtime tonight, perhaps feeling their mother's tension. It had taken both her and the au pair to get them settled, and with the au pair off duty for the night, Cynthia was anxious lest they awaken again. She lowered her voice another notch and changed her question slightly. 'Is no one doing anything to…to find out who's responsible for these horrors?'

Sir John took a sip of his drink and then put it down. 'The police have apparently dismissed both…events as accidents. Unless something else happens, I don't think they'll take any further action.'

'But they *must*!' Cynthia's voice rose a trifle, and a small protesting whimper sounded from the next room. Both parents froze, willing the child back to sleep. After a hushed period of waiting, with no further sounds of discontent, John lifted his glass again and Cynthia leaned over to pour herself some mineral water.

'Try not to worry too much, darling,' John said, reaching over to touch her hand. He was careful to speak in soothing tones that might reassure not only Cynthia, but any child who still hovered near the edge of wakefulness. 'We're doing all we can to get to the bottom of it all. I told you about the chief constable and his wife, and their friends are helping. It'll be all right in the end.'

'The end,' said Cynthia, 'is tomorrow.' Her voice was steady again, but her hand still trembled. 'John, we can't leave here without knowing. You know we can't.'

He shook his head, without speaking. There was nothing he could say to help her.

She lowered her voice still further. 'John, I know about her.'

He looked at her, alarm in his face.

'I knew the moment I saw her. You had described her to me, of course, but it was the look on your face that told me. You looked like…like the Lady of Shalott.'

'"The doom has come upon me".' His face now was grey, and he hid it in his hands. 'I didn't want you to know, ever.'

'John, it didn't matter. Not then. It didn't matter at all. We are legally married, and I know that, and I know you…that you and I…' Her voice was trembling now.

He raised his head and put out a hand. 'Cynthia…'

'No, let me finish. I'm all right. It's only that, if they never find out who did this, you will always be under suspicion. You, or I, or both of us. And I… I couldn't bear it!'

Her voice broke, finally, and with her tears came a wail from the next room, and then another.

'Mummy! Daddy!'

'It's all right, kittens. Daddy's here.'

He stood and gave Cynthia a hard hug before going to his children. Cynthia dashed away her tears and followed him. 'Now what are my bad kittens up to now?'

When the twins were finally soothed and settled, when hugs and drinks and teddy bears had been administered, without a word spoken the parents picked up the children and nestled with them, all four in the big bed together. This was a time for cuddling, for closeness, for comforting.

PART THREE

TWENTY

ALAN CAME IN as the three of us were sitting in the lounge, for once with nothing to eat or drink in front of us. We'd had our fill at the party, and we were too tired in any case to make any effort even at refreshment.

'You're a lively group,' he commented, surveying us as he walked into the room.

'We were waiting for you. Inga says she has some news, but she wouldn't tell us until you were here.'

'And here I am, and with news of my own. Ladies first,' he added, bowing toward Inga.

She nodded. 'I could tease you with it, but I won't. I think no one's in the mood for games. I know who Delia's lover was. Or who everyone says he was.'

No one spoke.

'His name is Ben Peterson. He's the concertmaster.'

It was a complete surprise, and, as we considered the implications, a severe blow. 'But...' I stammered. 'But if he murdered her...the festival... Oh, I suppose we shouldn't think about that, but...'

'The festival can't go on without the concertmaster,' said Nigel flatly. 'Almost anyone else can be replaced, but not him. He's in the top rank. Only someone like him could hold together a pick-up orchestra like this, and there are damn few like him. I admit I'd wondered why he'd agreed to be part of this. The Royal Phil is more up his street. But, if this is true...'

'We're getting ahead of ourselves,' said Alan. 'Inga, how sure are you of your information?'

'Pretty sure. With gossip one never knows, of course, but I had it from several sources, not all of them spiteful. The women, as one might expect, were inclined to scratch and spit a bit—don't look at me that way, Nigel, I meant it metaphorically. With the men it was more nudge, nudge, wink, wink. They didn't like Delia, but they wouldn't have minded a bit of what Peterson was apparently getting.'

'He'll have to be interviewed,' said Alan. 'The festival's made it hellishly tricky, though. Sensitive musicians who mustn't be put off their stride and all that. I'm getting damn tired of sensitive musicians! Present company excepted, Nigel.'

'I'm not a musician. I'm a techie. I don't count.'

Well, of course we all protested at that, and the atmosphere lightened a little.

'What does a man have to do,' said Alan, 'to get a drink in this place?'

'We have an assortment upstairs,' I said to the room at large, 'if someone younger than I would care to bring down whatever they'd like. I wouldn't mind some bourbon myself.'

Inga, who had helped her father at the bar of the Rose and Crown when she was a bit younger, did the honours efficiently, and we settled back very much more at ease.

'Now, Alan,' I said presently. 'You had some news for us as well.'

'I do indeed, though I've no idea how it's going to mesh with what Inga's rootled out. The trouble with this case,' he went on, his mood expanding as his whisky disappeared, 'is that nothing seems to fit with anything else. It's as if someone's dropped two jigsaw puzzles on the floor and muddled them up together.'

'Or three, or five,' I said. 'Never mind. Tell us. We'll sort it all out sooner or later.'

'It had best be sooner,' Nigel growled. 'May I remind you that in less than twenty-four hours the festival will be over, and everyone gone?'

'I don't think any of us has forgotten, Nigel. But what I've learned may be one of the important pieces of the puzzle, or puzzles. I talked to Larry Andrews. His sister was right, Dorothy. He does know something of importance, and suspects more.' Alan sipped at his drink. 'He told me that James hated Delia with a white passion, because he—James—thought Delia killed Daniel Green. And Larry thinks James somehow arranged Delia's death.'

'And that's why James has disappeared!' I said excitedly, waving my glass in the air and nearly spilling bourbon on Mairi's lovely carpet. I set my glass down. 'But what about Pat? Maybe we're wrong about the two of them going off together. I thought James and Pat were supposed to be at odds, James jealous of Pat and so on.'

'Ah, but that was before Dan died,' Alan went on. 'After that happened, according to Larry, the two were somewhat united in grief. Pat left the chorus, you'll remember, but James stayed on. Larry and several of the other singers thought that a bit odd, since James was as upset as Pat, and more demonstrative about it. He's Irish, of course, and they tend not to clamp a lid on their emotions the way we chilly English do. Probably healthier, but it can be rather trying to live with.'

'Rather,' said Nigel drily. 'James was raising pretty fair hell most of the time backstage, and putting away a good deal more drink than was good for him.' Nigel regarded his own modest glass of sherry, and put it down. 'I could easily believe him capable of the desire to do murder. But the problem remains, the one we've had all along. Delia simply could not have been murdered! All of you keep forgetting that I was *there*. I know no one was near enough to push her. I know she simply went mad and fell.'

'But why did she go mad? What caused that frenzy? I still think,' I said stubbornly, 'that it was engineered somehow.'

'How?' Nigel asked the question, but it came, essentially, from everyone in the room. And I had no answer.

'And what, if anything, did Ben Peterson have to do with it?' That was from Alan. 'If Delia was threatening to leave him… No, that won't work, will it? He might have thumped the other man, if there was one, but he'd hardly have killed Delia and thus made quite sure that she left him.'

'Especially,' said Inga, 'as it wasn't that sort of relationship. Ben Peterson is no fool—even if he is, Alan, one of your "sensitive musicians". He wasn't in love with Delia, not a bit of it. The women who talked to me thought she'd have liked to entangle him in her web as she had so many men, but with Peterson it was apparently just plain, uncomplicated sex. Good fun, but no emotional complications.'

'I've figured it out,' I announced. All eyes turned in my direction.

'How she was killed?' Alan inquired. 'Who did it?'

'No. I've figured out what we're dealing with here. There've been hints of it before, but now I'm sure. It isn't a puzzle at all. It's a grand opera plot, with hatred and revenge and lust and murder all over the stage. Donizetti would feel right at home, but I'm tired of dealing with it right now. Is anyone else hungry?'

WE HAD A quick meal at a nearby pub, but when we repaired back to Tower, I firmly set all the bottles aside and sent Inga upstairs for the tea trays, kettle and all. 'Because what we need now is some clear thinking. Coffee is called for.'

It was instant, but it wasn't awful, and thanks to the extra packets I always travel with, we could have enough to keep us awake all night if necessary.

'Now,' I said when we were all settled with steaming cups. I had pulled my little notebook out of my handbag. 'We need to get organized.'

'More lists?' Alan wasn't smiling, exactly, but his voice was.

'It's the way I think. All right. Alan, were you able to get a list of the boat passengers that day?'

'Yes. There were seventeen from the festival, not counting Nigel. The ones we're interested in, Delia, Dan, and James, and others whose names meant nothing to me, but whom we can question if necessary. There were no orchestral members among them, and none were absent from rehearsal that day.'

'So we can cross out the orchestra. Not that they were ever under much suspicion. Question number one, then. Do we agree with James's supposition that Delia pushed Dan off the boat?'

'What we have been told was James's supposition,' Alan interposed. 'We have only Larry's word for it.'

'All right, but let's assume for now that Larry's right. I repeat, do we agree with James?'

'Why?' Inga was sitting in the 'Thinker' position, one foot up on the couch, elbow on knee, chin propped on elbow. 'Granted that she could have done it. Almost anybody could have done it, what with the crush at that door. But why would she?'

'We may never know that,' said Alan. 'They're both dead. From all we know about Delia, she was the complete egomaniac. If Daniel stood in the way of something she wanted, she might very well have seized the opportunity to rid herself of him.'

'I wish we could find Pat. Daniel might have said something to her that would give us a clue.' I shifted discontentedly and drank some coffee.

Alan pulled out his mobile, found Pat's number, and punched it in. I, sitting closest to him, could hear a voice at the other end, but it was followed by a beep.

'Ah, Pat,' Alan said in clear tones. 'Alan Nesbitt here, from the music festival. We've been quite worried about you and would like to know that you're all right. Please ring me back, at any hour.' He gave the number of his phone, while holding out his hand for mine. 'Or you can also try my wife, on…' He pushed the right buttons for my phone to reveal its number, and quoted it to Pat. 'Do call, won't you?'

'She's taking messages now,' I said with some satisfaction. 'That's a good sign. Do you suppose she'll call?'

'It will depend on whether she thinks I'm a threat to James. Assuming James is in fact with her. Assuming James did in fact contrive somehow to murder Delia. Assuming James and she are still in a state of détente. A plethora of assumptions, with very little basis for any of them. However…' He spread his hands.

'Well, she'll call or she won't. Meanwhile my question remains. Even without knowing her motive, do we think Delia pushed Dan?'

Inga spoke. 'Always assuming—there's that little

snag again, Alan—assuming that she had a motive, I
think I believe it.' Inga was still 'Thinking'. 'It fits everything we know about the woman, and it fits with a
lot of the other things we've learned. It's a large chunk
of the puzzle falling into place, or a large piece of the
plot, if you prefer, Dorothy.'

'But it makes her relationship with Ben Peterson irrelevant,' Nigel objected.

'Maybe it is,' began Inga.

'Or maybe not!' I interrupted eagerly. 'I have an idea.
Wait a minute while I work it out.'

There was the kind of pause that used to be called
pregnant while I sorted out my thoughts.

'Suppose,' I said slowly, 'that Dan knew who Delia
was.'

'How?' It came in a chorus.

'Never mind how, for the moment. He was a singer.
He travelled around. We don't know where Delia's been
for the past ten years. Let's suppose, for the sake of the
argument, that he knew. Knew that Madame de la Rosa
was really Sir John's wife, or at least had been at one
time. And maybe he didn't know about the legalities
that had intervened.'

The response was grudging, but I ploughed ahead.
'All right. What would he have done with that knowledge? Never forget that he was a singer. According to
Nigel, singers all over the world admire, even revere
Sir John, not only for his skill as a conductor, but for
his sheer…goodness, for lack of a better word. So let's
suppose that Dan, also knowing Delia's reputation for
troublemaking, feared that she would try to make big
trouble between Sir John and his wife. What was Dan
like, Nigel? Did you have a chance to know him well
enough to judge his character?'

'Not really. We had only just begun rehearsals, you know, when he died. I don't know what you're getting at, Dorothy.'

'I'm trying not to lead the witness! But since you won't play, what I want to know is whether Dan was bold enough, brave enough, if you will, to confront Delia and ask her what she planned to do.'

Nigel shook his head. 'I can't answer that. The little I saw of him, he seemed wrapped up in Pat to the exclusion of any other ideas. But aside from that...' He shrugged. 'Certainly he never seemed to stick out from the crowd in any way. I think most of us were barely aware of his existence, except of course for Pat. And James.'

'Pat and James. It keeps coming back to those two.' I slapped the arm of the sofa in frustration. 'We need a talk with them, and we need it now!'

We all looked at our phones, Alan's and mine, which we had laid on end tables. They were stubbornly silent.

'But since we can't talk to them just now, you might as well go ahead with your theory, Dorothy.' Alan sounded wearily indulgent, and I might have resented the tone if I hadn't been so unsure of my theory myself.

'All right, but try not to poke holes in it until you've heard it all. I just want to know if it hangs together logically. We can try to find proof later. Okay?'

The nods were dutiful, if not enthusiastic.

I took a deep breath. 'What I think happened is this. Dan knew who Delia was, and found out she planned to blackmail Sir John on the strength of it. I think he overheard Delia talking about it, gloating about it, in fact, with Ben Peterson.'

Shaking heads and negative sounds all over the room.

'She didn't even show up at rehearsals until after Dan was dead,' said Nigel, with laboured patience.

'I know that! I also know, and so do you, that her story about a delayed flight from Brazil was sheer fabrication. She entered this country months before she made her appearance at rehearsals. We know that from her passport. We don't know where she was during all that time, but if her affair with Peterson had already begun, she was probably with him. And Dan saw them somewhere, and heard them laughing about what she planned. Oh, and it just occurred to me. At that point Dan didn't know she was the mezzo soloist for the festival. So he might not have understood some of the references she made until…no, that won't work, will it? He never saw her at a rehearsal.'

'No, I think it does work, Dorothy.' Alan leaned forward, becoming interested in spite of himself. 'Delia was on that boat; we know that for a fact. Peterson was busy that afternoon; there was an orchestral rehearsal, remember? So Delia was at a loose end and had to amuse herself somehow. Although a canal boat ride wouldn't seem to be her usual style of entertainment. In any case, finding herself in a nest of the festival singers, do you think she could have avoided boasting about her starring role?'

'Of course!' That was Inga, who abandoned her sculptural pose and leaned forward, eyes bright. 'That's why she chose to be on the boat in the first place; it was a place where she could be admired.'

'Yes, and when Dan heard her bragging all about her appearance at the festival, his uneasiness about her would have shot up about sixteen levels. Here she was, poised not only to wreck Sir John's life, but to wreck the festival at the same time. I think he would have said something to her, tried to reason with her—maybe on the bus, on the way to the boat. She would have laughed him off, or else used her feminine wiles to try to persuade him he was imagining things. But if he was as besotted with Pat as everyone says, she wouldn't have succeeded, be she never so wily. So then when everyone crowded to see the drop to the river, and she saw her chance…'

The silence this time had a different quality. They were considering.

'It hangs together,' said Alan at last. 'Of course it's hanging from invisible hooks, and we can never prove any of it.'

'And even if it's all true, every word of it—and I'll admit it's convincing—it doesn't matter,' said Inga. 'If Delia is a murderer, she's been punished, far more severely than she would have been by law.'

'It does matter, though,' said Alan, and he sounded grim. 'It matters because, if this tissue of assumptions we've woven has any strength to it, it provides a clear motive for James O'Hara to have killed Delia.'

'Which he could not have done,' said Nigel, but he said it very quietly. He sounded very tired of having to repeat his objection.

'The only thing we can do now, until Pat calls—if she does—is talk again to Ben Peterson,' I said with determination. 'Did you get his phone number, Alan?'

'I did.' He made no move toward his phone. 'Dorothy, have you any idea what time it is?'

I looked at the clock on the mantle, a lovely antique which, I remembered now, had showed five thirty-seven every time I'd glanced at it. 'No,' I said brandishing my empty wrist. I seldom wear a watch.

Alan opened his mouth to speak, but the tall clock in

the hall, which does still keep time, forestalled him by chiming sonorously, and for what seemed like forever.

'Oh,' I said. 'I suppose midnight is too late to call even a musician. Although I had an idea some of them kept very late hours indeed. Are you sure?'

'Quite sure, my love. If I were still an active policeman I might, with profuse apologies, bother the gentleman at this hour. As I can no longer claim police powers, and as we would like Mr Peterson's cooperation, we're going to have to leave it until morning.'

'Besides,' said Inga, yawning, 'coffee or no coffee, I can't keep my eyes open any longer.'

'You're right,' I said, raising a hand to Alan so he could help me out of the sofa's squashy embrace. 'But the time is so short!'

'Perhaps Pat will call before morning,' said Nigel. 'At least we'll all be fresh by then. I can't think any more.'

And when someone his age admits to weariness, the game is up.

We tidied up our coffee things and went up to bed.

TWENTY-ONE

THE PHONE CALL, the one that woke us a little after six, was not from Pat.

'Mr Nesbitt? John Warner here. Did I wake you?'

There is of course only one possible answer to that.

'Good. I'm afraid it's rather early, but I simply had to talk to you. I'm afraid my household is in rather a crisis.'

Alan was instantly wide awake. 'Not the twins!'

At those ominous words I was wide awake, too.

'No, no, at least, not in the way you mean. It's…look, I know it's a terrible imposition, but do you suppose you could drive over and have breakfast with us? There's been…a development.'

'I'll be there in twenty minutes.'

I was up and struggling into my clothes before he signed off. 'What?' I asked, trying to remember where I'd put my cleanest pair of slacks.

'I don't know. That was Sir John. Something's happened.'

'I gathered. But the twins are all right?'

'It sounded that way, though he was rather odd about it. Are you ready?'

There was a slight delay while we roused Mairi and Charles; we hated to do it, but the alarm system was armed, and we would have brought the police out had we opened the front door.

It was a lovely, fresh morning. The coots on the pond in front of the house were teaching their babies how to swim, and making a great fuss about it. Dew hung heavy on every rose, every oak leaf. I barely noticed, and Alan would have driven straight off without a glance if he had not had to wipe condensation off the windscreen.

There was another delay on the road while a herd of sheep, being transferred from one pasture to another, ambled along at their own leisurely pace and voiced their complaints about our presence. But it was, after all, not much more than twenty minutes before we rolled up to the entrance of Soughton Hall.

Sir John was waiting for us out on the gravel sweep. He looked as if he had slept even less than we had.

'I do apologize, Mr Nesbitt, but I couldn't think what to do. And I'm so glad you're here, too, Mrs Martin. My wife is in something of a state, I'm afraid.'

'Then suppose you tell us what's happened, before we go in.'

'We've had an anonymous letter. Our au pair found it when she came to see to the twins early this morning. She has left us in consequence.'

'And it said?'

'That I killed my wife; that I was a bigamist and the twins are bastards. That's the expurgated version.' He mopped his brow.

'Good Lord! I can see why Lady Cynthia is upset,' said Alan, shocked.

One of the reasons I love my husband so much is that, despite long years spent in law enforcement, having seen almost every evil that humans can perpetrate, he has never lost his compassion. He must, of course, keep a certain professional detachment, but he has never become calloused.

As for me, I was quite simply appalled. 'Where is she?' I asked Sir John.

'Upstairs with the twins. I'll take you through.'

Their room, large and luxurious, was at the moment in considerable disarray. The twins were huddled close to their mother on the big bed. All were still in their night clothes, and all were, or had been, crying.

'Oh, dear, this won't do at all, will it?' I sailed in, my years as a schoolteacher coming to the fore. 'Sir John, if you'll look after these darling children, I think they need a bath before they get dressed. Lady Cynthia, let me make you some coffee before you do another thing. Or would you prefer tea?'

She whispered something so softly I ignored it and busied myself with the kettle, filling it, arranging tea-bags, milk, sugar, cups. I could have ordered tea from room service, of course, but I thought watching the homely activities of tea-making might soothe the poor woman a little. I kept up a stream of chatter while the water boiled.

'My, this is a lovely hotel, or B & B, or whatever it is. Myself, I'd certainly call it a hotel, given the level of luxury. But of course it has the privacy of a B & B, almost the ambience of a private home. I've never visited Wales before, and I had no idea there were so many beautiful old manor houses in this part of the world. Do you know the history of this one?'

Obviously nothing could interest Lady Cynthia less at that moment, but she was a courteous woman. 'I… I'm not sure. There's a brochure somewhere.' She looked vaguely around the room.

'Goodness, never mind! The staff can undoubtedly tell me. Meanwhile, it's a lovely place to stay, isn't it?' I cast about for some other innocuous remark. I couldn't talk about the festival, or Sir John, or the twins, without precipitating more tears. 'And I believe the weather's unusually fine for this time of year, isn't it? Though as I say, never having been here before, I'm really not a good judge, am I?'

I sounded like a bad imitation of a nattering old woman. I was even boring myself. However, Lady Cynthia was quieter.

'I…it's very kind of you to do this for me, but I'm fine, really.'

The crack in her voice brought my real personality back. 'No, you're not. You're distraught, and have every right to be. You drink this right down, the moment it's cool enough.'

I handed her the brimming cup. She took a tentative sip, made a face, and set it down, perilously, on the bed. 'I don't take sugar, thank you.'

'You're taking it now. Come sit over here at the desk.' I rescued the cup and pulled out a chair for her. 'Sugar's good for shock, and you've had a bad shock.'

'How did you know that?' For the first time she seemed to focus on me.

'Your husband phoned my husband this morning. He thought we might be able to help.'

'I don't think anyone can help.' Another tear rolled down her cheek.

'Now that's just the shock talking. Of course they can help. *We* can help. For a start, I know what that letter said, and there's not a word of truth in it.'

'You don't know…'

'Yes, I do. I may know more about it than you do. I know you are Sir John's lawful wife, and those two lovely children are perfectly legitimate, and Sir John had nothing whatever to do with that awful woman's death.'

'I knew, you see,' she said, as if she hadn't heard.

'John tried to keep it from me, but I knew the moment I saw her. I've been so afraid…'

'My dear, there's nothing to be afraid of. You're a strong woman, and that wonderful husband of yours thinks the sun rises and sets on you. Anyone can see that. So just you drink that tea before it gets any colder than it already is, and then get dressed and see what sort of hash the men are making of getting the children bathed and dressed. Though from the noise, I'd say the twins are having a good time in the bath.'

The splashes and shrieks coming from the bathroom next door sounded happy, if not necessarily productive of useful cleansing. Never mind. The object had been to cheer the children up. Further washing could follow when they felt secure again.

'They are, aren't they?' A watery smile from Cynthia. 'I'd better tidy myself a bit so I won't terrify them again. I never meant to break down in front of them, but…'

'Now don't start again! You've got to think about young Snickelfritz there, for one thing.' I pointed to her bulging belly. 'We're going to find out the truth, and the truth, as the old saying goes, will make you free. Off you go.'

I said a little prayer as she made her way to the bathroom that I could make good on that promise.

That was when my phone rang.

I didn't know that was what it was, at first. I so seldom use the thing that I don't even recognize the jangly noise it makes, to me utterly unlike the way a phone should sound. Then when I did realize what it was I had to find the thing, and by the time I did, it had stopped. But I did remember how to make it call the last number that had called it. I pushed the appropriate buttons and waited, quite literally with bated breath.

'Hello? Is this Mrs Martin?'

'It is. And am I speaking to Pat—I'm sorry, I've forgotten the last name?'

'Stevens. Pat Stevens. I'm sorry it's so early, but I'm going out soon, and your husband did say that it—it was your husband who called, wasn't it?'

'Yes, and you can't imagine how glad I am to hear your voice. We've been really, really worried about you ever since you disappeared.'

'Disappeared?'

'Well, we couldn't reach you, and your phone wasn't taking messages, and then it wasn't working at all, and we were afraid something had happened to you. We knew you were…well, pretty upset about Dan's death, and…'

'I'd forgotten to charge the phone. Did you say you had something to do with the festival?'

'Only that we've come to hear the concerts, and one of the soloists, Nigel Evans, is a great friend. So, tell me, Pat, where are you? We thought you might have gone back home to Manchester.'

'No. There's nothing for me there any more, now that Dan…'

'What about your home? Your job? Your family and friends?'

'It's only a small flat, and a nothing job. I can find another easily enough. Daniel was my only friend there. I'm from the West Country, you see, and I hope I can find something here.'

'Where are you now, then? And are you really all right?'

'Look, I don't mean to be rude, but I have to go. I'm meeting someone in a few minutes. And I don't know you, and I don't know what business it is of yours where

I am and what I'm doing. I'm fine, I tell you, with a friend to look after me. Thank you for your concern, but you can tell everyone not to worry about me. Goodbye.'

'No, don't hang up!' But it was too late. She was gone. And far from being reassured, I was more worried about her than ever. There had been a note of near-hysteria in her voice.

The splashing sounds next door had ceased, and two small naked bodies burst into their parents' bedroom, chasing and squealing. They stopped abruptly at the sight of a stranger instead of their mother.

'Well, don't you two look lovely and clean!' I said warmly.

The little girl stuck a thumb in her mouth and stared at me. 'Mummy?' she said doubtfully.

'Your mummy is getting all nice and clean, too. Shall we go and find some clothes for you to put on?'

'No,' said the boy firmly.

'*There's* my naughty Tom kitten,' said his father, snatching him up under one arm. 'And you, too, Thomasina.'

'That's not my name, Daddy,' said the girl, giggling.

'No? Well, we'll go in and get you dressed, and both of you can tell me what your names are.'

'You *know*, Daddy,' said the boy. 'I'm Jack and she's Jill.'

'*Really*? Just like the rhyme? Can you sing it?'

Jack slithered to the floor and hand in hand the three of them skipped into the children's room singing the nursery rhyme. On pitch, I noticed.

I noticed, also, that I had tears in my eyes. I dashed them away.

'You're slightly damp, my love,' I said, surveying Alan, who looked as if he'd fallen into the tub with the twins. 'I don't suppose you had a chance to ask Sir John anything.'

'He asked us to drop the Sir and Lady. They both find the titles slightly embarrassing except for formal occasions. And no, we couldn't talk in front of the children.'

'You certainly did a lovely job with everyone's mood, anyway.'

'That's all very well, but my mood will improve only when we make some headway with this mess!'

'Mine, too. And I'm afraid I have some bad news on that front. Pat called, just a few minutes ago, but I couldn't make her tell me where she is. She said over and over again that she's all right, but…'

'But?'

'She was so emphatic about it that it almost sounded as if she was trying to convince herself.'

'Mmm. Not good. Did you ask her about James?'

'No. I thought it might scare her off. She did say she was with someone—"a friend to look after me"—but she didn't say who, and I didn't have time to ask. If James ran away because he killed Delia somehow… but she got spooked anyway. She definitely didn't want to tell me where she was, and when I tried to press her, she hung up. She sounded… I can't put a finger on it, but unsettled, at the very least. I'm sorry, Alan. I'm sure you would have handled it much better. I wish she'd called you instead.'

'She might have done. Unfortunately I left my phone back at Tower. Don't worry, love. I'll phone her right now.'

'She said she was going out.'

'She'll still have her phone, presumably. Especially if you're right and she's uneasy about something.'

'I wish there were a way to track cellphones. Mobiles, I mean.'

'There is, but it's quite sophisticated, and not available to us poor civilians. Don't worry. We'll find her.'

'We'd better do it soon!'

That remark didn't deserve a reply, so Alan made none, but opened the door into the hallway.

'Where are you going?'

'You sound almost as panicky as Cynthia. I'm going to find a landline, or to borrow someone's mobile. I don't want to call from yours; she'd know the number and might not answer.'

'Use Sir John's. She won't know that number, and if his name shows up, that might not hurt anything, either.'

He considered that. 'Do you think she has any idea about the connection between him and Delia?'

'Why would she?'

'Someone does. Witness the anonymous letter.'

'Oh, Lord! Do you know, I'd positively forgotten the letter for the moment! I can't imagine how anyone found out, but maybe you're right. Better use the hotel phone. Oh, but before you go, did Sir John show you the letter?'

'There wasn't time. I certainly want to see it.'

'So do I. I'll ask him about it. Go make that phone call.'

The children were making a noisy game out of getting dressed. I tapped on the door, walked in, and approached their father.

'Sir John,' I said quietly, under cover of the shouts of the twins, 'do you have that letter? Alan and I would like to see it, if you don't mind.'

'It's just John, please, and certainly you may see it.' He pulled it out of his breast pocket, holding it gingerly between thumb and forefinger. 'It doesn't make pleasant reading.' He handed it over with a little shudder of distaste, and I grabbed a tissue before accepting it.

I suppose I had expected the usual plain envelope, printed in block capitals. This wasn't like that at all. The envelope was thick and expensive, and was addressed twice. The first address, somewhere in Kent, was typed, or probably printed from a computer. That one was crossed out, in pen, with the Soughton Hall address handwritten in a rather irregular scrawl beside it.

I looked up questioningly.

'It was sent to our home and redirected here. We have a gardener who comes over occasionally, and a woman to help with the cleaning. One of them must have sent it on.'

I peered at the postmarks. The top one was yesterday's, but the one underneath it was smeared too badly to be legible. 'I wonder,' I said, 'how long this has taken to reach you.'

'That's one of the things I mean to find out as soon as I can. I had to deal with poor Cynthia first. I can't thank you enough—'

I waved a hand. 'There'll be time to sort all that out later. Right now we need to learn as much as we can about this letter. It must, of course, be turned over to the police. This is the first tangible evidence we have of criminal activity, and it's the kind of thing they're very good at tracing. You'll note I haven't touched it, nor do I intend to take out the enclosure until Alan is back. I imagine Cynthia has a pair of tweezers with her?'

'I imagine so. Tom kitten, what *are* you doing with that shirt? It goes on the other way round, don't you think?'

'Fraülein always does it for me. I want Fraülein!' His lip began to tremble.

'I'm Fraülein for today,' I said, giving the envelope carefully back to Sir John. 'Now let me zee,' I went on in what I fondly imagined to be a German accent. 'Vass heff ve here?' I clumsily inserted Jack into the shirt. With neither children nor grandchildren of my own, my experience in dressing kids was limited.

Jack put up with my uncertain ministrations for a moment or two, but a tantrum was imminent when Cynthia walked into the room, bathed, dressed, and looking much more like the cool, soignée self I'd seen before.

'What's this, then, kittens? Nearly all dressed? What grown-up kittens you're getting to be, aren't you, darlings? Mummy's very proud of you!'

'Did it myself!' proclaimed Jack. 'Nearly,' he added with a sidelong glance at me.

I winked back in a tacit promise not to give him away.

'Splendid, both of you. Now I don't know about you, but Mummy's starving, so I'm going to take you down to breakfast while Daddy and Mrs Martin talk.'

'Want Daddy, too.' Jack's lower lip became prominent once more.

That little boy knew what he wanted, and was certainly shaping to be the troublemaker of the two. But Cynthia knew how to deal with him. 'Poor Daddy has to do some boring work while we have our lovely eggs. He'll be down in five minutes. Now let's creep downstairs like little mice, because other people are sleeping and we don't want to wake them up. Ssshh!' She put her finger to her lips and began to creep in stage-villain fashion, the children aping her.

TWENTY-TWO

THE DOOR CLOSED behind them and Sir John sank into a chair, looking twenty years older than he had a moment before.

'It's better to have something to do, isn't it?' I said. 'Someone to look after. I knew that well when I was a teacher. I remember one day when there was a terrible storm. It was late spring and there were tornadoes all around us. The sky turned green and the classroom windows rattled and the children were terrified. So was I, but I couldn't show it. I knew we'd be told if a tornado was actually approaching, and meanwhile it was best to go on with what we were doing. But it was useless to try to make anyone concentrate on long division. So I decided on an art lesson, the messiest, most absorbing activity I could think of. We got out paper and crayons and paste and paint and modelling clay, and I told them to make pictures of the storm, using any medium they liked.'

'Was the distraction effective?'

'Oh, yes. Some of the efforts they produced were more expressions of their own emotions than literal representations of a storm, but that's probably closer to real art, anyway. It took their minds off their fears, and did the same for me. The storm had cleared before we were done, and they hadn't even noticed the sun was out.'

'I wish our particular storm would clear.'

'It will. We'll take this letter to the police and they'll

track down the sender, and we'll be a long way toward solving the problem. And Alan left a little while ago to phone Pat Stevens. You remember, the fiancée of the singer who fell off the boat?'

'Ah, yes. The young alto. How will she be able to help?'

'We think her fiancé might have told her something that would confirm some of our theories. I'd rather not say more, because it's all in the realm of guesswork just now, but…and here's Alan back. Any news?'

'Quite a lot, actually.' Alan looked moderately satisfied with himself. 'But do you think we could discuss it over breakfast? I'm rather hungry, and the children are getting fractious. I think Cynthia would appreciate your help, John.'

The hotel people were cooperative about providing two extra breakfasts, and the twins were cooperative about eating theirs, now that they were once more securely surrounded by their family.

I was more interested in what Alan had to say than in bacon and eggs, so I drank my coffee while he, in between bites, told us what he had learned from Pat.

'She's in Penzance, for a start. She's from those parts, and though her family are all gone now, she says she used to have friends and connections there. She's staying at a B & B for now, and looking for a place of her own. James is no longer with her.'

'But he was?'

'He was. They left together. Pat was a bit cagey about where they went first, and where he is now, but I got the impression they quarrelled. Not hard to do, I'd have thought, given James's temper.' He finished his bacon and picked up his coffee cup.

'But did she tell you anything about…' I looked over

at the twins, now absorbed in finishing their toast soldiers, and lowered my voice. 'Anything about what we discussed earlier?'

'I asked her if she and Dan had talked at all about the diva,' said Alan blandly, his eye also on the twins, 'and she said they had, and he had told her some surprising things.'

We waited for him to continue.

'And she'll be here in—' he looked at his watch— 'about an hour to answer any questions we or the police want to put to her. That missive you received, John, may be the best thing that's happened in this case, because it puts the matter firmly in the hands of the authorities.'

'But doesn't take it *out* of your hands, I hope,' said Cynthia, with enough anxiety in her voice to disturb the children. Their balance was still pretty fragile— as, I thought, was hers. They turned their heads toward her with worried looks on their small faces, and she immediately pulled herself together, ruffled their hair and pointed to their plates. 'Have you finished, darlings? You've more crumbs on your plates and on your faces than in your tummies, I do believe. We'd best go and get you clean and tidy again.'

'Daddy?' said Jack, predictably.

'I'll be there soon, Tom-kitten,' he said. 'Go with Mummy now and be a good boy.' There was a firmness to his tone that Jack had heard before, judging by his reaction. I could see the small boy decide it would be safest to do as he was told.

'Now,' said Alan as soon as Cynthia and the children had left the room, 'I'd like to see that letter. Ah, carefully wrapped, I see.'

'Your wife did that,' said Sir John. 'I'm afraid I'd handled it by that time; so had Cynthia and Frieda.'

'No matter. It'll be easy to get all those fingerprints. At least, you said Frieda had gone?'

'Not far, not yet. She said she was going back to the house in Appledore to get her things, and then she was going home. She was quite hysterical. Said she wanted nothing to do with such a family.'

'You'll need to head her off. Can you phone the house?'

'She might not answer, or she might not have arrived yet. Train connections aren't terribly good from here to Appledore, and it's still only—good Lord, not even eight o'clock. I'll ring Mrs Stokes, who does cleaning for us.'

While he did that, Alan studied the envelope carefully. 'Redirected,' he commented.

'Yes, Sir John—John, I keep forgetting—said the gardener or household helper probably sent it on. He was just going to phone when you came back upstairs.'

'Good. We'll need, or rather the police will need to try to find out when it was originally sent. Now, let's have a look at the letter itself.'

He used a table knife to ease out the folded sheet and then to lay it flat.

It, too, was a neat computer printout. Times New Roman in a large, bold size, about twenty point if I was any judge.

'Computers have made this sort of thing much more difficult, haven't they?'

'You're telling me! I positively long for the good old days of words cut from newspapers. The experts can tell what kind of printer was used for this, but as there will be twenty thousand of them within a fifty-mile radius of wherever this was sent from, it's precisely no help at all.'

'The paper?'

'That's rather more helpful. Good quality bond, not

your standard computer paper.' Holding it with the tissue, he lifted it up to the light. 'Watermarked, too. That'll gladden the Inspector's heart somewhat.'

He put the letter back on the table and we studied it. I was glad I'd had nothing to eat.

'You've destroyed your slut of a wife and wrecked your family,' it read in its nice, neat, bold print. 'You're a fucking bigamist and your brats are bastards. You'll get what's bloody coming to you.'

I swallowed. 'This is vile,' I whispered.

'It's all of that,' said Alan soberly. 'It's also very interesting, for several reasons.'

I nodded. 'Not one mistake of spelling, grammar, or punctuation. Someone slipped up there.'

'Perhaps, though it's hard to fake illiteracy convincingly. But this tells us that it was written by a person who is either educated, or knows how to use the spelling and grammar tools on a computer. Either way, not someone stupid.'

'Not much help,' I said. 'Presumably this was sent by someone connected with the festival, and most musicians are reasonably bright.'

'I'm not sure your assumption holds water, Dorothy. Very few people connected with the festival knew about Delia's connection with John. Yesterday I would have said no one, except for Delia herself.'

'But we thought probably her lover knew. The violinist. And probably Dan Green.'

'Perhaps. But this letter…frankly, though ugly and distressing, it may well be largely irrelevant to the larger issues at hand. But nasty as it is, it has one great virtue, and that is that the implied threat is enough to bring the police into the matter.'

'But too late, too late! In less than eight hours, everyone will be gone.'

'Gone, yes, but not out of reach of authority. We were worried because we had no right to detain or pursue anyone once they have left the festival, but now... Ah, John.'

'Mrs Stokes says that Frieda has not yet arrived. She worked out the rail connections on her computer, and reckons she can't get there before noon, at best.'

'Her computer?' I queried.

Sir John was mildly amused. 'She's a very modern char, you know. She runs a cleaning service, and keeps her schedule on her computer. She fits the old model in some ways, though. She doesn't care much for foreigners, especially Germans. I believe one of her grandparents, at least, was killed in the Blitz. At any rate, she's never got on well with Frieda. She says she'll make sure "that girl" stays at the house until the police can come to take her fingerprints. I suspect she'll lock her in, if it takes that.'

'And did you ask her about the letter?'

'Yes. I told her nothing about what was in it. It would upset her greatly. She was a bit exercised about it in any case.'

'And what did she tell you?' Alan asked patiently.

'She blamed the gardener, you see. They're old enemies. He never comes on the same day she does, so they won't encounter each other. It's an old feud, over I don't know what, from years ago. Anyway, apparently he came to work on the garden a day or two after we'd left to come here. He went to the front hall for reasons Mrs Stokes does not excuse. Sheer curiosity, I'd say. He snoops a bit. At any rate, he picked the mail up off the mat and put it on the side table, and for some reason covered it with a road atlas we keep there. By the time Mrs Stokes noticed the pile of mail, he'd done this several times. The pile had grown high and unstable, and cascaded to the floor, where Mrs Stokes found it. I had asked her to glance through the mail and forward anything that looked important on to me here, and so, this morning...'

'You didn't have the post office forward everything?'

'No. I didn't want to have to deal with masses of junk mail, which is most of it these days. And I trust Mrs Stokes' judgement. She was, as I said, most upset. She hoped there wasn't anything terribly important in what she sent, because she knew some of it might be weeks old by now.'

'I don't suppose she had an idea where in the pile this particular letter was.'

'I didn't ask. She said it was all in a muddle on the floor when she found it. And of course by the time she'd sorted through it, it wouldn't be in any real order in any case.'

'No. It's a pity the postmark can't be read, but the police might be able to decipher it. They have some pretty sophisticated equipment these days.' Alan stood up. 'Unless there's something else we can do for you here, I think the sooner this gets into the hands of the police, the better. And you're not to worry about any of this. I do think we're very near a solution.'

'You've done a great deal, both of you, and I appreciate it more than I can say. Mrs Martin, Cynthia is feeling much more like herself, thanks to you.'

'It's Dorothy, and I didn't do a thing. She's a very resilient lady, your wife, as well as being beautiful. And your children are darlings.'

We shook hands, Alan tucked the letter safely into his breast pocket, and we hurried down to the car.

'Whew!' I said when we were out of earshot. 'I feel as if I've lived several lifetimes since we got up. And I'm starved. I was too busy worrying to eat breakfast. Those poor people. Um…are you sure we're on the right road? I thought we turned back there for Tower.'

Alan grinned. 'For once, dear heart, your sense of direction is accurate. We're going to the police station in Wrexham, to give the Inspector this letter.'

'But isn't Pat due at Tower any time?'

'She is. I phoned Nigel earlier to expect her. He'll cope.'

We were longer at Wrexham than I had anticipated, since everything had to be explained, and the Inspector was a painstaking man. I was on tenterhooks the whole time. What if Pat felt threatened somehow, and fled again? What if Nigel asked her too many questions? What if she'd changed her mind and never came at all?

When we finally, finally, got back to Tower, however, we found Nigel, Inga and a girl I assumed to be Pat sitting at the breakfast table drinking coffee.

Pat would have been a pretty girl if she hadn't looked so miserable. Her dark, curly hair framed a face that was meant to be round and cheerful. Instead, she looked gaunt, with dark circles under her eyes. Her clothes gave the same impression. They were attractive and unusual, a blue T-shirt and jeans, both trimmed with elaborate and unusual black crocheted lace, but they had the air of being thrown on without thought.

'You'll be Pat Stevens,' I said, holding out a hand. 'Dorothy Martin. And I have to say, my dear, that I've never seen such an interesting outfit. Casual and dressy at the same time. Wherever did you find it?'

'Oh.' She looked down at her clothes as if she'd never seen them before. 'I made them. Made the lace, I mean.'

'I'm impressed,' I said truthfully. 'I'm no good at that sort of thing.'

I plumped down at the table, gazing with longing at the one remaining piece of toast, and Mairi poked her head in as if reading my mind.

'All right?' she asked.

'Mairi, we're being perfect nuisances, and I'm so sorry.'

'No, no. What can I get you for breakfast?'

'Just coffee for me, thanks,' said Alan, 'but I think Dorothy would like the lot. It's been a rather…interesting morning.'

'Right,' said Mairi. 'I'll just be a moment.'

'It's nearly ten,' I said, 'and that poor woman undoubtedly has other things to do besides cook me breakfast. But thank you. I wouldn't have had the nerve to ask. It's a pity one doesn't tip at a B & B.'

'When this is all over, we'll take the two of them out to the finest dinner we can find, and tell them the whole story,' said Alan. 'Meanwhile, Pat, we're eager to hear what you have to tell us.'

She shrugged, a little helplessly. 'I don't know what you want from me. Nigel's told me I might know something about what's been happening, that woman's death and all, but I can't imagine what. I never even met her.'

'We'd like to know what Daniel told you about her,' said Alan. 'I do realize this may be painful for you, and I wouldn't ask if it weren't terribly, terribly important.'

She swallowed. Alan poured her a glass of water and waited.

'He told me a lot of stuff, most of it months ago. Do you want all that?'

'Please. Everything you can remember.'

'Well, when we both auditioned and were accepted

for the choir, Dan was really excited. He sings—sang—in the cathedral choir in Manchester. It has a really good choir, did you know?'

'An excellent choir,' said Nigel, nodding.

'And Dan thinks—thought—Sir John's the next thing to God. He just couldn't get over how wonderful it was to be singing for him. We were both over the moon, actually. So we went out to dinner to celebrate. We didn't do that a lot, because neither of us had much money, you know? But we were both so…' Tears welled up, but she brushed them away impatiently. 'Anyway, Dan took me to this really expensive place, and there was this other couple there, and we could hear them talking, and Dan got really upset, because they were talking about Sir John.'

Mairi slipped into the room with my breakfast, and I tried to eat noiselessly while Pat went on with her story.

'The woman was being really cruel, talking about how she was going to make him pay, make him sorry he'd ever left her, and so on. So I asked Dan who she was, and he said her name was Delia something or other, and she was Sir John's first wife.'

'How did he know that, Pat?' asked Alan.

'I'm not sure. He was rather jibbering, because he was nearly beside himself with anger. I think he'd seen her before at some concert he sang in way back when he was a treble, just a kid. It must have been before that shipwreck, because he kept saying that she was supposed to be dead, and what a…witch she was, and what this would do to Sir John and his family, and…well, it spoiled the evening for us.'

'I'm sure it must have done. When was this, by the way?'

'The middle of February, because that's when the audition results were announced.' Another tear escaped.

'You're being very brave about this, Pat, and we appreciate it. I have only a few more questions. Did Dan talk to you any more about this incident?'

She sighed. 'He talked of nothing else! At first he wanted to find this woman and try to talk her out of what she was planning, though he didn't have any clear idea of what that was. He'd wanted to do that even that night, just walk over to their table and… I don't know, scream at her, I suppose. I'd managed to drag him away before he could do that, but he wouldn't stop talking about it. Then he wanted to go to Sir John and tell him his wife was still alive and planning mischief, but I persuaded him to wait until after the festival. He finally agreed to that, because I kept telling him how it would upset the man, and ruin the festival he'd worked so hard for. Sir John, I mean, but of course Dan too, and me, for that matter, and all the musicians. It was in aid of such a good cause, and it meant so much to everyone involved. So he let the subject drop, most of the time, but I knew it was still weighing on his mind.'

'I have a question, if you don't mind, Pat, about that first evening, when Dan recognized the woman. Did either of you know who the man was, her dinner partner?'

'Not then, but we both thought we recognized him later, when rehearsals began. He looked a lot like the concertmaster, Ben Peterson.'

TWENTY-THREE

'RIGHT,' SAID ALAN, after we all exchanged glances. 'Now I know you've had enough, Pat, but there's one more question I'd like to ask. Before I do, though, I should tell you that we know that the woman you and Dan saw in the restaurant that night was indeed Sir John's first wife, but the marriage had long been legally dissolved. Her real name was Delia Warner, but she had adopted the stage name of Madame de la Rosa.'

Pat gasped.

'Yes. The mezzo soloist for the festival, the one who died. Further, we do not know, but we believe, that she was responsible for Dan's death.'

'So that's... James kept talking about Madame...but I didn't know...'

'No one knew the two were one and the same, except of course Sir John, perhaps Dan, and presumably Mr Peterson, if he was the man you saw with her in April.'

'But if James thought she killed Dan,' I said gently, 'it wouldn't have mattered to him what her name was. He would have hated her for killing his friend.'

Pat sat up straight. 'Are you saying that James killed this woman? Madame de la Rosa, or Delia, or whoever she was?'

'We have no evidence whatsoever,' said Alan, with a warning look at me, 'that Delia's death was anything but accidental. We do believe that she was responsible for Dan's fall from the canal boat, either by accident or by design. We think James must have seen her push him, and we'd very much like to talk to him about that in order to put the matter to rest. Can you tell us where he is?'

'We quarrelled. He... I...' She made a little face and clasped her arms around her chest in a classic defensive pose.

'He became possessive?' I suggested gently.

'He seemed to think because he was Dan's friend, and Dan was gone, that he owned me now! And I don't even like him! He was bloody awful to me before Dan died, but then he turned to me afterwards, I suppose because we were both grieving. I went with him because I felt sorry for him, but when he started...well, I told him to bugger off!'

Anger had replaced her tears, but the tears wouldn't be long in coming back, and this time she'd really break down, if I was any judge.

'Pat, you have no reason to protect him,' I said urgently. 'When did you and James O'Hara part company, and where is he now?'

'I pushed him out yesterday, and if I had to guess, I'd say he's back in Wicklow, and be damned to him!' And she buried her face in her hands and began to sob.

Alan had arranged with Mairi for Pat to stay at Tower for a night or two, if she wished, and as she was plainly in no state to drive back to Penzance, Inga and Mairi helped her up to her room. Inga stayed with her while the rest of us put our heads together.

'My heart aches for that child,' I said with a sigh. 'She seems to be quite alone, and she's at an age when even a small crisis can seem like the end of the world, let alone the death of a beloved. I hope she'll be all right. But what are we going to do now?'

'I'm going back to the police with all this,' said Alan. 'We have enough now to request a review of the whole case, and enough to ask Inspector Owen to bring James O'Hara in for questioning. Nigel, when do you have to be at the castle?'

Nigel glanced at his watch. 'Not till two. The concert's at three today. Sir John wants to go over the *Pié Jesu*, but most of us know it quite well, so it's just a matter of balance and his own interpretation, that sort of thing. It's only ten thirty, so we've piles of time.'

'Good. Then I'd like you to phone the festival office—you'd better ring Sir John first, so you won't run into roadblocks—and find the Andrews twins. You know where they're staying, yes? Then go and talk to them about, first, James and what led Larry to think he might have engineered Delia's death, and second, what either of them might know about Ben Peterson. If I can get back to the castle by one I will, or a little earlier if possible, because I want to talk to the twins too, and to Mr Peterson. Dorothy, if you will, I'd like you to come with me. I'll drop you off at Soughton Hall, and you can make sure all is serene there. Tell them not to worry any more. Oh, and you might say I think I know who sent the letter.'

'What? Who?'

'What letter?' asked poor Nigel.

'Later,' shouted Alan, heading for the front door.

Nigel turned to me. 'What letter?'

'I can't tell you just now. I'm beginning to have a glimmer, but… I'm sorry, I can't tell you. It's not my secret. I have to go.'

And I hustled to the car. I sincerely hoped I'd have time to change clothes before the concert. Jeans and sneakers aren't my idea of proper concert attire, even an al fresco one. I could have asked Inga to bring me something if I'd thought of it. Never mind.

'Who?' I asked Alan the minute I was settled in the car.

'Haven't you worked it out?'

'Maybe. It all depends on the postmark, doesn't it?'

Alan beamed at me. 'I knew you'd get it.'

Soughton Hall, which had been slumbering peacefully when we left it earlier, was now bustling with activity. A marquee had been set up in the back garden, and the staff were carrying tables and chairs and china and cutlery and flowers out to it.

Somebody was getting married. Well, they had a beautiful setting for it.

When I inquired after the Warners, the desk clerk told me she thought they had taken the children for a walk in the garden. It must, I thought, be difficult to keep two active toddlers busy and happy for such an extended stay away from home, and now that their nanny had flown the coop, Cynthia certainly had her hands full. Not for the first time, I wished I were better with small children. School-age ones, the middle grades, I could deal with, but the little ones...

I had wandered past the marquee by now and into the gardens, which were formal and not, I thought, terribly child-friendly. For one thing, there was a pond which any right-minded child would find irresistible.

Sure enough, there they were at the other end of the pond. Jack was throwing bits of gravel into the water, while Jill was leaning over it, gazing intently. Her father squatted beside her, a firm hand on the waistband of her skirt.

'No fish,' said Jill in a tone of disapproval.

'No, darling, I don't think this is the kind of pond with fish.'

'Jack's scaring them away. You stop, Jack!' She tried to move toward her twin, but her father's grip kept her where she was. 'Let go, Daddy!' she commanded.

'Let's go see what the chipmunk is doing, shall we?' He scooped her up in his arms, and turned and saw me.

'Getting just a little bored, are we?' I said. 'Hello, Jill.'

She buried her head in Sir John's shoulder.

'Bored and restless. Frieda had promised them a little jaunt to the seaside today, and they're not very happy about missing it.'

'I wish I could help, but I'm terrified at the idea of supervising two active children at such a hazardous place as the seaside. Oh!'

Sir John raised his eyebrows. 'Is something wrong?'

'No. I've just had an idea. Inga and Nigel have a little boy almost exactly the same age as your two, and I know she's missing him dreadfully. Well, they both are, but Nigel has such a lot to do, and Inga's more or less along for the ride. What if she were to take the children out today? She's perfectly reliable, I can attest to that, and I know she'd love to do it.'

'Want to go to seaside!' Jill cast her vote in favour of the proposition.

'Let's ask Mummy, shall we?'

Cynthia, who was looking frazzled, agreed with enthusiasm, so all that remained was to phone Inga to see if she was agreeable.

'Oh, I'm glad you called. Of course I'd love to take the kids to the beach. Nigel can take us, on his way to talk to Larry and Laurie, and we'll get a cab or a bus or something when everyone's tired. I don't mind missing today's concert; *Carmina* isn't one of my favourites. And I think we should take Pat along. She's feeling better, having got all that off her chest, but she needs some distraction, and I could use a second pair of hands and eyes. We'll be there in…half an hour? And would you like me to bring you some smarter clothes? I thought of it after you left.'

I thanked her for everything and reported to the Warners, who were delighted. The twins, of course, were overjoyed. The halfhour sped past as we got the children ready and assembled all the necessary paraphernalia. We spent the last few minutes outside watching the final preparations for the wedding.

'Birthday party?' queried Jill.

'Even nicer,' said her mother. 'A wedding.'

'With cake and games?'

'Cake, but probably not games.'

'Birthday party's better,' she said with finality.

There were a few sticky moments when the children realized they were going off with people they didn't know, without their parents, but Inga and Pat dealt with them competently, and when they'd left both parents heaved a great sigh of relief.

'Now, I may have to impose upon you for a ride to the castle,' I said as we went back inside. 'Alan's off to Wrexham to talk to the police and set some things in motion. And I was to tell you not to worry, that everything's under control, and he thinks he knows who wrote the anonymous letter.'

'Who?' they asked in unison.

'He didn't say. He can be terribly annoying at times. And I think I'm beginning to have an idea, but I'd better not say, in case I'm wildly wrong. But we really are on the right track at last, I think, and truly, this night-mare is nearly over.'

They looked at me searchingly, but I simply smiled. Alan could tell them the whole story, if we ever did work it out. I wasn't going to tantalize them with hints and guesses.

They treated me to an excellent early lunch at The Stables, then I changed clothes, begged a toothbrush from the management, said goodbye to Cynthia, who had decided to stay behind and rest, and was ready to go back to the castle.

For the last time. The last concert. I found myself hoping with ridiculous fervour that it would go well, that there would be no untoward incidents to spoil it, that the musicians and the audience alike would be lifted to that exalted state of consciousness that only music can evoke. I wanted to learn who had killed Delia, and how. I wanted the Warners out from under the cloud of doubt and suspicion. But I wanted none of the solution to cast a pall over the concert.

John cast a wary eye at the sky as we set out. 'I hope the weather holds. We've been unbelievably lucky so far, but this fine weather can't last forever. Those clouds…'

I peered out the window. 'They look like fair-weather clouds to me. I'm sure it'll be all right.' But there was a heaviness to the air that, back home in the States, might have boded a storm.

Things are different here in Wales, I reminded myself.

We were very early. Alan had arrived, but the only musicians there were Nigel, the Andrews twins, and a disgruntled concertmaster, who was inclined to be snappish.

'I have a demanding concert to play this afternoon, in case it had escaped your notice,' he snarled.

'I need only a few minutes of your time,' said Alan, but his tone was in no way conciliatory. 'I believe the late Madame de la Rosa was a…good friend, shall we say, of yours?'

'I don't see that that's any business of yours.'

'Oh, but it is, you see. It bears on an investigation I have undertaken at the request of Sir John Warner. I understand that you knew who the lady really was, and that she discussed with you some plans for…embarrassing Sir John, to put it mildly.'

Peterson opened his mouth, but Alan held up a hand. 'You needn't bother to deny it. You were seen, and overheard, and recognized, and I can produce a witness to that effect if necessary.'

'Why should I bother to deny it? The lady never carried out her plans.'

She did too, I wanted to answer. *She tried to blackmail Sir John, and caused him and his wife great distress, and if this man thought that was nothing, he could think again!* But I kept my mouth shut while Alan continued.

'I'm not particularly concerned with that aspect of the problem just now, though there might be an interesting point of law at issue. However, my question is this: exactly when did you post a letter for Madame?'

'There's no law against posting a letter!'

'Not unless it contains a threat. When did you post it?'

'A few days ago. I don't remember.'

'Before or after Delia—to use her proper name—before or after she died?'

'After! And I had nothing to do with her death! How could I, when I was sitting here playing first fiddle in front of a hundred other people?'

'And that,' said Alan, turning to me, 'disposes of the letter.'

'Delia wrote it herself.'

'Of course she did. It was meant to soften up Sir John before she started her blackmail, only Mr Peterson forgot to mail it.'

'Fortunately. But it said he killed his wife. That makes no sense. When she wrote it, she was obviously alive.'

'The letter said he had *destroyed* his wife and family. Delia was referring to his present wife and children, who, she thought, would be destroyed if it were learned that she was still alive.'

I shook my head in disbelief. 'She really was a piece of work, wasn't she? I wish I could be sorry she's dead, but I can't find it in my heart.'

'A thoroughly nasty person,' Alan agreed. 'She could sing like an angel, though.'

'That doesn't excuse her, any more than…' I didn't finish the sentence, but I glared at Ben Peterson's back as he stalked off, his violin under his arm.

TWENTY-FOUR

'HE'LL PAY FOR IT,' said Laurie, who had heard part of the conversation. 'Whatever he tried to do to Sir John, word will get around that he's trouble. Yes, he plays a fine violin, but he's already had a few problems with temperament. That's why he doesn't have a permanent job with a good orchestra. I can't stand him, myself, and there are a few others in the orchestra who think he's an arrogant son of a…gun. Now when the scuttlebutt goes around that he tried to sabotage Sir John, he's going to find it harder and harder to get good jobs. Trust me. I'll be the first to make sure it gets to Chicago.'

Larry, who had been lurking unhappily nearby, came up to Alan. 'Sir, I don't know what you want with me. I don't know any more than I've told you. I don't know where James O'Hara is.'

'That's not what interests me at the moment. We think we may know where to find him. What I need from you now is a little more information about your conversation with him. He gave you cause for concern. Why?'

Larry shuffled his feet and bit his lip. 'Look, I don't mean to be rude or anything, but is this really your business? You're not the police.'

'No, I'm not, not now, though for many years I was. But Sir John has asked me to find the reasons for the terrible events that have so interfered with this festival, and if possible name the person or persons behind them. In order to do that, I must ask questions you may find intrusive. And may I remind you that we have very little time before everyone leaves the area, and even, in some cases, the country?'

Larry made a face and spread his hands. 'Okay. Shoot.'

'I want you to tell me what passed between you and James O'Hara. Exact words, please, so far as you can remember them.'

'I'm not likely to forget.' He took a deep breath. 'See, it was on the Saturday, the first full rehearsals after that awful boat ride and the accident.'

Alan nodded. 'The day before she died.' He glanced at his watch.

'Okay, I'll hurry it up. Anyway, some of us went out afterwards for drinks, and James was drinking quite a lot more than other people, and carrying on about Dan, getting pretty loud. And…well, I guess I'd had a little too much, too. Anyway, I got sort of maudlin, and I said…' He paused and swallowed. 'I said what a great thing it would have been if somebody had pushed Gracie in the drink, instead of Dan.'

'Larry!' It was out of my mouth before I could stop it.

'I know, I know! Do you think I haven't kicked myself around the block about it? I was sorry I'd said it even then, but I never thought… But then when she fell the next day I got to wondering. She was awfully close to Dan on the boat; I saw her. What if James thought she'd pushed him? What if I'd planted an idea in his head? He was so furious about Dan's death. I tried to talk to him, find out what he was thinking, but he was drinking way too much and never made much sense. And then you started nosing around and making everybody wonder if she really was murdered somehow, though none of us could see how. And then when he and Pat disappeared together…'

Larry ran down, and Alan looked at his watch again. 'All right, that's been very helpful, and it'll have to do for now.' He addressed the small group around us. 'Go get ready to perform. I won't ask you to forget about this; that's not possible. But use the hurt or anger or whatever you're feeling and turn it into music.'

'That,' I said, linking my arm with my husband's, 'was one of the wisest things I've ever heard you say.'

'It's the only thing to do with negative emotions, isn't it? Use them to make something positive.'

And that simple philosophy, I thought as we strolled around the castle waiting for the rehearsal to finish and the performance to begin, could do away with terrorism and most other crime in a heartbeat, if more of the world would adopt it.

But we couldn't do it. I, for one, couldn't do it. If I could take all the worry and fear and anxiety and doubt I'd experienced this week, all my loathing for Delia's selfishness and Ben's callousness, if I could roll them up into a ball of positive energy, I could light up all of North Wales with it. But no. I had to hug those feelings to myself, cherish them, feed on them, poisonous though they were.

But then, I wasn't an artist. Artists, of whatever stripe—painters, musicians, actors—had an outlet. They could take whatever was boiling inside them and make it into something meaningful. And for the rest of us, perhaps, I thought as the lovely strains of the *Pié Jesu* reached my ears and my heart—perhaps that was part of what the Christian rite of confession was all about. Get rid of all the negativity, all the poison, lay it in the hands of him who could transform it into something positive, something wonderful.

In that rather exalted mood I followed Alan into the pavilion to claim our seats for this last of the festival concerts.

The orchestra took their seats. The chorus filed in and sat down. The concertmaster walked on. Applause, applause, applause, in which I pointedly did not join. There I was, hugging my resentment. *Mea culpa,* I whispered to myself, but Alan heard, and smiled as if he knew exactly what I was thinking. The concertmaster nodded to the oboe, who sounded the A, and the orchestra did their final tuning.

Then Sir John entered, and this time I joined in the applause whole-heartedly. He bowed and then held out his hands for silence.

'Ladies and gentlemen, as we have come to the last concert of our music festival, I want to thank you very sincerely for your support of our efforts. We have raised a goodly sum for the benefit of the RNLI, and I'm sure they thank you, too.'

Applause.

'Many of you know,' he went on, 'that we have been saddened by the death of two of our musicians in the course of this festival. In their memory, therefore, we would like to offer tonight, as a special tribute, Andrew Lloyd Webber's *Pié Jesu.*'

Without giving time for anyone to applaud, he turned and raised his baton. Nigel, seated next to the concertmaster, rose, as did the choir, and the gentle, lovely strains of the violins began.

I've said before that music often makes me cry. Even the ragged dissonances of an unrehearsed high school band playing 'The Stars and Stripes Forever' at a July

4th parade will make my throat close up. So when a group of professional musicians, under a superb director, performed one of the loveliest of contemporary music works, I was hard put not to sob.

Pié Jesu, qui tollis peccata mundi, dona eis requiem... Blessed Jesus, who takes away the sins of the world, grant them rest...

At some point Alan took my hand and squeezed it hard, and handed me his handkerchief when my tissues proved inadequate.

'That was perfect,' I croaked over the applause, blowing my nose one last time. 'Just what we all needed.'

'Better now?' said Alan. It wasn't really a question.

There was a brief interlude while the musical forces regrouped for the major work of the evening, which requires a huge orchestra, a team of percussionists, two pianos and a celesta, and a boy choir, along with the usual choir and four soloists. Resetting all that took a little time.

'We're almost there, aren't we?' I asked Alan quietly.

'All except for the one little detail of who killed Delia, and how.'

'You think it was James, don't you?'

'I would think so, if I had one single shred of evidence that she was murdered at all.'

'We both know she was.'

'Knowing it and being able to prove it are two very different things.'

'It'll work out,' I said serenely.

He studied my face. 'You really are feeling better, aren't you?'

'The music. And the words. I'm not worried any more. I've given it up.'

Not many people would have understood. That I am

married to someone who nearly always does understand is one of the great blessings of my life.

'Have you had any word about James?'

'No. I'm hoping they'll find him and get him here before we leave tomorrow, but it doesn't matter very much. It doesn't even matter if I question him or leave it to Inspector Owen. It's his case now, anyway. I can make a full report to Sir John without… And here we go.'

Carmina Burana is a long and tempestuous vocal-orchestral work that defies description. If you know the piece, you know what I mean. If not, nothing I could say could begin to convey the flavour. Actually, it's a bit like trying to describe a flavour. You can say of a fruit that it's both sweet and tangy, with a little bite to it, but none of those words evoke pineapple. At any rate, we all sat back to enjoy the bombast and the lyricism, the glee and the poignancy, and for over an hour we revelled in the musical fireworks.

At last it was nearly over. The last few minutes rose to an almost frenetic conclusion, with the full forces employed *fortissimo*, drums and cymbals clashing, voices soaring to a triumphant climax.

It was no wonder, then, that in that instant before the audience burst into applause, I thought I was hearing an echo. Surely that wasn't an anguished shout from somewhere outside the castle.

'NO!!'

TWENTY-FIVE

'LET'S GO.' Alan half-pulled me from my seat.

'What…?'

'I don't know.'

The rest of the audience was on their feet, applauding and cheering. We pushed our way through them, earning a few glares.

'Was that really someone shouting?' I asked, panting in Alan's wake.

'Yes.' He was saving his breath.

I stumbled over one of the cables, but Alan caught me and hurried on. I had no breath left for questions.

I don't suppose it was actually more than a minute or two before we reached the exit, though it seemed longer. And there, standing just under where the portcullis used to be, was one James O'Hara, struggling in the firm clasp of two burly policemen.

'NO!!' he shouted again. 'It was meant to be a joke! I only wanted to frighten her. She was a right bitch, and she killed me best mate, and I'm glad she's dead, but I never killed her!'

'The Inspector said you wanted to question him. Sir.' The last was added in a tone that narrowly skirted insolence, and I saw that the officer was my least favourite sergeant.

'I do,' said Alan, ignoring the disrespect. 'But this isn't the place to do it. Several hundred people will be streaming out of here in a moment. And for heaven's sake take your hands off the boy! He's not going anywhere!'

'We was told to keep him under control. Sir.'

'And he is now under my control. Quickly, Mr O'Hara. This way, unless you want to be trampled to death.'

Alan led him into the gift shop, just in time, as the first of the joyful horde flooded out of the castle. They were in a bit more of a hurry than usual, I thought, because the sky was now definitely threatening. I hoped we could get home before the storm, and then forgot about the weather as I followed Alan and James, the two policemen close behind.

'Now then,' Alan said calmly to the two clerks on duty. 'Ladies, I believe you deserve a tea break.' He handed one of them a twenty-pound note. 'I'm afraid we need this room for a few minutes.'

'But we can't—the till—we're not allowed...'

'As you see, the till is well protected.' Alan gestured toward the policemen. 'And I will take personal responsibility in case your supervisor is upset. Now go and have yourselves a lovely tea, and come back in...shall we say forty-five minutes?'

'Well, I suppose...'

'Thank you very much.'

Alan eased them out the door and then pulled one of their chairs out from behind the cash desk and gestured to James.

I took a good look at him. He was good-looking, in a flamboyant sort of way. Lots of black hair, lots of muscle, very blue eyes and a very florid complexion. He seemed almost a stage Irishman. And he did, as someone had remarked, smoulder.

'You might as well make yourself comfortable,' said

Alan. 'How did you get here so quickly? I wasn't expecting you until tomorrow.'

'Flew me here in a bloody helicopter, didn't they? Mindin' me own business, havin' a drink or two with me mates, and two feckin' coppers haul me away before I can even finish me pint! And who the bloody hell are you, if you don't mind me askin', me lord?'

His Irishness was even more pronounced and, I thought, just a trifle exaggerated. I also revised my opinion about his looks. When he opened his mouth, where there should have been a flash of white, he displayed instead teeth that were broken, stained and, in some cases, missing. A pity, I thought, because otherwise he really was handsome. Except in manner, that is.

'I don't mind your asking,' said Alan, 'though I'd prefer you moderated your language a bit. There is a lady present. My name is Alan Nesbitt. This is my wife, Dorothy Martin.'

The punctilious courtesy damped James's bellicosity somewhat. He mumbled an acknowledgement of the introductions. 'But what the bloody... I mean, what are you doing here? What do you have to do with all this? You're not a copper.'

'No, not any more. I was a policeman for many years, but I am now retired. Sir John requested that I look into the deaths of Daniel Green and Madame de la Rosa, events which disturbed him profoundly.'

'They did, did they? Well, Dan's death disturbed *me* profoundly! He was me best mate, and that bitch killed him! She deserved anything she got!'

'Why do you think that Madame de la Rosa killed Daniel?'

'I saw her, didn't I?' James wiped his hand across his

mouth. 'There wouldn't be anything to drink around this place, would there? A man gets dry, doin' all this talkin'.'

'Dorothy, would you mind getting Mr O'Hara something to drink?' He held out an assortment of coins and gestured toward the vending machine. 'Would you prefer water or a soft drink?'

James looked at him, aghast. 'Never mind. Get on with it, mate.'

'You say you saw Madame de la Rosa kill Daniel Green. I'd like to know more about that.'

'I was on that bl—that boat. I saw the bitch crowding up next to Dan. I saw him go over. I couldn't get to him. Oh, God!'

He buried his face in his hands and wept.

Killer though I was sure he was, I felt sorry for him. He was in genuine pain. I wondered briefly if he and Daniel had been lovers, and decided it didn't matter. Whatever the nature of their relationship, plainly James had loved Daniel, and was devastated by his loss.

Alan gave him time. When James had recovered somewhat, Alan reached for a handkerchief and realized he had given it to me. I found a packet of tissues on a rack, opened it, and gave a handful to James.

'Ta,' he said, and blew his nose.

'I'm sorry,' said Alan, and meant it. 'I know this is hard for you. But when did you start to believe that Madame had pushed Daniel? Right then, when it happened?'

'No, it was later. I heard a lot of talk about her the next day. See, I hadn't known she was with the festival. She hadn't bloody bothered to show up on time. And when she came and started acting like she owned the place, and people started talking about her, I started to wonder. And then Ben Peterson—the first violin, y'know?—said something to her, and she laughed and said not to worry, that she'd solved a problem. And somethin' about the way she said it... I knew. And I knew I had to do somethin' about it.'

'And just what did you... Yes?' Alan looked up with irritation at the clerk, one of the two he had sent away.

'Very sorry, sir, but Sir John asked me to give you a message. He's gone off in a hurry. His wife has fallen and they're taking her to hospital and he'd like you and your wife to come.'

'Which hospital?' he asked on his way out the door.

WE DIDN'T SPEAK on the road, Alan because his full attention was focussed on driving as fast as was safely possible through the heavy rain that was now starting to fall, and I because all I could think of was the baby. I, who had so badly wanted babies and never could have them. The thought of Cynthia losing her baby was unendurable. I could only pray.

The emergency room was crowded, but Alan found me a seat while he went to try to find someone in charge. Sir John was nowhere in sight; I assumed he was with his wife.

'They won't tell me much,' said Alan, returning. He was fuming. 'These places give bureaucracy a bad name. They're so confounded taken up with their own petty regulations and their own self-importance—'

He was interrupted by a nurse, or an aide, or somebody in a white uniform, at any rate. 'Would you come with me, please, Mr Nesbitt?' Her sour face made it evident that she had overheard him. I didn't ask if I could come, too. Best not to push our luck. I could fret just as well here in the waiting room.

What if the accident cost not only the baby's life,

but Cynthia's, too? What would Sir John do? He was a sensitive man, a musician, obviously in love with his wife. How would he be able to cope with a double loss, on top of everything else? And there were the twins to look after... I prayed some more.

And how had the accident happened? Was it... Oh, dear heaven, was it another non-accident? Surely no one could have wanted to harm Sir John's pregnant wife!

Had anyone thought to tell Inga and Pat, at the seashore with the twins, and probably getting drenched? Sir John would want them back near him, no matter what happened. He would be imagining all the terrible things that could happen to them, too.

I've always been an expert fretter.

Alan came back into the room and forestalled my questions. 'She's gone into labour. John is with her, of course. She wasn't badly hurt in the fall, only a sprained ankle, but she's only a month away from her due date, and the baby decided to start things a bit early.'

'Will the baby be all right? Will she be all right?'

'They think so, but of course it's too soon to tell for sure. They're not going to try to stop the labour, since the baby's heartbeat is strong, and they think it has an excellent chance of survival. They may perform a Caesarean section if the baby seems to be getting stressed. And that's all I know, love.'

'It's good news as far as it goes,' I said, weak with relief. 'How's John?'

'Coping rather well, actually. Of course he wants to be strong and calm for Cynthia, but that's not all of it. He's a man of strong faith, Dorothy.'

I was reminded of how weak my own faith can sometimes be, all that fretting. I took a deep breath. 'I wondered if anyone had thought to get in touch with Inga.'

'Oh, Lord, yes, she's off with the twins, isn't she? Or at least she might be coming home at this point, especially with the rain. I think John had meant to go and pick them up, but of course… Do you have her number?'

I was scanning my phone's memory as he talked. 'Yes, here it is.'

'You'll have to take that outside, madam,' broke in the officious voice of the attendant whom Alan had annoyed earlier. She pointed to a somewhat tattered sign prohibiting mobile use in the hospital.

'Yes, of course. Alan, is there anything else we can usefully do here, for the moment?'

'I don't think so. It may be hours before there's any change.'

'Then let's go. We can pick up the girls and the twins and bring them back. That at least will be some help to John.'

Alan paused to leave a message at the desk in case John should start worrying about the twins, and then we left, and I pulled out my phone.

TWENTY-SIX

INGA ANSWERED IMMEDIATELY. 'Dorothy! Where is everybody? I've tried ringing Lady Cynthia and Sir John, but no one answers. We're just about ready to climb on a bus. The twins have had a glorious day, but then the rain started, and besides, they're more than ready for their naps.'

'We'll tell you when we get there. Here's Alan; you can give him directions.'

One is never far from the sea anywhere in Great Britain. In North Wales it's only a few miles away. Alan told Inga we'd be there in fifteen minutes, rang off, and set out.

'How did Cynthia happen to fall?' I asked, finally able to think beyond the immediate crisis.

'John didn't know, and I didn't press it. Cynthia was in too much distress to tell him, and it wasn't his chief concern at the moment.'

'No, of course not. But I wonder...'

'So do I. Far-fetched as it may seem, so do I, though we're probably both being foolish. But at the moment I'm more interested in how Delia fell, which I think James was about to tell us.'

'Oh! James! I forgot all about him! Oh, good grief, do you think he'll have run away again?'

'Far more likely that Sergeant Blimp has clapped him in irons and thrown away the key. I wish I didn't dislike that chap so much.'

'He's an idiot!' I said warmly. 'He'll alienate James so much, he won't say a word when you talk to him next.'

'Unfortunately, you could be quite right. We'll face that when we come to it.' Alan peered through the rain-streaked windscreen. 'Did that sign say Prestatyn?'

'It said something unlikely in Welsh. We were past it too fast for me to read the English underneath. You'll have to turn around.'

Despite a couple of such diversions, we got there in very little more than the fifteen minutes Alan had promised, and none too soon. The twins were hot, tired, and cross, and both Inga and Pat were looking frazzled. They had waited in the bus shelter, but everyone was rather wet.

'I promised them ice cream,' said Inga, 'but I'm beginning to regret it. They've reached the stage where nothing is right, nothing is what they want, and of course the rain has rather spoiled things.'

'Ah, yes,' said Alan, the experienced father and grandfather, 'and their favourite word is "no". Right, then,' he said, addressing the children. 'Into the car you get. We'll stop for ice cream on the way home. There's not a lot of room, so you'll have to sit on laps.'

'Don't want to sit on a lap!' wailed Jack. 'Want ice cream now!'

'It's a lap and ice cream, or neither,' said Alan, fixing both children with a stern eye.

Men, I've always thought, have an unfair advantage when it comes to dealing with peevish children. There's something about that baritone voice that we women simply can't match. Jack's lower lip still protruded, but he scrambled on to Inga's lap with no further protest as Jill settled in with Pat.

'Are we really going to stop for ice cream?' I murmured as Alan took off down the road.

'If they're not asleep by the time we find a place, yes. I keep my promises. Within reason,' he added.

But as Alan had predicted, the children were sound asleep in five minutes. The threatened storm had failed to materialize, but the rain persisted. Inga, speaking in a soft and soothing voice, said, 'All right. What haven't you told us? Where are their parents?'

'Cynthia took a fall,' I said in the same tones. 'She seems to be okay, but she's gone into labour. John is with her. So far everything seems to be coming along well.'

'She looked to be pretty far along.'

'Eight months, I understand. So the baby has a good chance.'

'One more accident,' said Pat, and her voice was so full of sadness I feared it might rouse the sleeping twins, but they were exhausted and slept on.

'I know what you're thinking,' said Alan firmly, 'but this time it does really seem to have been an accident.'

Alan had nothing whatsoever on which to base that opinion, I thought as we drove on through the rainy, sleepy afternoon. But if it made anyone feel better, what was the harm?

Inga phoned Nigel to tell him what had happened, and to expect her when he saw her. The twins, oblivious to everything, didn't wake even when we got to Soughton Hall. The girls carried them up to their rooms and laid them in their big double bed, damp clothes and all. 'They can have a bath when they wake up,' said Inga softly as she pulled the door nearly shut. 'Right now we all need some rest.'

'And some tea,' I said firmly. 'I'm starving. Lunch was a very long time ago.'

'We can't leave the children,' said Inga.

'Of course not.' I picked up the phone. I had to explain why I was calling and ordering tea from the Warners' room, but once that was sorted out, the meal was quick to arrive, delivered by none other than the proprietor.

'We were so worried about Lady Cynthia!' she said as she arranged the tea things. 'We hadn't heard anything since the ambulance took her to hospital. Is she... will she be all right?'

'We think so,' said Alan. He nodded toward the door of the twins' room and kept his voice low. 'She's gone into labour, but when we left the hospital about half an hour ago, all the vital signs, hers and the baby's, were good.'

'Oh, I do hope so! We were so upset! She's such a lovely person, and so is Sir John. And the twins are a delight.'

'What happened, anyway?' I asked. 'Sir John didn't know.'

'We don't either, really. One of the wedding party—you know we had a wedding here today?'

We nodded. 'I hope it was over before the rain.'

'Barely. Everyone was leaving when one of the groomsmen heard her scream and found her lying in the garden, by one of the paths. There didn't seem to be anything she could have tripped over, but there she was. He tried to help her up, but she couldn't manage to stand or walk, so he laid her in a more comfortable position and ran to us. We rang the ambulance and then Sir John and...you probably know the rest. You went to the hospital with Sir John, then?'

'He asked us to follow him.'

'Oh, I see.' She sounded as if she didn't, really. 'Had they finished the concert?'

'Just,' said Alan. 'It was a great success.'

'Oh, good. She was worried about that, kept saying she couldn't interrupt him while he was on stage.'

'She's a musician herself, of course,' I said with a smile. 'The show must go on, and all that.'

'Well,' she said after a fractional pause, 'I'll leave you to your tea. Just ring up if there's anything else you need. And of course there'll be no bill. We're just happy to hear that Lady Cynthia is doing as well as she is.'

'Thank you so much. This looks splendid,' said Alan, carefully closing the door after her.

'She was wondering why John wanted us at the hospital,' I said. 'And to tell the truth I wondered myself. Do you think she thinks he thinks… Let me start over. She probably knows who we are, and that we've been looking into the incidents that have plagued the festival. I'll bet she's worrying that John thinks something peculiar happened with this accident, and he's wanting you to investigate. Which might lead to liability issues for the hotel.'

'Convoluted though that statement is, I managed to make my way through it,' said Alan. 'And I suspect you're right.'

'That's why she's treating us to the tea.'

'Right again. If I were still a policeman, I couldn't have any of this, since it constitutes a bribe. However, as I'm not…' and he polished off a small crustless sandwich in two bites. Inga followed his example, making a good meal, but Pat was listless and ate little.

'Wouldn't you like a sandwich?' I asked, offering her the plate.

'Thanks, but I'm not hungry. I'm tired, I think.'

'And no wonder! But some food would help, really it would.' I looked at her drawn face and her restless hands.

'I couldn't,' she said with a shudder. 'But thank you. You're...very kind.'

Well, if she wouldn't eat, she wouldn't. I changed the subject. 'Why *do* you think John wanted us at the hospital?' I asked Alan, taking a couple of sandwiches myself.

'I think he wanted you, particularly, because you seem to be a calming influence on Cynthia. But then she was out of anyone's reach except his. I was superfluous, I think.'

'Never,' I assured him, and ate a scone.

The children slept through our tea, but woke shortly afterwards and wanted their own. We'd saved some for them, and the food kept them occupied for a little while, but then they wanted their parents. They wanted their nanny. It took all our efforts to get them calmed down, bathed, and changed into fresh clothes. But then they wanted entertainment. None of their toys were of interest. Jack, indeed, threw his Thomas the Tank Engine across the room, narrowly missing a very nice lamp. Much as I hate the electronic babysitter, I tried a couple of the videos John and Cynthia had brought along. The twins didn't want to watch them. We were out of ideas.

Alan said, 'I'm terribly sorry, but I do really need to go back to the hospital and see how Cynthia's getting along. And then I should make sure James is safely on ice for the night. I think tomorrow will be soon enough to question him again. I hate to leave you with this, though.'

He gestured at the twins, who were using the very expensive mahogany bed as a trampoline and doing their best to destroy the duvet, shrieking all the while.

'It's all right,' said Inga. 'We'll manage. Go do what you have to do.'

He had barely left when I had an idea. 'Listen, Inga, Pat. These kids are usually pretty good, but their world has been upset. They want their parents, and they want to go home, and there's no chance of any of that for a while yet. I'm opposed on principle to bribing children, but there comes a time. I'd like to take them to a toy store and turn them loose. Do you think Nigel could come with the car?'

He could and would, Inga told us after a brief phone call. So we quieted the twins (with some difficulty), straightened their clothes and tidied the disturbed bed, and had them ready to go when Nigel pulled up to the front door.

The hotel people had told us where to find a big toy store. It was exactly the kind of place I dislike, a big store with lots of plastic toys and little to stimulate a child's imagination. Never mind. What the adults needed just now was a diversion, something to keep the kids amused until we could figure out what to do next.

And it worked. With two adults to supervise each child, we managed to maintain more or less civilized behaviour. Nigel and Inga, experienced parents, set boundaries on what the twins could have, and they, like the good children they basically were, accepted the limitations. They took a long time to choose the two toys each wanted the most, and I gladly proffered my credit card to the cashier. It was a small price to pay for some peace and quiet.

Back at the hotel, the two settled down like angels to play with their new acquisitions, and the adults to a conference. 'What they need,' said Inga, 'is their own familiar surroundings. With their parents and their nanny here, they did reasonably well in a hotel. Now that everyone's out of reach, they're bound to be disoriented and scared. I wonder if there are some grandparents who could be prevailed upon?'

'I suppose we could ask John. It depends upon how things are going with Cynthia.'

'You could phone Alan and find out,' Pat suggested.

'I can't, though. That is, I could try, but if he's at the hospital still, he'll have the mobile turned off. They're very pernickety about the rules.'

'Hospitals always are,' said Nigel. 'But he might not still be there. Why not try? The kids are okay now, but they won't be for long. If they're anything like Nigel Peter, they have an attention span of about ten minutes.'

'If that,' said Inga.

I was, therefore, greatly relieved when Alan answered his phone.

'What's going on?' I asked. 'Where are you?'

'In the hospital car park,' he said. 'Jack and Jill have a new baby brother!'

'Oh!' *It's a boy*, I mouthed to the others. 'That was quick.'

'They decided on a Caesarean. Both mother and baby are doing well. He's small, only a little over five pounds, but healthy, and the doctors say he'll be fine. He's still in the special care unit, but that's just a precaution, because of his low birth weight. And Cynthia, when I left, was just coming out of the anaesthetic and quite happy. I'm just headed for the police station to check on our fiery Irishman.'

'Before you do that, do you think you could go back and talk to John for a moment? Now that he's over most of the anxiety, we need to know if there are any grandparents, or aunts, or anyone who could take over the care of the twins. They're being somewhat difficult, and I don't know how much longer the hotel people are going to put up with them.'

'Oh, Lord, yes! Even Mike and Dennis, perfect grandchildren though they are, could be hellions at that age, especially when they were upset. You poor darling! There's hope, though. Frieda's arrived in Appledore.'

'To stay? Or only to pack up her things?' I couldn't keep the hope out of my voice.

'To stay, John thinks. He talked to her on the phone, told her it was all a mistake, and she'd soon have another baby to look after. Apparently she adores babies.'

'So what should we do?' In the background, the twins were growing noisy. Apparently one of the new toys was in dispute between the two of them.

'If you can bear it, I'd suggest taking them home at once. I'll check with John, of course, but it seems the only sensible solution. Look, you won't all fit into that tiny car of Nigel's, so suppose I drop everything else and come to help.'

'No, I don't think that's a good plan. You need to talk to James, and I want to be with you when you do. I have a better idea. I'll find out what the train connections are, while you talk to John. Between the three of them, I think Nigel and Inga and Pat can manage, if there aren't too many changes. You can delay your visit to the police station long enough to take them to Chester, and someone can surely meet them at the station in Kent.'

'Well, perhaps. You check, and I'll go talk with John.'

I let the hotel staff do the checking for me. They were eager to cooperate, probably because they were looking forward to the imminent departure of the twins. The news, though, was discouraging. 'It's direct from Chester to London Euston, madam,' said the clerk who rang me back. 'Every half-hour. But then they'd have to get to St Pancras, which isn't far, but with two children and luggage, it could be a trial. Then they would take a train to Ashford, and then change to another to get to Appledore. The connections aren't good, I'm afraid, and there are reports of delays on the line.'

I rang off, discouraged. 'You can't get there from here,' I said with a sigh. 'Not travelling with two whirling dervishes.'

'I begin,' said Inga, 'to understand the nineteenth-century appeal of laudanum.' For the twins by that time were whining with sheer exhaustion and resisting all persuasion to better behaviour. They were unhappy, and they wanted the world to know about it.

It was fortunate for our sanity that Alan called back very quickly. 'Forget about trains, love.'

'I already have. They're impossible. I guess you're our only hope.'

'No, the best solution of all will be at your door in five minutes or so. John agrees that the twins must be taken home, and has hired a car and driver for the trip. If Nigel and Inga and Pat will accompany them, they can return in the same car, and John would like to pay them for their trouble. He's most grateful to you all for seeing to them, and apologizes for leaving it to you.'

'There's nothing to apologize for. Tell him I want to see that new baby as soon as we can, and thank him for making this so much easier. And I'll see you shortly?'

We made quick work of packing the twins' things, and when we told them they were going home to Fraülein, they became far more cooperative. The driver of the Bentley helped, too. I had some misgivings about two small children and all that expensive upholstery, and then decided to stop worrying about it. Doubtless John would reimburse the company for any damage.

Alan arrived before I'd finished seeing off the little party, and he helped, too. When they had finally gone, I turned to him, shoulders sagging. 'I'm too old for this sort of thing. They're adorable children, really, but...'

'But you've had enough of them.'

'At least for now. I have new respect for Nigel and Inga.'

'And they have only one to cope with. Now, my dear, we are going to repair to The Stables for a drink and some dinner, courtesy of John, who told me to put it on his bill.'

'But James...' I protested, weakly.

'James can stew in his own juice a little longer. Come on. You need a rest.'

The dinner was excellent, and I stood up from it, refreshed and ready to face the next thing. 'Just let me brush my teeth. I hate furry teeth.'

One doesn't expect to be struck by a major revelation in the ladies' room of a restaurant. I was attending to my teeth, trying to hurry, when suddenly I saw it all.

I only needed confirmation, and we were on our way to get it.

TWENTY-SEVEN

'YOU'RE VERY QUIET, Dorothy,' said Alan on the way to the police station. 'Still tired?'

'No. Just thinking.'

He darted a quick, quizzical look my way, but I closed my mouth firmly. I wasn't ready yet to talk about my brilliant idea.

James was not in the best of tempers when we were admitted to the lock-up. In fact, he reminded me of the twins at their worst. He was petulant, aggressive and stubborn, all magnified by his Irish disposition. In short, he was in no mood to cooperate with anyone about anything.

Alan, with commendable patience, put up with his fury and his language for some time before saying, 'All right, Mr O'Hara. I've listened to you. Now you listen to me for a moment.'

'Why should I?'

'Because if you don't, I'll leave you here until Inspector Owen releases you. That could be some time.'

'I've not bloody done anything!'

'Then you'd do much better to answer my questions and prove that to me. Or shall I leave now?'

'I don't have to talk to you!'

'True.' Alan stood up. 'I think we're wasting our time here, Dorothy.'

We didn't even get to the end of the corridor. 'Ah,

bloody hell,' said James. 'Come and ask your feckin' questions.'

We went back.

'No promises to answer them, mind.'

'No, of course not.'

'Don't you have to tell me I can have a lawyer?' he asked truculently, when we had sat down again in the cramped cell.

'You've been watching too much American television,' said Alan amicably. 'Here in the UK, the caution doesn't say anything about legal representation. Of course, you're entitled to have a lawyer present if you want. It would be at your own expense, though. And I remind you that I'm not a policeman, so this is not an official interview.'

'Ah, hell. Get it over.'

'Very well, then. This afternoon when we first talked, you talked about wanting to get even with Madame de la Rosa—'

'Might as well call her Gracie. Or bitch.'

'Gracie will do nicely. To get even with Gracie, then, for what you thought she did to your friend Daniel Green.'

James said nothing. Alan gave him a moment, and then went on. 'And you made a further, very interesting statement. You said you only meant to frighten her. What was it that you did to try to frighten her?'

Again he remained silent, though his eyes darted from one of us to the other like a frightened animal.

'Did you give her something to eat or drink just before she fell?'

We both knew the answer to that one: no drugs had been found in her system. But James didn't know that. 'No!' he shouted. 'I tell you, I didn't mean to kill her. Only...'

And then he firmly closed his mouth again.

I decided it was time to explode my little bomb. 'James,' I said, leaning toward him, 'when did you find time to do it? It must have been tricky, with all those stagehands and musicians milling around. Anyone could have seen you.'

'Time to do what?' He still looked surly, but his voice gave him away.

'Time,' I said gently, 'to tape the dental floss to the top of the balcony.'

The look he gave me showed astonishment mixed with admiration, mixed, I could have sworn, with amusement.

It took some time for him to tell us the whole story. How he'd become increasingly sure that Gracie, to use his name for her, had pushed Daniel to his death. How Larry's thoughtless remark had festered in his mind until he decided to do something to get even. How he'd seen Gracie shy in terror at a spider on that ill-fated morning at the castle, before the weather forced the transfer of the rehearsal to the church.

'At first I thought I'd buy one of those fake tarantulas,' James had said. His speech had changed, his accent less evident, his language far less crude, reinforcing my opinion that much of his Irishness was put on for effect. 'But I couldn't find one readily, and anyway it might have been seen too soon. So then I thought that a web would be just as good, and I knew just the way to create that effect.'

'How did you hit on the idea?' I couldn't resist asking. 'It was brilliant, but it took me forever to figure it out.'

'Ah, but you never terrorized your little sister, did you? I learned that trick when I was ten. It was useful in other ways, too. Me mum thought I was being such a good boy, flossing me teeth every time. She used to brag about how often she had to buy the floss!'

He told us about planning every move, how he'd bought the super-sticky strapping tape 'because your sellotape would never stick to stone'; how he'd cut the lengths of floss ahead of time, painstakingly painted them with black marker so they wouldn't be easily seen, and attached them to the tape, which he'd then lightly attached to some aluminium foil to make it easy to carry. How he'd chosen a moment to 'go to the loo' when everyone's attention was elsewhere, sneaking up to the balcony to affix the tape to the lintel of the window opening. He'd even brought along someone's cello case to stand on, so he could reach high enough.

'It was a lot of trouble to go to for a joke,' I said to Alan back at Tower later as we were getting ready for bed. The house seemed very quiet and empty without Nigel and Inga.

'It wasn't a joke,' said Alan soberly. 'It was revenge. And it succeeded beyond his wildest dreams.'

'You don't think he really meant to kill her, then?'

'No, and I think he was terrified by what happened. He thought his only chance was that everyone would think it was an accident. And we very nearly did accept that explanation.'

'If I weren't so afraid of spiders myself, he might have got by with it. That was the only thing that made me believe she was somehow frightened to death. What will happen to him?'

'That depends on what view a jury takes of his actions. There's little doubt he caused her death, but I can't see them deciding it was purposeful. He'll probably be reprimanded severely and told to take more consideration of his actions in future. Beyond that, not much, I shouldn't think.'

'And do you think he will? Consider his actions in future, I mean?'

'I very much doubt it.' Alan yawned, and his phone rang.

I looked at the bedside clock. Eleven thirty. My stomach lurched. No good ever comes of a call at that time of night.

'Yes. Surely. Goodnight.'

'Not another crisis?'

'No, dear heart. That was Nigel telling me they arrived in Appledore safely, the children are tucked up under the watchful eye of Frieda and Pat, and he and Inga are going to sleep at home tonight before the driver brings them back tomorrow to pick up their car and say their goodbyes here. The drama is over, my dear. Sleep well.'

'EXCEPT OF COURSE he didn't do it.'

Alan was awake, but only just. He turned over, sat up, and accepted the cup of coffee I handed him. 'What did you say?' he asked in a rusty, early-morning voice.

'James didn't do it. Or at least not that way. I was so much in love with my theory last night that my common sense deserted me. Alan, have you ever looked at that man's teeth?'

'Hmm.' Alan sipped his coffee. 'I see what you mean.'

'Yes. I doubt if a toothbrush touches them very often, let alone dental floss.'

'So why did he say he did?'

'He didn't. I did. I thought at the time there was some amusement mixed with the surprise in his reaction. Now I understand why. I'd come up with a perfect solution to his dilemma.'

'His dilemma being?'

'How to confess to something when he had no idea how he had supposedly done it.'

'But…but why did he want to confess if he hadn't done it? Is there more coffee?'

'Coming right up. I asked Mairi to brew us a potful. And you obviously need it. Think, dear heart! All those years as a policeman…'

He had downed most of the second cup before he replied, 'He's protecting someone.'

'Of course! And we know who, don't we? Who was it he dragged away from here as fast as he could get her? Who was it he stuck to like a burr until she'd had enough of him?'

'And who is it,' Alan added grimly, 'who is now helping to look after the Warner twins?'

'Exactly.'

Alan handed me his cup, got out of bed, and headed for the shower.

We breakfasted quickly on toast and cereal while we discussed what to do. Notify John first, or head for Kent? Call Nigel and Inga and ask them to go back to the Warner home to keep a watching brief?

We decided to do all those things. Alan called John while I phoned Inga and explained the situation.

'We were just about to leave for Tower,' said Inga, 'and bring Nigel Peter along for a treat. He won't be happy about us leaving him again, but I suppose…'

'Don't,' I said, thinking quickly. 'Stay with him. Send Nigel to the Warners' in that hired car, to keep an eye on things. We'll join him as soon as we can get away from here. You'll just have to pick up your car later. We'll work that out.'

'Right. And Dorothy...be careful. Pat was acting a little odd last night, I thought. Maybe she was just tired, but...'

It only needed that, I thought as I rang off.

'John's frantic,' Alan reported. 'He can't leave Cynthia and the new baby, but he's worried sick about the twins. I tried to play down the danger, but it was only right he should know.'

'Yes. Let's go.'

It's a long drive from Mold, North Wales, to Appledore, Kent. Alan borrowed Mairi's computer and took five minutes to look it up online, then handed me a sheaf of bewildering directions, and we set out.

The first few miles, on local roads and through villages, were maddening. I sat tense, directions in hand, pushing the car every foot of the way. 'You know,' said Alan, 'we won't get there any faster if you give yourself a headache.'

'I know, but... I'm going to phone Nigel.'

'Not until we reach the motorway, if you please, my dear. I don't know these roads, and I don't want to get lost.'

I tried to relax my shoulders, but it wasn't easy. It seemed hours before we found ourselves on the M6 bound for Birmingham, and I could finally call Nigel. I was, as Alan had predicted, getting a headache.

The connection wasn't good. We must have been passing through an area ill-served by transmission towers. Nigel didn't answer for several rings, and when he did, his voice didn't sound at all like himself.

'Nigel? Is that you? It's Dorothy.' I paused. 'Speak up, dear. I can't hear you.'

'…not easy…bad…hurry…hostage…'

The last word came through quite clearly, even though Nigel was apparently whispering.

'Nigel! Are you telling me you're involved in a hostage situation?'

Alan swerved, narrowly missing a huge lorry that was roaring past. And I lost the signal.

TWENTY-EIGHT

'NIGEL! NIGEL?' I frantically pressed redial, but there was no response.

Alan meanwhile had pulled into a lay-by. 'What did he say?'

'Almost nothing I could make out, except a few words. "Hurry", he said, and "bad", and "hostage".'

'You're sure about that last?'

'It was very clear, the clearest of anything. Alan, the signal was terrible, but I think he was whispering!'

'Right.' Alan had pulled out his own phone and was punching in a well-remembered number.

'Inspector Morrison, please. It's very urgent. This is… Oh, yes, Sergeant. Thank you.' There was a very brief pause. 'Derek? Alan here. I have a favour to ask. We have word of a potentially dangerous situation in Appledore, down in Kent. It may involve two very young children as hostages, and we have reason to believe a young woman of unstable mentality might also be involved. No details as yet, and we're hurrying to get there as fast as we can, but we're hours away on the M6. I don't know who's in charge down there any more.' Pause. 'Ah. Well, will you ring him and tell him the children of Sir John Warner may be at grave risk. Yes, the conductor. Keep me posted. Oh, and Derek, see if you can pass the word to the motorway authorities to keep an eye out for my car, and let me maintain some speed.'

He put the phone back in his pocket and eased back into traffic.

We were lucky in a way, I suppose. There were no major traffic jams on the motorways, even around Birmingham and London, and nobody stopped us, though Alan was certainly going far faster than the speed limit. He's an excellent driver, but he is seventy, after all, and his reflexes can't be what they were. My knuckles were white for a good part of the way, but I wasn't sure whether it was the speed or fear of what might meet us at our destination.

The Kent countryside, when we finally reached it, basked in the sunny June afternoon. Appledore was a pretty little village in a county full of pretty little villages. I scarcely noticed it. 'Which house?' I asked.

'I don't know.' He pulled to a stop outside the village shop, which a small sign identified as also the post office, got out of the car (with some difficulty) and went inside.

I was suddenly aware of my urgent need for a loo. I looked down the street and found the expected pub. Alan would understand. I got out of the car even more slowly than he had, stiff and sore after five hours of tense sitting, and toddled to the pub.

I met him, bound on the same errand, on my way back to the car.

'The big house at the end of the street,' he said, pointing. 'We'll walk, I think. Less conspicuous, in case…'

He didn't say in case of what. He didn't have to. I waited for him, suddenly wishing myself far away.

There was no obvious activity around the big house, but as we approached the drive, a man materialized from behind a bush. 'I'll ask you to move on, sir,' he said, very quietly.

'I am Alan Nesbitt, retired chief constable of Belleshire. I asked Inspector Morrison, Sherebury Constabulary, to notify your chief of this perhaps dangerous situation.'

'Ah. That would be me. Superintendent Curtis of the Kent Constabulary, sir.' They shook hands. 'Can you tell me what you know of the matter, sir?'

'Not a lot, to be perfectly honest. We believe the Warner children, three-year-old twins, to be inside with their nanny and another woman. It's the other woman who might be the problem. We believe her to be guilty of a rather ingenious murder in Wales a few days ago, and to be emotionally unstable. I hasten to add that nearly all of this is supposition, except that we spoke, some hours ago, with the third adult in the house, a friend from Sherebury.' Alan nodded at me and I took up the tale.

'The connection was very poor, and I caught only a few words, but they frightened me badly. He quite clearly said "hostage", also "bad" and "hurry".'

'I see.' The Superintendent frowned. 'This was how long ago, did you say?'

'About three hours,' said Alan. 'We were just approaching Birmingham on the M6. I phoned Derek immediately.'

'And he rang us, and we've been here ever since. We've taken no action, not knowing quite what the situation was, but we've kept watch. No one has entered or left the house, and there has been no noise of any kind.'

'Right.' Alan considered. 'You're in charge here, sir. But I have been close to the situation, and I know the people involved, all except for the nanny. One of them is a close friend. I'd like to make a suggestion.'

'As it happens, I know Sir John rather well, and the

twins, of course, and I have their interests very much at heart. But I'd welcome anything you'd care to mention.'

I stood there, my heart in my mouth, wishing they'd dispense with the courtesies and get on with it.

'I'd like, first, to try to phone Nigel. I know him best, and he was the one who alerted us to the situation.'

'He may not feel free to talk to you.'

'I realize that. But I think I could communicate with him. I think it's worth a try.'

He held his hand out for my phone, with Nigel's number the first on the list.

We waited. And waited.

'Number not in service,' he reported, finally.

'He's turned it off.' I wasn't surprised, but I was deeply disappointed, nevertheless.

'Yes, someone probably made him do that after your phone call,' said Alan. 'All right, let's try the next thing.'

'And that would be, sir?' The superintendent was cooperative, but was making it quite clear that he was in charge.

'Subject to your approval, of course, I'd like to pretend that everything is normal, and simply go up to the front door and knock. It might work, you know, Superintendent. We may be making a great mountain out of a molehill.'

'You're forgetting what the young gentleman told your wife, sir. I think we must assume that someone is being held in that house against their will, and that the situation might prove dangerous for the children, if for no one else.'

I couldn't contain myself any longer. 'Superintendent, may I make a suggestion?'

'Certainly, madam.'

'I spent most of yesterday with Pat and the twins.

Struggling to deal with anxious agitated children can form a bond. I began to feel very close to Pat and her troubles. I think I might be able to talk to her. I'd like to try.'

'We cannot place civilians in danger, madam,' said the superintendent at the same time that Alan said, 'It's out of the question, Dorothy. The risk is too great!'

'The risk to whom? If you think there's a chance that Pat might harm the children, I'll concede. But I don't think she would. In fact, I don't really know why she's holed up in there at all. Yes, she wants to save her own skin, if she thinks we've worked out what she did. But we don't know what she's thinking, about Nigel or Frieda or the children or any part of the whole mess! I'd like to talk to her and find out what she wants. Surely that's a reasonable thing to do.'

Alan and the superintendent looked at each other. Finally Alan said, 'Very well, Dorothy. But I insist that you take some precautions. Talk to her through a window, if we can find one open. And we will have some men— you have other men stationed here, Superintendent?'

'Three.'

'You will have some men near you, just in case.'

'No,' I said flatly. 'I go up to the house and knock on the door and go inside. It all has to seem normal and ordinary and non-threatening. That's the only way it'll work. And it's the only way I'll do it.'

'I don't like it,' Alan muttered.

'Alan, listen to me. If I weren't your wife, if I were just someone who knew Pat and was likely to be able to talk sense into her, you'd accept in a minute. Wouldn't you?'

Superintendent Curtis had remained tactfully silent during this exchange. Now he cleared his throat and said, tentatively, 'The lady has a point, Mr Nesbitt. Of course, as she *is* your wife, you and she must decide. I think, myself, that it's worth a try. Now that she's explained further, I feel the risk may be negligible.'

'I'll be careful, love, I promise I will. And if I think I'm in the slightest danger, I'll skedaddle.'

Of course he argued some more, but I won my point in the end. I knew I would. He's a sensible, intelligent man except for that one attitude about overprotecting me. He can't help it, poor dear. He's an Englishman, and the Code was drummed into him from infancy.

He had the last word. 'If you're not out in ten minutes, I'm coming in, boots and all!'

I kissed him on the cheek and, trying to appear more courageous than I felt, pushed open the gate and walked into the grounds.

The house was an imposing one, almost coldly symmetrical, in the Georgian style. It wore a forbidding look, with all the windows tightly shut, despite the June heat. I craned my neck, while I was still hidden behind the shrubbery, and saw one window they had overlooked, high at one end of the top floor. There was no chance at all of anyone save a mountain climber entering by that one.

I took a deep breath and crunched along the gravel sweep, announcing my presence as loudly as if I'd hired the town crier. The front door, a massive mahogany affair, was firmly and intimidatingly shut. There was an old-fashioned bell pull in the wall of the house, to the right of the door, and a large lion's head knocker on the door itself. There was also, tucked discreetly away on the left, a modern electric buzzer with an intercom. That was the button I chose to push.

The house was too solid for me to hear it buzz inside.

After an interval, with no response, I spoke into the intercom, quietly, gently. 'Pat. Pat, dear, it's me, Dorothy Martin. I dropped by to see how the twins were doing. May I come in?'

Nothing. I pressed the buzzer again, holding my finger on it for a good three seconds, counted in my head.

'Pat!' I said more loudly. 'Pat, do let me in. I've travelled for hours and I'm awfully tired, and…well, to tell the truth, I need to use the loo.'

I don't know if it was the pathos in my voice, or a woman's response to another woman's need, but the door, quite soundlessly, opened a crack and Pat peered through the gap.

'It really is you,' she said in a voice devoid of expression. I was reminded of Mrs Danvers, and a chill ran down my back, but I pushed in anyway.

'Yes, and I'm so glad you're home! I've been thinking about the children, and hoping you and—Frieda, is that her name?—have been coping. I'm sure they're happier now that they're back in their own home. Goodness, what a lovely house! And I'm embarrassed to waltz in here and ask for the loo first thing, but…' As I talked I was walking farther into the house, looking and listening. 'I suppose it would be upstairs in a house this age,' I continued brightly, and was halfway up the imposing staircase before Pat could react.

'No!' she said loudly. 'I mean, there's one just off the hall, down here.'

'That's all right, dear. I've been sitting a long time and I need a little exercise.' It wasn't a very good excuse, but I didn't have time to think of a better one. And I was determined to get upstairs, because when Pat shouted at me, I thought I'd heard a faint cry from somewhere in the upper regions.

A child's cry, immediately hushed.

It was lucky for me that all the doors off the hallway on this floor were shut. It meant I had to open every one in my supposed quest for the bathroom. I didn't find anything or anyone interesting, however, except an elegant, beautifully equipped bathroom, complete with bidet and whirlpool bath. By this time nerves had made my need real, so I used the toilet, but I didn't flush it immediately. I wanted time to think.

The nursery was probably on the top floor. If all the old English mysteries I'd read were accurate, the nurseries always were at the top of this sort of house. I suppose it kept the children farther away and less apt to be either seen or heard.

How was I to get to the top floor?

Keep it simple, Dorothy. Tell the truth. I flushed the toilet. The old-fashioned (though quite new) water closet produced a great rush of water, easily heard downstairs. I stepped out of the room and called down the stairs. 'Pat, I'm longing to see the children. I thought I heard them just now, so they must not be napping. I'll just go on up and pop into the nursery.'

To my own ears I sounded perfectly convincing, but Pat must have been even more on edge than I supposed, because she was at my heels before I had taken two steps up the steep, narrow staircase that led to the top floor.

'No! You mustn't! That is, I don't want—Frieda and I don't want the children disturbed. They've been upset. We've only just got them settled and you mustn't—'

'Why, Pat! Whatever is the matter?' I kept on climbing, wondering if she was going to try physically to stop me. 'You sound distraught. I'm sorry the children have been such a handful, but as you say, they've had a trying time. I'm sure they'll be fine now that they're in familiar surroundings. Is it this way?'

'No! Stop! I don't want…you mustn't go in there!'

I had reached the top floor. I stopped. I was disturbing an already disturbed woman, more with every step I took. It occurred to me, belatedly, that this was not wise. I turned to face Pat.

'My dear, something's wrong. I'm sorry I didn't notice until just now. What is it?'

'I…nothing, it's only…oh, what's the use?' And she collapsed against the wall, her head in her hands, sobs racking her body.

The noises from behind the door at the end of the hall were becoming louder every moment. Muffled young voices blended with quieter adult ones. I looked from Pat to the door, torn between ministering to this deeply distressed woman and checking on the twin situation.

The twins won out. I left Pat where she was, moved to the door, and put my hand on the knob.

It was locked.

'Open the door, Frieda, or Nigel, or somebody,' I called over the increasing noise from the children. 'It's Dorothy Martin.'

'We can't,' said a voice I recognized as Nigel's. 'Pat's locked us in!'

'Are you all right in there?'

'We are fine,' said a clipped German voice, 'but we want to get out!'

I looked at Pat, who was showing signs of recovery. I looked back at the nursery door, behind which the children were beginning to wail loudly. Back at Pat. Back at the nursery.

'DOROTHY!' The bellow from the downstairs hall was the most welcome sound I've ever heard.

EPILOGUE

'So, DOROTHY, HOW did she do it? I gather she still hasn't told the police very much, except that she's not sorry she did it, that Delia ruined her life and deserved what she got.'

It was a month later. We were gathered around the remnants of a lavish meal at the Rose and Crown in Sherebury's Cathedral Close, Alan and I, Nigel and Inga, and John and Cynthia, along with Inga's parents Peter and Greta Endicott, owners of the inn, and my next-door neighbour and good friend Jane Langland. Nigel Peter was sound asleep upstairs and the Warner children were safely at home with Frieda. Now Jane (my pet-sitter) and the Endicotts (babysitters for Nigel Peter), who had missed out on all the action, wanted to be brought up to date, while the rest of us traded details to complete the story.

'How did she do it?' Inga persisted.

'Oh, didn't I tell you? She told me a day or two ago when I went to visit her in the jail. I'm glad you managed that for me, Alan. I really do feel sorry for her, despite everything.'

'I'm growing dangerous, Dorothy,' said Inga, looking about as dangerous as a month-old kitten.

'It was so absurdly simple. I should have figured it out at once, but no, I had to go inventing elaborate plots about violin strings and dental floss. Yes, I'm getting there, Inga! You know how we admired that crocheted lace she had all over her clothes? And she told us she made it? It was unusual, because it was black.'

I waited for them to get it.

'Crochet thread,' said Jane, slapping her hand on the table. 'Black crochet thread. Heavy enough to hang nicely, fine enough to be almost invisible, easy to tape even to stone.'

I nodded. 'And she said she bought a small plastic spider at a novelty shop in Wrexham, to stick at the top of one of the strands of thread, just to reinforce the illusion. You remember how Delia looked up as she hit that high note, just before she started screaming? She must have seen the spider then, and then felt the threads as she waved her hands around, and then…'

'And speaking of violin strings,' said Nigel, 'I wonder who did steal them from Laurie. I don't think she ever found out.'

'This is guesswork,' said Alan, 'but it wouldn't surprise me at all to learn that it was Delia herself. We don't know that she had anything against Laurie, but Laurie and Ben didn't get along any too well, and I can see Delia thinking she'd play a spiteful trick on Laurie just to please Ben.'

'I don't think,' said Cynthia, 'from what I've learned of Delia, that she ever in her life did anything to please anyone else. It's certainly no thanks to her that she didn't succeed in ruining our life.' She put out a hand to John, who clasped it with a smile that warmed even me, old and long-married as I am. 'And I hope nothing very dreadful happens to Pat.'

'That's up to the judge, of course, assuming she's convicted of malicious mischief, as charged. But she's not displaying very rational behaviour at the moment, so I suspect the problem will be dealt with medically.'

'She told me a lot, while she had us cooped up in your house,' said Nigel soberly, nodding to John and Cynthia. 'She was rambling, really, but it was quite clear that she'd always been a loner, with music her only joy in life. Her family hadn't been very stable, moving about a lot, not taking much notice of her.'

Well, I thought, Nigel, whose family background had also been troubled, could certainly sympathize with Pat there.

'Then she got fed up with her family, such as it was, moved to Manchester, and met Daniel. Another musician, you see. She thought her life had finally turned around. So when Daniel was killed, there seemed to be nothing left for her.'

'But what I still don't understand,' said Inga, 'is why James tried to make us believe he'd set up the trap for Delia. Why would he bother to protect Pat? We could all see how jealous he was of her, coming between him and his friend Daniel.'

'I didn't see that for a long time, either,' I said, trying to swallow the lump in my throat. 'James was certainly jealous. But of Daniel, not of Pat. He and Daniel had been best friends, and then they both met Pat. And both fell for her. And Daniel won out. James, being Irish, raged about it, but the trouble was he was still bound by strong ties of friendship to Dan. So he didn't do much of anything about it, except drink too much. But when Dan died, he thought maybe he had a chance with Pat. And when he realized what she'd done, he thought he could protect her and…'

'And make her love him,' said Greta softly. 'And instead she rejected him. And still he tried to protect her.'

'Unrequited love,' said Alan. 'Another stock situation in grand opera.'

'As in real life,' said John. 'I've always thought that one reason for the perennial popularity of opera is that it does deal with genuine human problems, genuine emotion. Oh, writ larger than life, perhaps, magnified and enhanced by the glorious music, but with a firm basis in reality.'

'That's a new idea for me,' I said thoughtfully. 'I'd always considered opera plots, tragic opera at least, to be the purest melodrama. That's why I've preferred to listen to them in what someone called the decent obscurity of a foreign language.'

'You're right about the melodrama,' said Alan. 'But that's the point, surely. Most of us, at least we English,' he said, patting my hand, 'have been brought up to suppress our violent feelings about love and betrayal and death and revenge. Opera lets us experience those feelings vicariously.'

'I think all music does,' said Nigel. 'A great catharsis.'

'A healing.' I nodded, remembering the way the *Pié Jesu* had healed me. 'So I'd like to propose a toast.' I raised my glass. 'To the beauty and power of music, and to the musicians who make it so.'

'To music!' they chorused, and if there were some tears mixed with the smiles, it seemed only right. Lives had been lost. Other lives had been tragically changed. *Dona eis requiem sempiternam.* Grant them rest eternal.

* * * * *

REQUEST YOUR FREE BOOKS!
2 FREE NOVELS PLUS 2 FREE GIFTS!

⊞ HARLEQUIN®

INTRIGUE

BREATHTAKING ROMANTIC SUSPENSE

YES! Please send me 2 FREE Harlequin® Intrigue novels and my 2 FREE gifts (gifts are worth about $10). After receiving them, if I don't wish to receive any more books, I can return the shipping statement marked "cancel." If I don't cancel, I will receive 6 brand-new novels every month and be billed just $4.74 per book in the U.S. or $5.49 per book in Canada. That's a savings of at least 12% off the cover price! It's quite a bargain! Shipping and handling is just 50¢ per book in the U.S. and 75¢ per book in Canada.* I understand that accepting the 2 free books and gifts places me under no obligation to buy anything. I can always return a shipment and cancel at any time. Even if I never buy another book, the two free books and gifts are mine to keep forever.

182/382 HDN GH3D

Name _____ (PLEASE PRINT) _____

Address _____ Apt. # _____

City _____ State/Prov. _____ Zip/Postal Code _____

Signature (if under 18, a parent or guardian must sign) _____

Mail to the **Reader Service:**
IN U.S.A.: P.O. Box 1867, Buffalo, NY 14240-1867
IN CANADA: P.O. Box 609, Fort Erie, Ontario L2A 5X3
**Are you a subscriber to Harlequin® Intrigue books
and want to receive the larger-print edition?
Call 1-800-873-8635 or visit www.ReaderService.com.**

* Terms and prices subject to change without notice. Prices do not include applicable taxes. Sales tax applicable in N.Y. Canadian residents will be charged applicable taxes. Offer not valid in Quebec. This offer is limited to one order per household. Not valid for current subscribers to Harlequin Intrigue books. All orders subject to credit approval. Credit or debit balances in a customer's account(s) may be offset by any other outstanding balance owed by or to the customer. Please allow 4 to 6 weeks for delivery. Offer available while quantities last.

Your Privacy—The Reader Service is committed to protecting your privacy. Our Privacy Policy is available online at www.ReaderService.com or upon request from the Reader Service.

We make a portion of our mailing list available to reputable third parties that offer products we believe may interest you. If you prefer that we not exchange your name with third parties, or if you wish to clarify or modify your communication preferences, please visit us at www.ReaderService.com/consumerchoice or write to us at Reader Service Preference Service, P.O. Box 9062, Buffalo, NY 14240-9062. Include your complete name and address.

HI15

REQUEST YOUR FREE BOOKS!
2 FREE NOVELS PLUS 2 FREE GIFTS!

ℍHARLEQUIN®

ROMANTIC suspense

Sparked by danger, fueled by passion

YES! Please send me 2 FREE Harlequin® Romantic Suspense novels and my 2 FREE gifts (gifts are worth about $10). After receiving them, if I don't wish to receive any more books, I can return the shipping statement marked "cancel." If I don't cancel, I will receive 4 brand-new novels every month and be billed just $4.74 per book in the U.S. or $5.49 per book in Canada. That's a savings of at least 12% off the cover price! It's quite a bargain! Shipping and handling is just 50¢ per book in the U.S. and 75¢ per book in Canada.* I understand that accepting the 2 free books and gifts places me under no obligation to buy anything. I can always return a shipment and cancel at any time. Even if I never buy another book, the two free books and gifts are mine to keep forever.

240/340 HDN GH3P

Name _____ (PLEASE PRINT) _____

Address _____ Apt. #

City _____ State/Prov. _____ Zip/Postal Code

Signature (if under 18, a parent or guardian must sign)

Mail to the **Reader Service:**

IN U.S.A.: P.O. Box 1867, Buffalo, NY 14240-1867
IN CANADA: P.O. Box 609, Fort Erie, Ontario L2A 5X3

Want to try two free books from another line?
Call 1-800-873-8635 or visit www.ReaderService.com.

* Terms and prices subject to change without notice. Prices do not include applicable taxes. Sales tax applicable in N.Y. Canadian residents will be charged applicable taxes. Offer not valid in Quebec. This offer is limited to one order per household. Not valid for current subscribers to Harlequin Romantic Suspense books. All orders subject to credit approval. Credit or debit balances in a customer's account(s) may be offset by any other outstanding balance owed by or to the customer. Please allow 4 to 6 weeks for delivery. Offer available while quantities last.

Your Privacy—The Reader Service is committed to protecting your privacy. Our Privacy Policy is available online at www.ReaderService.com or upon request from the Reader Service.

We make a portion of our mailing list available to reputable third parties that offer products we believe may interest you. If you prefer that we not exchange your name with third parties, or if you wish to clarify or modify your communication preferences, please visit us at www.ReaderService.com/consumerschoice or write to us at Reader Service Preference Service, P.O. Box 9062, Buffalo, NY 14240-9062. Include your complete name and address.

HRS15

REQUEST YOUR FREE BOOKS!

2 FREE NOVELS
FROM THE SUSPENSE COLLECTION
PLUS 2 FREE GIFTS!

YES! Please send me 2 FREE novels from the Suspense Collection and my 2 FREE gifts (gifts are worth about $10). After receiving them, if I don't wish to receive any more books, I can return the shipping statement marked "cancel." If I don't cancel, I will receive 4 brand-new novels every month and be billed just $6.49 per book in the U.S. or $6.99 per book in Canada. That's a savings of at least 19% off the cover price. It's quite a bargain! Shipping and handling is just 50¢ per book in the U.S. and 75¢ per book in Canada.* I understand that accepting the 2 free books and gifts places me under no obligation to buy anything. I can always return a shipment and cancel at any time. Even if I never buy another book, the two free books and gifts are mine to keep forever.

191/391 MDN GH4Z

Name	(PLEASE PRINT)	
Address		Apt. #
City	State/Prov.	Zip/Postal Code

Signature (if under 18, a parent or guardian must sign)

Mail to the **Reader Service**:
IN U.S.A.: P.O. Box 1867, Buffalo, NY 14240-1867
IN CANADA: P.O. Box 609, Fort Erie, Ontario L2A 5X3

Want to try two free books from another line?
Call 1-800-873-8635 or visit www.ReaderService.com.

* Terms and prices subject to change without notice. Prices do not include applicable taxes. Sales tax applicable in N.Y. Canadian residents will be charged applicable taxes. Offer not valid in Quebec. This offer is limited to one order per household. Not valid for current subscribers to the Suspense Collection or the Romance/Suspense Collection. All orders subject to credit approval. Credit or debit balances in a customer's account(s) may be offset by any other outstanding balance owed by or to the customer. Please allow 4 to 6 weeks for delivery. Offer available while quantities last.

Your Privacy—The Reader Service is committed to protecting your privacy. Our Privacy Policy is available online at www.ReaderService.com or upon request from the Reader Service.

We make a portion of our mailing list available to reputable third parties that offer products we believe may interest you. If you prefer that we not exchange your name with third parties, or if you wish to clarify or modify your communication preferences, please visit us at www.ReaderService.com/consumerschoice or write to us at Reader Service Preference Service, P.O. Box 9062, Buffalo, NY 14240-9062. Include your complete name and address.

READERSERVICE.COM

Manage your account online!

- Review your order history
- Manage your payments
- Update your address

> *We've designed the*
> *Reader Service website*
> *just for you.*

Enjoy all the features!

- Discover new series available to you, and read excerpts from any series.
- Respond to mailings and special monthly offers.
- Connect with favorite authors at the blog.
- Browse the Bonus Bucks catalog and online-only exculsives.
- Share your feedback.

Visit us at:
ReaderService.com

REQUEST YOUR FREE BOOKS!

2 FREE RIVETING INSPIRATIONAL NOVELS
PLUS 2 FREE MYSTERY GIFTS

Love Inspired®
SUSPENSE
RIVETING INSPIRATIONAL ROMANCE

YES! Please send me 2 FREE Love Inspired® Suspense novels and my 2 FREE mystery gifts (gifts are worth about $10). After receiving them, if I don't wish to receive any more books, I can return the shipping statement marked "cancel." If I don't cancel, I will receive 4 brand-new novels every month and be billed just $4.99 per book in the U.S. or $5.49 per book in Canada. That's a savings of at least 17% off the cover price. It's quite a bargain! Shipping and handling is just 50¢ per book in the U.S. and 75¢ per book in Canada.* I understand that accepting the 2 free books and gifts places me under no obligation to buy anything. I can always return a shipment and cancel at any time. Even if I never buy another book, the two free books and gifts are mine to keep forever.

123/323 IDN GH5Z

Name _____ (PLEASE PRINT) _____

Address _____ Apt. # _____

City _____ State/Prov. _____ Zip/Postal Code _____

Signature (if under 18, a parent or guardian must sign)

Mail to the **Reader Service:**
IN U.S.A.: P.O. Box 1867, Buffalo, NY 14240-1867
IN CANADA: P.O. Box 609, Fort Erie, Ontario L2A 5X3

**Are you a current subscriber to Love Inspired® Suspense books
and want to receive the larger-print edition?
Call 1-800-873-8635 or visit www.ReaderService.com.**

* Terms and prices subject to change without notice. Prices do not include applicable taxes. Sales tax applicable in N.Y. Canadian residents will be charged applicable taxes. Offer not valid in Quebec. This offer is limited to one order per household. Not valid for current subscribers to Love Inspired Suspense books. All orders subject to credit approval. Credit or debit balances in a customer's account(s) may be offset by any other outstanding balance owed by or to the customer. Please allow 4 to 6 weeks for delivery. Offer available while quantities last.

Your Privacy—The Reader Service is committed to protecting your privacy. Our Privacy Policy is available online at www.ReaderService.com or upon request from the Reader Service.
We make a portion of our mailing list available to reputable third parties that offer products we believe may interest you. If you prefer that we not exchange your name with third parties, or if you wish to clarify or modify your communication preferences, please visit us at www.ReaderService.com/consumerschoice or write to us at Reader Service Preference Service, P.O. Box 9062, Buffalo, NY 14240-9062. Include your complete name and address.

LIS15